THERE'S FREEDOM IN
REMEMBERING.

AMNESTY

CAMBRIA HEBERT

ISBN: 978-1-946836-06-9

Cover design by Cover Me Darling
Edited by Cassie McCown
Interior design by Cover Me Darling
Formatting by Athena Interior Book Design

Published by: Cambria Hebert
http://www.cambriahebert.com

AMNESTY

CAMBRIA HEBERT

There's freedom in remembering.

My past is a double-edged sword.
Damned if I remember; damned if I don't.
Recollection beyond the horrors I already have will change me. Change us.
But what if I'm living a lie? What if everything I believe is wrong?
What if *who* I thought I was isn't real?
If not her, then…
Who am I?
Eddie says it doesn't matter, but deep down, I'm terrified it does.
I'm trapped. Held prisoner by a past I can't remember and a future that may not belong to me.
There's a light, though not at the end of the tunnel…
It's wavering in the distance, calling to me from Rumor Island.
That light, it scares me far more than darkness. Am I brave enough to confront it?
So many questions, so few answers.
I don't have a choice; the truth always finds a way to the surface.
Finally learning who I truly am will be a permanent life sentence.
Total punishment or absolute amnesty.

for Kaydence
You inspired me again.

CHAPTER ONE

AMNESIA

I thought I was safe.

Widow West was still in the hospital, still unresponsive and immobile. She wasn't able to come for me. Not anymore, at least not right now. I let my guard down with a false sense of security... And now I was regretting it.

I don't know why, but I assumed the man who sent the widow after me wouldn't come. It seemed he was content with having someone else do the kidnapping. Or perhaps he just wanted to remain out of sight. Regardless, the idea he would come to finish what she started didn't occur to me.

Until, of course, he did.

Just as I was finishing my workday at Loch Gen—a job, as it turned out, I really loved—there was a sound toward the back of the store. Maybe I wouldn't have noticed the noise at all except for the fact my fingers were still on the locks; the sign I just flipped over to "closed" was still moving against the windowpane.

No one was in here.

No one but me.

Eddie ran out to drop off a grocery delivery to one of the town people who called needing a few essentials but was too sick to come in. Being the man he was, Eddie jotted down the order immediately and bagged it up. These small details here at Lake Loch were never lost on me. I knew there were other places in the world where things like this didn't happen. Things like neighbors counting on neighbors and everyone pretty much being your friend. It was something I would never take for granted, especially since recalling some things that proved this world could be a cruel place.

After assuring Eddie I could close up and start a few restocks before we called it a night, he took off and I was left alone.

At least I thought I'd been alone.

Still standing with my back to the store, hand paused over the lock, I listened. The ceiling fans, which were always on, hummed slightly, creating a sort of warbled whirring overhead. The low drone of the coolers on the other side of the place kicked on, and I wondered if perhaps that's what I'd heard.

But the sound that made me pause came from the other direction. Back toward the stairs and the tiny bathroom. Back where all the Lake Loch merchandise was, including the little stuffed Loch Ness monsters I loved so much.

The sound of hangers knocking together, as if someone bumped into a rack of clothes and caused everything on it to collide, was fairly distinct. It wasn't a noise that could be easily explained away. At least not in that moment, not as my ears searched for another reason and my fingertips trembled.

"Hello?" I said, brazenly calling out in my fear.

No one replied as I turned fully away from the door and stared out across the section of store I could see.

"Is anyone here?" I called out. "I'm closing up."

The sudden trill of the phone near the register made me leap off the floor. With a gasp, I pressed my palm to my chest and scurried around the counter to pick it up. "Loch General," I said, partially out of breath.

The sound of static greeted me. Nervous energy crackled along my limbs, buzzing beneath my skin. "Hello?" I asked.

Nothing.

Replacing the receiver, I began closing out the register, trying to evade the uneasy feeling coiling inside me.

The distinct scuffle of feet against the floor brought my head up. Instantly, my heart began to pound. Leaving the cash drawer wide open, I crept cautiously around the counter toward the back of the store where the noises were coming from.

I was just being paranoid. After everything that happened, it was understandable that I'd react this way to intrusive noise. That every single sound would take my imagination to the furthest point and panic would build. I should probably mention this to Dr. Kline.

The merchandise section came into view; everything looked okay. I saw no hulking figure standing there ready to attack.

My sigh of relief was so strong it lifted my shoulders to my ears, and as I released the tension, I rested my hands on my hips. Shaking my head at my own paranoia, I started to spin back toward the register.

That's when I saw it.

Out of the corner of my eye, a familiar shape, small and dark, had my feet stopping, my lips pulling down into a frown.

One of the small Loch Ness toys was on the floor. It lay there against the wood planks, on its side, completely out of place. The rack where all the toys were displayed wasn't even near where it lay. It was as if someone had accidentally dropped it there as they'd been shopping.

Or placed it there on purpose…

Brushing off the thought, I told myself to stop being so sinister. Why would someone deliberately place a harmless stuffed animal on the floor?

There was no reason.

I didn't like seeing the little guy there, though. I had an affinity for those toys, considering they reminded me of this town that was my solace and of Eddie… the man who completely stole my heart.

The one he'd given me was at home, on my bed, right atop the colorful quilt I loved so much.

Smiling at the warmth that suffused my heart at just seeing the little guy, I went over and bent to pick it up.

"How'd you get way over here?" I murmured, lifting it, brushing it off after I straightened.

A sudden creepy feeling stole over me. Gooseflesh rose along my arms and legs, a chill working its way up my spine.

With my heart suddenly in my throat, my stomach weighing the same as a bag of lead, I spun around, glancing behind me toward the tiny bathroom under the stairs.

At the very same moment, the wooden door burst open and something launched out of the small space right at me.

A shriek ripped out of my throat as the dark figure barreled into me, knocking me backward. I sprawled out on the floor, the hot, heavy figure weighing me down. I was caught up in the folds of the black cloak they wore, and I began to panic, feeling as though I'd been captured in a net.

The stuffed toy went flying as I fought the fabric, desperately trying to get free.

"No!" I screamed, struggling.

The figure grabbed my wrist and pinned it to the floor, and a sudden burst of rage, an emotion so powerful I didn't even understand, lit up my insides like a bolt of lightning cracking through a dark sky.

"Nooo!" I roared again, this time sounding like a completely different person. Adrenaline gave my leg power as I jackknifed it up between my attacker's legs.

He fell off me sideways, sliding to the floor like a puddle. Shoving up, I scrambled away. A hand caught my ankle, and I screamed and kicked, managing to get free.

The front door was already locked, but the back door was still open. Since I was near the back, I raced that way, not looking behind me at all. My feet slapped over the hard floors as I wheezed and rushed, so desperate to get outside I pushed on the door when I should have pulled.

I heard him behind me, and I muttered a cry when the door opened, the wintry air slapping me in the face when I lunged outside.

A hand grasped at my hair, caught the short strands as it floated out behind me, and yanked so hard I cried out. My body jolted backward as I was pulled against a chest, a strong arm latching around my torso so tight I was unable to breathe.

He began walking backward, as if he had all the time in the world and he wasn't worried I would escape again.

He's going to torture me. The things he did in the past are nothing compared to the punishment I'll get for daring to live my own life.

With perfect clarity, I recalled something Eddie had taught me, a defensive move. Without thinking too much, I brought my foot up, hurtled it down over the attacker's, and stomped hard. His body jolted, and I used my arm, lifted it, and brought it down to disengage the hold I was caught in.

Free, I took off running. I ran as fast as my legs would carry me over the expanse of tall grasses, against the biting wind, and through the rocky section that led to the lake.

The sound of water crashing against the shoreline was loud but welcoming, and the air was fresh and clear this close to the water.

My lungs screamed for air. Body halting, I bent at the waist to suck in great gulps and try to catch my breath.

Still scared for my life, I straightened and looked over my shoulder.

"Ahh!" I screamed. The figure was right there on top of me. His hands grabbed me like shackles, and instead of towing me back toward the store, he reversed direction and went to the water.

"No!" I protested, trying to struggle. Calmly, he dragged me backward, my heels rubbing over the ground, leaving a trail through the beach.

Water that had to be very close to freezing stole my breath the second it splashed up my legs and soaked my pants.

Terror made me fight harder. Memories of nearly drowning clawed at my head almost as strongly as the man dragging me into the frigid water.

All at once, I was freed of his clutches. My body was lifted and tossed. I plunged beneath the surface. It swallowed me in one big gulp. Bubbles escaped my nose and raced to the surface as I tried to follow.

Before I could manage, I was yanked up by the front of my shirt. I barely had time to gasp before I was plunged back under. This time his hands stayed on me, pressing me under... keeping me down.

I struggled and fought. He brought me up only to plunge me back down.

I was drowning.

He was drowning me.

I was going to die in this lake at the hands of someone whose face I'd never seen.

My fingers dug into the arms holding me, my fingernails cutting into them, even through the fabric covering his skin. Forcing my eyes open, I stared up at the hulking dark figure, water making everything blurry.

With another rough yank, I was above the surface. I blinked, gasping. "Wait!" The word ripped out of me, and whatever he heard in my voice gave him pause.

"Look at me," I gurgled.

Still keeping that impenetrable hold on my shirt, he ripped the fabric back from his head and stared down.

I jerked, eyes wide. "No!" I screamed, struggling anew. "No!"

"You wanted to die," the voice, which was mine, insisted.

I shook my head.

The girl—me—gazed down with short, dark-blond hair, freckles, and brown eyes, which I never thought of as evil until this very moment, and threw back her head and laughed.

"It's time to finish the job you started," she told me. "It's time."

With force I had no idea she even possessed, she shoved me back beneath the brown waves.

All this time I'd been running from that dark, faceless figure... a stalker. Someone who lurked above the waves, waiting for me to drown.

All this time, I'd been running from the person who tried to kill me.

I'd been running from me.

A huge gasp shook me from the lifelike dream. My body lifted with the force of it as I grappled at my throat with my hands, clawing at the skin as if that would somehow make it easier to breath. Reality came forward as the room around me came into focus, and my fingers gentled on my body. Slumping forward a bit, I breathed a sigh of relief. My entire body trembled, skin slicked with sweat. Every part of me was flushed and uncomfortable. The horrid pictures I'd just dreamed still flashed in the back of my mind as though they weren't quite ready to let me go.

It's just a dream. I assured myself. *Just a dream.*
A terrible, terrible dream.

With a shuddering breath, I looked beside me where Eddie was sprawled against the mattress, blankets around his waist, bare chest on full display. I thought of burrowing against him, letting him wrap his arm around me. I wanted to. Almost desperately.

I didn't.

I wasn't sure I deserved the comfort.

Tossing aside the covers, I winced slightly when the bottoms of my bare feet came into contact with the cold floor. Moving as quietly as I could so as not to wake Eddie, I crept down the hallway and into the kitchen. It was the middle of the night, still dark outside, with no promise of day yet.

My hoodie was on the end of the kitchen counter, and I snatched it up as I unlocked the door and let myself out onto the small porch. Once the soft fabric of the sweater enveloped me, I leaned my elbows on the railing and glanced across the yard, down to the water.

The sound of the waves lapping against the shore was comforting, even though it was endlessly dark out there on the surface. The water looked impenetrable, like an unmatched obscurity that concealed a veiled threat. The stars that usually dotted the sky were hidden, and the moon was currently dulled behind a cloud.

The bare skin on my legs was no match for the cold air coming off the water, my toes even less so. But I didn't retreat inside. Instead, I ignored the cold, huddled a little farther inside the shirt, and stared out over the landscape, eyes scanning the enigmatic water.

My empathy was dwindling.

I knew the widow of Rumor Island (was she even really a widow?) suffered. It was clear in the physical injuries I witnessed on her body. It was evident in the words she hurled at me with hate. And then, of course, when she attacked us. Now she sat catatonic in the hospital.

I got the feeling she was somehow brainwashed by the man who I partially remembered. The one who tortured me—and probably her, too. It made me wonder if I was brainwashed, too, you know, before my brain forgot it all.

Did that make us sort of kindred? Victims of something horrible, of the same man? Is that why, after everything, I felt sorry for her? Because really, no one should have to endure what she did, what *I* did. I wouldn't wish it upon anyone.

In spite of it all, the more time that passed, the more the nightmares stole my sleep, the more I dwelled on everything that had happened, and the less compassion I felt.

He loves Sadie. Not you. You aren't Sadie.

Those words haunted me more than the terrible memories that resurfaced in my mind. Those words threatened my future, the life I wanted so desperately, the one I now had.

But how long would I keep it?

I wasn't a liar, yet I told a lie. To Eddie, the man I loved. The lie, even though already spoken, hung in my throat, threatening to choke me, reminding me every moment of every day what I didn't say.

I'd been so angry when I found out he suspected all along I was Sadie, the girl he lost. I told him I couldn't trust him because he refused to tell me the truth.

And now here I was doing the same.

Widow West told me I wasn't Sadie, but I didn't tell anyone at all.

I was afraid to.

Afraid if I did, I'd lose everything.

"Am." Eddie's voice startled me. Straightening off the rail, I looked over my shoulder to where he stood on the other side of the screen door, gazing out. "What are you doing out here?"

"I had another nightmare," I murmured, turning back toward the water.

The hinges creaked as he let himself out. From behind, his arms encircled me. Instead of pulling me back into his chest, he moved close to mold himself around me. "You should have woken me."

If I woke him every time I had a nightmare, it would be every single night. Ever since the widow tried to kidnap me, I hadn't had one full night of sleep. My insides churned just as much as the lake on the cusp of a storm.

I felt as if my very life were on the cusp of a storm.

"Wanna talk about it?" He cajoled, kissing the side of my neck.

I turned my cheek toward him, taking the solace he offered.

"No," I whispered.

His chin settled on my shoulder, and he said nothing more.

We stood there for a while, silent, gazing out across the lake. My stare always went to Rumor Island. I became more curious about it with every passing day.

Part of me was terrified of that place, but the other part wanted to go there.

Even in the darkness, I could make out the outline of the ominous suspended patch of land. The distinct shape it made was undeniable, even in the dark. If anything, it was darker there, as if it were shrouded by evil, disguised only by daylight.

"Let's go back to bed," he murmured, fingertips caressing my stomach. "I'll warm you up."

I allowed him to draw me backward, away from the railing. As I went, a disruption in the inky night stopped me my tracks.

There was a light.

It bobbed around in the air, almost like a firefly on a warm summer night. It wasn't summer and there were no fireflies out.

Even if there were, I wouldn't be able to see one at such a distance.

I watched it moving, a golden orb traveling through the shadows.

I squinted, wondering if perhaps my imagination was playing tricks on me. If maybe I was still dreaming, yet to awaken.

"Baby," Eddie whispered, nuzzling the side of my neck again. "C'mon."

My eyes drifted shut for a moment, the sound of his voice an aphrodisiac. I smiled, loving the way it felt to be in his arms.

Eddie swept me off the ground, cradling me against him. Before carrying me back into the house, I craned my neck around to glance back one last time toward the water, to seek out the floating light.

It was gone.

As though it hadn't even been there at all.

CHAPTER TWO

EDWARD

Time is its own type of currency, universal in value, and once it's spent, it can never be earned back.

Twelve years ago, it seemed time was on my side. Some moments, hell, some days I wished away to get to the next, to the better.

Then Sadie disappeared, and the time I spent living and dreaming screeched to a sudden halt. Though time continued to pass, spent right from my account, I sat in limbo.

A man who sits waiting becomes a victim of time.

Waiting, wondering, blaming… things that make time feel more like a burden than a blessing.

Now that I was no longer a boy, I understood time was priceless, not guaranteed. Some people were richly blessed with it, but for others, time ran out too fast.

None of us knows our wealth. Only the universe knows, and the universe is the best secret keeper there will ever be.

Maybe that was why now, in the back of my mind, I heard a clock ticking away, counting down the seconds, reminding me I wasn't waiting anymore and time was speeding up.

It didn't matter how much the universe would give me; it would never be enough.

My life before Amnesia hadn't been bad. On the contrary. My life was pretty charmed. Born into a family business, two parents who were almost old-fashioned in this day in age because they remained in love. Our small town, while suffocating and cumbersome at times, was also a safety net and relief when I needed it most.

Here in Lake Loch, I had friends. Family. A job I actually liked and that paid enough for me to live on the lake and gradually fix up my tiny house into a place I would never want to leave.

But…

Something had always been missing. Someone.

The night Sadie vanished, she took a part of me, too. When she was lost in that lake, in many ways, I had been, too.

I felt that missing piece, that chunk carved right out of me, endlessly. I hid it after a while, covered it with my dimples, curly hair, and charming smile. People didn't want to see my emptiness, even though I had a feeling some knew it was there.

That missing piece was back, though. It walked around outside my body in the form of a woman. I didn't feel empty anymore; I was consumed.

Consumed with love and lust and energy.

The second I fished Amnesia out of the lake's greedy clutches, my world began to grow complete, and the ticking of the clock increased.

Maybe that was why I was tired of waiting. I'd already spent too much time waiting for my life to start.

Truth was my life started long ago. Even when it felt it was on pause, life still played.

I was just ready to participate again.

Not just ready… *willing.*

Whatever the widow told her that night in the hospital, whatever words the crazy woman hurled at her while still somehow in her catatonic state, were like the swell of a wave on a stormy night. Pushing and pulling Amnesia to and away from me. Making her cling in certain moments but drift away in others.

I hated it.

I was a patient man, but my patience was wearing thin.

Not necessarily with her, but with the situation. How much more would Amnesia have to go through? What if I lost her again, this time forever?

The nightmares that woke her almost nightly were proof she was haunted. But she didn't want to talk. She wouldn't. Instead, it stayed rolled up inside her like a message trapped in a bottle. Floating… drifting through a sea of what she couldn't remember and the flashes of what she could.

I couldn't make it better; that much I knew. Still, I yearned to try.

I wanted these clouds gone, the ominous storm to vanish. Time was precious, and I was greedy. Now that I had Amnesia, I wanted as much time with her as possible. And I wanted her to be able to enjoy it, too.

Is she really Amnesia, though... or is she Sadie?

I told myself it didn't matter, but the question was always there. I'd been so convinced it was her, then changed my mind... And now I was stuck somewhere in between, wondering like everyone else.

It gave me some sort of insight on what it must be like to have amnesia, to not know anything about yourself. The woman I loved was a riddle.

The thought made me guilty.

Amnesia had no more control than I did.

I was frustrated. I wanted her to open up to me. To trust me enough to tell me whatever it was that gave her nightmares and put that faraway look in her eyes on an almost daily basis.

To me, those were stolen moments. Time that would never be given back. Taken from her, taken from me.

I was tired of people taking from us. I wanted to fight back. The thing was I couldn't fight until she told me exactly what I was up against.

So I continued to wait.

It had been over a week since that night the widow tried to haul my girl out into the secretive waters. Amnesia was a little more withdrawn than before. It pained me, but I tried not to push. Seemed to me I shouldn't apply to much pressure to something with a crack in it.

Instead, I just loved her, tried to be there... tried to bide my time.

Sometimes it was harder than milking an elephant, but then others, like right now, it was simple as pie.

Beneath the blankets, Am shifted, and instinctively my body followed. We lay spooned together, me curled around her. She fit into me like that missing piece I spoke of earlier, the final piece of a puzzle, except she was the final piece of *me*.

The thick waves of her light-colored hair brushed across the lower half of my face, tickling my nose, and if I were a mouth breather, they'd likely be trying to floss my teeth.

Good thing I wasn't a mouth breather.

I didn't move away, though. Instead, I just wiggled my nose until it no longer tickled, pulling her in tighter along my body.

She sighed softly, and my lower belly quivered with the low sound. Automatically, my hips rocked forward, pressing against her round ass.

I should have let her sleep. She'd been up again last night. Waking up alone was nearly the worst alarm clock a guy could ever have. Reaching for your girl. Coming up with air… After everything that happened?

Hell to the no.

I wasn't surprised to find her outside, though I hated when she went out there at night alone. I was drawn to the lake, sometimes desperately, but even so, I knew it wasn't always safe.

Odd to feel this was where I belonged—where *we* belonged—yet have the kind of history with the shore that would drive most away.

She was just as drawn to Lake Loch as I was, something else I often suspected was a telling clue to her true identity.

Her warm, supple ass pressed against me, wiggled, and all early morning ponderings fled my brain like cockroaches beneath a kitchen light. A low groan rumbled deep in my throat, vibrating into her neck as I nuzzled against her.

A soft sound of appreciation permeated the bedroom. Her hand stretched up and behind her, fingers delving into the hair on the back of my head and flexing until they were good and tangled.

Using my chin, I scratched lightly over her neck until her hair was pushed aside, then fastened my lips against her skin with soft enthusiasm. Her chin tilted against the pillow, and I sucked deeper, pulling her satiny skin past my lips to massage it with my tongue.

My hips moved again, rocking into her ass, again and again, creating a slow rhythm that my lips matched against her throat. My cock was stiff between us. The more it brushed against her, the harder it became.

Still gripping my head, Am twisted her upper body, turning her face so our lips could collide. We kissed deeply, as if we'd been apart weeks instead of right beside each other, only parted by a few hours of sleep.

My hunger for her never waned. It only grew like an insatiable craving. My palm dragged down her body and over her side to clamp onto her hip. Using gentle pressure, I held her lower half in place as I continually rocked into her ass, my tongue getting to know her mouth all over again.

It didn't take long for her to wiggle against me, which flared my already lit fuse into a full-on inferno. Releasing her hip, I pushed up the hem of her T-shirt, allowing my hand to slide between her legs. Her core was warm, the fabric of her panties felt damp, and the second my fingers stroked over the space between her thighs, her legs quivered.

After a few tugs, Am's hand was free of my bedhead, and she reached between us, grasping the waistband of my boxers and giving them a tug.

She didn't have to say anything else. I knew exactly what she wanted.

Pulling my hand out from between her thighs was maddening, but I did it, hurrying to shove the boxers down just enough so my rod could spring free.

Amnesia wiggled against my cock again, her sweet ass sending jolts of pleasure rocking through my entire lower half. With a moan, my teeth scraped over her shoulder, tugging at the T-shirt covering her skin.

One of her legs lifted, my hips surged forward, and my cock slid between her thighs. My length lay along her core, resting along her opening, my head brushing against the area near her throbbing clit.

Her leg dropped, effectively trapping me between her thighs. Her butt wiggled, the action causing the soft fabric of her panties to brush over my head.

Dipping my hand beneath the hem of her shirt, my fingers trailed across her abs, crawled up her ribcage, and teased the underside of her breast. She pushed against me again, and my hips rose to meet hers.

Palming her bare breast, I tweaked her nipple until it was hard and she arched into my palm. My tongue slid along her ear while I massaged the flesh, and the sound of her increased breathing filled the room.

My heart hammered beneath my ribs, so hard she could probably feel it against her back. I hoped she could feel it. After all, it beat for her.

"Am," I crooned against her ear, leaving her breast and moving down.

"Yes," she said. "Yes."

Impatient, I didn't bother pushing her onto her back and yanking down the panties. Instead, my fingers delved between her thighs, yanking the fabric to the side.

My dick was met by her slick moisture, and I nearly growled against her back. Am lifted her leg, tilting her hips so I would have the access I desired.

I slid into her, and her body went languid against the mattress. I wrapped her in both my arms, held her tight against me, and made love to her from behind.

Her hand found mine and squeezed just a little tighter with every thrust.

"Okay?" I whispered, breathless, against her.

Her response was to rock against me, pushing my dick deeper into her heat.

I lost it a little then, pumping into her with abandon.

Am reached around, palmed my ass cheek, and spurred me on.

My breathing turned ragged. The climax built inside me until my lower abs shook with the need to let it all go. I wasn't ready, though. I didn't want to go alone. I wanted her to tumble over that edge with me.

My hand slid down the front of her body as I pumped into her from behind. Using some of her own liquid, I swirled my finger around her clit, then rolled it between two fingers.

Her body tightened instantly. My hips had to surge forward for me to stay inside.

My name fell from her lips. I smiled into her hair.

"With me," I told her, pushing deep and rubbing against her sweet spot.

Her body started to shudder, and I let go. We exploded together, our bodies shaking as one, as I held her close through the shattering climax.

Soon, we came back down, and she wiggled until I let her roll to face me. Freckles scattered over her nose and cheeks; full eyebrows framed out her very expressive brown eyes. Her lower lip was red, and I knew it was because she'd been biting it while I'd made love to her.

I brushed the hair off her cheek, leaned forward, and kissed her fully on the mouth.

She smiled when I pulled back. My heart had never felt so full.

These were the kind of moments I wanted to spend my time on. When I was with Amnesia, it didn't matter it was time I would never get back, because it was currency well spent.

"Move in with me." I hadn't planned to say that. The request was a complete surprise.

Okay, maybe not a surprise. It wasn't as if I hadn't thought about moving Am in here. I thought about it a lot, but I knew the timing was all wrong.

Screw time and what it dictated. I wanted her.

Her eyes widened, a little of the sex-induced haze cleared. "What?"

"Move in. I want to wake up to you every single day."

Her lips curled up. That soft expression returned. "Really?"

I made a show of rolling my eyes. "Duh."

"Duh?" she teased.

I shrugged against the pillows. "It's all that reality TV you make me watch."

Giggling, she twirled a few curls lying over my ear. As she twisted, she sighed. "I wish I could."

"Oh, baby, you can."

Her eyes grew sad for a moment, a wistful smile tugging at her lips. "No, I can't. Not right now."

"Why?" I demanded, surly.

She tugged my hair. "I don't want to do something you might regret."

A rude sound erupted from my mouth. "The only thing I regret is not asking sooner."

"It's just not a good time right now."

I had to ask. There was no stopping the question. "If I had asked you last week, what would you have said then?"

Her eyes skirted away, her body language changed. I'd hit the nail on the head. It didn't feel good to be right. In fact, it was fucking painful.

Her voice was soft, maybe because her face was now turned away. "A lot has happened in a week."

Gently, I reached out, grasping her chin to carefully bring her face back around. "Nothing has changed the way I feel. Can you say the same?"

Her eyes widened, so much so the whites around the brown orbs of her irises were on full display. "Of course I can." Her voice cracked as if my words pierced something inside her that was already raw.

"Hey," I murmured, palming her hip and urging her back around to face me. I felt like a complete dick. Questioning the way she felt about me wasn't what I meant to do, but that's the way it came out, and now I'd made it seem as though the way she showed her love wasn't enough.

It was enough.

"Am, I'm sorry." I began, tugging her fully against my body. The way her nose nuzzled against my chest caused my throat to constrict. "I know you love me. I just got frustrated."

The words sounded stupid to my ears. Useless. Some words were more powerful than others, and sometimes it seemed the words that hurt weighed more than any apology.

"I do love you," she said, the softness of her mouth brushing over my skin as she spoke. Her voice was muffled, but I understood every word. Amnesia pulled back, enough to tilt her head up and look me in the eyes. I still saw traces of hurt there, but more than that wariness. "I don't even think I can explain how much you mean to me." Her voice faded. "I just—"

"Stop," I cut her off. "You don't have to say anything else." I rubbed my palm over her shoulder, hoping it was a soothing gesture. "You've been through so much shit. It's literally not even funny. And it's even less fair of me to push you to move in here when you aren't ready."

"I wish I was," she whispered. Her throat worked to swallow.

"The second you are, just say the word. The offer never expires."

The guarded veil dropped over her eyes again. Amnesia somehow convinced herself I was one day not going to want her. That there was something out there with the capability to change the beating of my heart.

Or…

Am wasn't the one who convinced herself. Someone else did it for her.

More specifically, that old bat lying unresponsive in the hospital.

Fuck not pushing. Fuck biding my time. If that bitch was somehow manipulating my girl's head, even in her "catatonic" state, I was going to put a stop to it.

PS: I used quotations around catatonic because, let's get real, the psycho was probably faking.

"What did she say to you?" I demanded, though I tried to do it gently.

Amnesia's eyes moved away. "Who?"

"Am," I growled.

She sighed. "I—"

The doorbell rang.

I swore to all that's holy I was going to rip that ringer right off the side of the house. And then I was going to beat whoever it was that pushed on it with the broken pieces.

"Why do people always show up when we're in bed?" Am wondered.

I made a rude sound. "Because people are assholes."

Am giggled, and the sound lifted the darkest of the black settling over my mood. "Or maybe it's because we spend too much time in here."

I screwed up my face in horror. "I should make you eat a banana for saying that."

She cringed.

The doorbell rang again. Repeatedly.

Instead of jumping off the mattress, I wrapped an arm across her waist and kissed her loud and sloppily all over her cheek. Her laughter floated out the door behind me as I finally stormed toward the front of the house.

"This better be good!" I roared and flung it open.

"What the hell, man!" someone roared back.

"Robbie?" I asked, even though he was standing right in front of me.

"Are you still in bed?" He scoffed, taking in my undressed state and glowering.

"What are you, my mother?" I retorted.

"If I was, I'd be half blind, because, dude…" He glanced down. "You need to adjust your junk."

I glanced down and frowned. "I already adjusted it."

"Made you look!" He announced and smacked me on the shoulder. His palm made a slapping sound against my skin.

"What are you, in fifth grade?" Even as I asked, a grin tugged at my lips.

"Those were the days." He reminisced. "Cindy Vans was so hot for me."

I rolled my eyes. "She still is."

He smirked. "I know."

"What the fuck are you doing here?" I asked. As fun as this was, I had better things to do than shoot the shit with him while I stood around in my boxers.

He laid a hand over his chest. "You wound me."

"You should seek counseling." I deadpanned and started to shut the door in his face.

His palm thumped against the wood when he slammed it down to push the door wide again. "You stood me up."

"Eddie?" Amnesia's voice called out from behind me. Both Robbie and I spun around as though we'd been caught doing something we weren't supposed to.

"Um, whoa." Robbie whistled below his breath behind me.

In the center of my back, I felt my shoulder blades slam together. I glanced around, giving him a hard look. "You better keep those eyes up." I warned.

"You think so low of me."

"That's because I've known you for a long ass time."

"And this is why it's so painful you stood me up today." He made a sound like he might cry. "On our annual date day."

Shit. "That's today?"

"What's today?" Amnesia asked.

"Second Tuesday of every October." Robbie tapped on the pretend watch around his wrist.

I cursed. "Sorry, man. I haven't been able to keep up with time lately."

His eyes went past me toward Am. "You have a good reason."

I glanced back around to see her watching him curiously. I sighed. "Am, Robbie. Robbie, Am."

Robbie let himself into my house, across the living room, and shoved his hand out to Am. "Nice to meet ya, finally."

I growled. "Do not even think about touching her when she's not wearing pants."

Amnesia gasped. Robbie laughed.

"What happens on the second Tuesday of every October?" she asked.

"Paintball," Robbie answered.

I watched her mind work, brow furrowing. Seconds later, she looked at me. "What's paintball?"

Robbie and I looked at each other.

He grinned. "Oh, this is going to be fun."

CHAPTER THREE

AMNESIA

"This is ridiculous." I said, still not even sure what we were doing.

Eddie paused in his task, the rattling of the plastic bag silenced when he stopped to give me his trademark grin. "But fun, yeah?"

His smile was infectious, and even though I was standing in the middle of some cornfield while he strapped a plastic grocery bag over my casted wrist, I found myself beaming just as wide. Though I knew my grin wasn't as ornery. Or able to make people literally stop and glance my way.

People actually did that. The more I went out in public with Eddie, the more and more I realized just how drawn to him everyone was.

His chuckle was low and deep as he returned to making sure my cast was completely covered.

"Can I even play paintball with one hand?" I asked, entirely skeptical.

He tilted his head to the side. "Can't wait to find out."

I mock gasped.

He threw back his head and laughed.

The fact I seemed so clueless about this so-called sport only made Eddie and Robbie more intent to bring me along, though I tried really hard to get out of it. Okay, not so hard. Just a little. I'd probably follow Eddie just about anywhere.

I could tell he wanted to go by the way the blue of his eyes sparkled with mischief and the wide smile Robbie wore when he tried to explain what paintball was.

Basically, it was when a bunch of people dressed up in old clothes, ran around a field, and literally shot balls of paint at each other. Of course, the object was to not get hit with said balls, but when you did, you were instantaneously splattered with paint.

For some reason, I didn't see this as something a lot of women did. Yet here I was, dressed in a pair of jeans, sneakers, and some old Loch Gen shirts. Oh, and let's not forget the uber-attractive grocery bags being duck taped around my arm.

"That should do it," Eddie said, admiring his taping skills.

I felt the sharp edge of my teeth sink into my lower lip. He laughed softly, swung an arm around me, and pulled me into his side. "I got you, Am. If I didn't think you could do it, I would never have brought you."

"I trust you," I replied.

His thumb and forefinger grasped just beneath my chin, lifting my face. The intensity of his eyes when they connected with mine sent a jolt of energy all the way to the bottom of my feet. Instead of using words, his face lowered, capturing my lips with his. I pushed up onto my tiptoes, our mouths locked in a sweet yet fierce kiss.

"There's no kissing in paintball," Robbie announced, coming up behind us.

Against my lips, Eddie smiled. "Rules are there are no rules." He countered, lifting his head.

Robbie made a sound, shifting all the stuff piled in his arms. "Here's the rest of the gear." He let it all fall at his feet, giving me a smile. "Better suit up. Times a'wastin'!"

I watched Eddie and Robbie "suit up" as though they were preparing for war. Over their old, already paint-splattered clothes, they dressed in what looked like sensible onesies. The kind auto mechanics wore to protect their clothes from grease.

I don't know how I knew what auto mechanics wore. Seemed that was some odd detail my brain shouldn't identify, right? I was beginning to accept that as my reality, though—my brain filled with a ton of useless information and nothing about me.

Once they zipped up the suits, they strapped on wide belts with a bunch of canister-looking things hanging off them. Eddie winked when he pulled up the hood attached to the suit and covered all his dark, spirally curls. Once it was tied beneath his chin (seriously, how did he still look sexy in that getup?), he pulled a helmet with a full-on face mask over his head. It had thin vents so I could hear his voice when he talked.

"Is this war or a game?" I asked, dubiously looking between them.

"What's the difference?" Robbie cracked.

"I'll help you," Eddie said, chivalrously holding out the suit for me to step in. Once I was dressed just as horribly as the men, they both laughed, the sounds muffled by the headgear.

"What?" I said, noting they were staring at me.

"You look like you're about to fall over," Robbie answered.

"Not all of us can look like Rambo."

How do I know who Rambo is?

Robbie laughed again. "Dude, I like you."

"I'm not so sure about you yet."

"I grow on people," he remarked, and I was pretty sure he winked at me behind the mask.

"Is that too much weight on your hips?" Eddie said, drawing my attention as he stepped forward and reached for the canisters filled with what I now knew was my ammunition.

"I think it's okay," I said.

I saw the frown in his voice. "Maybe I should carry some of it for you." Before I could say anything else, he was relieving me of my paintball stash and putting it on his own belt.

"What the hell is this?"

Eddie made a rude sound. "She's on my team." He reminded his friend, as if that somehow made it all right.

Maybe it did, because Robbie didn't argue.

We stood at the edge of what I thought of as the battlefield. Before us, other people ran around, and the sound of paintball guns going off and people squealing echoed all around the field. Apparently, this wasn't just any old paintball game.

This was Lake Loch's fall edition. That meant the barricades and walls to hide behind were giant hay bales all covered in bright-colored paint. Not only that, but they created a maze-type play zone, so not only did you have to worry about not getting shot, but also about not getting turned around.

There were large pumpkins sitting around everywhere, all of them splattered with paint. Some of them had actual holes in them. When we first came in, there was a tent where all the gear was rented as well as a smaller tent beside it with apple cider and donuts.

The air today was crisp and almost cold, not that I could feel it with all this gear piled on me. Not an ounce of my skin was actually exposed… well, except for my *one* hand.

"Just stay near me," Eddie said, drawing my attention. "We play until we run out of ammo."

"He means the balls," Robbie explained. He just wanted to say balls.

Eddie snickered inside his helmet. It was nice to see this side of him. More carefree almost. I wondered why he never mentioned Robbie to me before. "We're red; he's blue."

"I'm coming for you, Sa—" Robbie began, but Eddie moved so fast it caught us all off guard. He shoved his friend back with a full body check. Robbie stumbled, but didn't fall.

"Her name is Amnesia," Eddie growled.

Robbie didn't shove back or even seem mad over Eddie's actions. Instead, his shoulders slumped a little. "I'm sorry, for real. It was an accident."

Eddie's shoulders were so tense he practically vibrated. He wasn't going to let his friend off so easily.

Rushing forward, the canisters banging against each other as I went, I hurried to say. "It's fine! No big deal."

Did Robbie know Sadie, too? He must think I'm her.

"Am." Robbie came forward.

I held up my hand. "Don't apologize again."

We all stood there awkwardly, a few tense moments floating in the air. I hated it. It always came back around to this… I wanted a break. I needed one.

Eddie, too.

I bent down and picked up a nearby gun. "Who's going to show me how to shoot this thing."

"You're holding it backward," Eddie informed me.

"Like this?" I adjusted.

"Sure, if you want to shoot yourself." Robbie cracked. "FYI, I wouldn't recommend that. From that range, you'd be hurting for days."

Eddie materialized beside me, gently relieving me of the gun, spinning it around and demonstrating how to hold it.

"Does it really hurt to get hit?" I asked.

"It stings." He glanced at me through the helmet. "Don't worry, baby. No one's going to hit you today."

"Isn't that the point, though?" I wondered.

"The point is to shoot *other* people." After finishing his demonstration, Eddie handed me the gun.

"You and Robbie do this all the time?"

"Not as much as we used to."

"How long have you been friends?" I asked, taking the weapon.

"Since kindergarten."

I paused, swinging around to face him. "That's a lot of history!" I couldn't even imagine… To have memories that went that far back. "You're lucky to have a friend that long."

Something passed behind his eyes, but it was unreadable.

"C'mon, let's do this!" Robbie called.

After they both gave me a few more pointers, the three of us stepped out onto the field, and the game began.

I learned something about myself. Something to add to the list of things about me.

I sucked at paintball.

In all likelihood, I sucked at *all* sports, but I wasn't yet ready to put that broad of a statement on my list.

Also, I didn't get it. We literally ran from hay bale to hay bale, diving behind them for "cover" while balls of paint flew at our heads. Eddie and Robbie took this game seriously, though.

It was almost funny. Actually, it *was* funny. At one point, I started laughing at them and nearly got my head blasted with a random paint bullet. Eddie stepped in front of me, though, shielding me with his own body and taking the hit.

His body jerked in front of me when it hit him, and a sick feeling wormed into my belly, making me lightheaded for a moment. But then he was there, wrapping his arm at my waist and tugging me behind the next blockade.

Even though I stunk at the game, it was still kind of fun. I got some shots off. None of them hit anything, but that was okay with me. It was nice just being outside, listening to the guys trash talking each other, and listening to everyone else laughing and screaming around us.

It almost felt normal.

Like a normal fall day in Maine. Like maybe these were the kind of days I missed when I'd been missing... the days Sadie should have had.

You aren't Sadie.

Eddie made a loud whooping sound, bringing me out of my dark thoughts. "That was the money shot!" He celebrated. "You see that, baby?"

I blinked, looking up from where I leaned against the hay.

"Am?" he said, suddenly serious. His body bent close, our eyes connecting. "You okay?"

"Of course," I said, offering a smile he probably couldn't see. "Nice shot!"

The corners of his eyes crinkled with his smile. He was covered in paint. Most of it was blue. Some of it was yellow and green, because at one point we all teamed up against another team.

We all teamed up = Eddie and Robbie ran in front of me and let me make poorly aimed shots that hit no one.

"Dude, I'm out of ammo," Robbie said, coming around to where we stood.

"Good game." Eddie offered his fist and they bumped them together.

Robbie glanced at me, his low whistle echoing beneath his helmet. "Didn't even get hit once."

"No one wanted a piece of this," I said, tapping my chest with the gun I was holding.

They laughed.

How rude.

"C'mon, we're done." Eddie reached for my gun, and I handed it over. The three of us wandered through the path until it opened up into the field. As we were walking toward the rental tent, my mind wandered once again to Sadie and if Robbie had known her, too.

Something hard slammed into me from behind. A sound erupted out of my throat as I pitched forward. A sharp stinging sensation exploded across my lower back, an ache forming beneath it.

"No!" The word ripped roughly from my throat, and for endless seconds, the world as I knew it slipped away, another one taking its place.

The sharp sting of leather cut into my back, making my eyes water and ears fill with the distinct sound of my ragged breathing. Don't cry. Don't cry. He likes it when you cry. *Another slice of pain slashed through me and my knees buckled.*

"This is all your fault, Sadie. All your fault."

I would have crumpled to the ground, but Eddie lunged forward and caught me, tucking me right into his chest. "Am," he called. His voice seemed so far away. "Amnesia."

Sunlight broke over the memory that had plunged me into darkness. His voice that had seemed lightyears away was right here now, as close as his body. "Eddie."

"What happened?"

Pushing back the horrible memory, I swallowed. Suddenly, my mouth felt desert dry. "Something hit me." I frowned. Or maybe it hadn't. Maybe it was just a memory.

Before I could voice my confusion, Eddie placed me on my feet, and he and Robbie glanced at my back, which actually was still throbbing. I craned my neck over my shoulder, seeing a splatter of bright green covering the back of my suit.

"Oh, it was just a paintball," I said, relieved. Being shot with a paintball was much better than the memory it unknowingly induced.

"What. The. Fuck?" Eddie growled. His voice was wild and untamed, dangerous even.

The sound of laughter and victorious crooning erupted nearby. "Nice shot!" someone called out.

"Bull's-eye," a man yelled. He was holding a gun in his hand, loaded with green balls.

"Did you just take a cheap shot at my girl?" Eddie confronted him, stepping away from me.

"Shouldn't turn your back on the game." The man tsked.

"It was an unarmed woman, dick face," Robbie yelled. "She was leaving the game."

He shrugged. "Still points for me."

Everything happened at once the second the idiot spoke. Eddie ripped the helmet off his head. It made a loud thumping sound against the hard ground when he threw it down. Crouching low, he scooped up both the guns he'd dropped to catch me when I stumbled.

Holding one in each hand, he opened fire, shooting ball after ball right at the man who'd shot me. The sound of the gun releasing the "bullets" filled the air.

"Hey!" the man roared, stepping back as ball after ball hit his body. "Fuck! Ow!" He moved back, but Eddie kept going, walking calmly, almost as though he were strolling, but with eagle-like focus as he fired over and over.

One gun ran out of pellets. He tossed it down without missing a beat, still firing with the other.

The man on the receiving end fell back, chest heaving. Eddie walked right up beside him, staring down.

"Fuck, man, I'm going to have bruises for a month!" he rasped.

"Points for me," Eddie said, giving him a hard look.

I stared in shock. His dark hair was wild around his head, the very ends fluttering around when the wind blew. At the base of his neck, some of the strands were damp with sweat and stuck out. His profile looked to be carved from granite, his jaw locked, the muscle protruding. Even though he was no longer using the gun, his eyes were still firing bullets.

He bent down, shoving his face close to the man. I saw his friends hovering nearby, unsure if they should intervene.

One looked ready to jump in. Robbie noted it, too. He made a sound beneath his breath, caught the man's eye, and simply said, "I wouldn't if I were you."

"You owe my girl an apology," Eddie spat.

"It's a fucking game!" the man roared, beginning to sit up.

Using his foot against his shoulder, Eddie pushed him back down. He spoke low, so low I didn't hear what it was.

Whatever it was definitely was effective.

"I'm sorry!" the man yelled.

Eddie stared at him a second longer, the tick in his jaw still strong, before relenting and stepping away.

Everyone within range of the scene was watching now, silent. Even Robbie, the guy who had a wisecrack for everything.

I couldn't tear my eyes off Eddie. The power he exuded was unmatched. There was most definitely solid steel beneath his friendly, easygoing appearance.

When he was almost to my side, his eyes slipped to mine. The glittering blue shards softened, and a small smile tugged at the corner of his mouth. I felt my own eyes widen. He winked.

He winked at me. Went from killer to cuddly in two seconds flat.

I was still trying to recover when he reached my side. His arm slipped around my waist, holding me firmly, but without any force. "C'mon, baby, time to go."

"We better not get banned," Robbie cracked. "This is a tradition. Can't mess with that."

"We aren't going to get banned," Eddie retorted, his voice dry.

"It was just a paintball," I said, still trying to catch up. "That's what we were here to do."

"Men who shoot women in the back are assholes," Eddie declared. "He deserved what he got."

Robbie made a sound of agreement.

After we stripped off all the gear, Eddie piled it in his arms and glanced at Robbie. "Stay here with Am. I'll turn this in."

The second Eddie walked off, I turned my full stare on his friend. "How come he never mentioned you?" I blurted out.

Surprise flickered across his face. Then he glanced in the direction Eddie went. I waved my hand in front of his face, drawing his attention once more.

"Maybe he didn't want the competition." Robbie wagged his eyebrows.

I rolled my eyes.

"A lot's been going on." His voice turned serious. "Maybe he thought it was too much too soon."

I cut right to the chase. "You knew Sadie."

"Yeah," he said, glancing down at his shoes. "I knew her."

"Do you think I'm her?" I asked.

His eyes widened. Once again, he looked back in the direction Eddie went. As though he were afraid to say too much.

I sighed and reminded him, "You almost called me by her name."

Robbie cocked his head to the side. "So you don't think you're her?" He answered my question with his own.

I shrugged. "I'd like to get your opinion, you know, from someone who once knew her."

Robbie stared at me for a moment. "You mean from someone who isn't as biased as your boyfriend?"

It was my turn to shrug. "Maybe."

"All right, I'll play," Robbie mused, his dark eyes settling on me. I felt them measure me in a way he hadn't before. After a moment, he relented. "Could be."

"That's all you got?" I said, disappointed.

"Sorry, honey, I left my crystal ball at home today."

"Funny," I noted, but I was pretty letdown. I thought maybe Robbie would see something or recognize something no one else did.

"You do look like her in a lot of ways, but it's been over ten years… People change, especially from teens to adulthood."

"Yeah," I answered, forlorn. I knew that, but it wasn't enough to keep me from hoping.

"You seriously have no idea? No memories at all that would even give a clue?"

"I have a few brief memories… But it's hard to trust my own mind right now."

"Eddie seems convinced." Robbie pointed out. "He'd know better than anyone."

I glanced up, a little surprised. "How close are you and Eddie?"

"I don't stalk the guy, but I mean, we're tight. Been through some shit together and still managed to keep it together. That's sort of why we do this paintball every year."

"Eddie isn't completely convinced I'm Sadie. He didn't tell you that?" I probed.

"Nope. Haven't talked to him much since you washed into town." He cleared his throat. "He's been pretty busy."

"What am I missing here?" I pressed, unable to shake the feeling there was something between Eddie and his friend I didn't know.

Robbie averted his gaze.

"You never came to the hospital during all the months I was there." My voice turned thoughtful. "He never once mentioned you…"

Robbie remained mum, but the way he shifted told me I was onto something.

"I'll just ask Eddie," I said, starting in the direction he went off in.

"Wait." Robbie caught my wrist. I glanced back at him.

"I was the one…" He began, his voice dropping.

"The one?"

"The one who dared Eddie to go to Rumor Island, the reason he and Sadie got in the boat that night. The reason she—maybe you—disappeared."

CHAPTER FOUR

EDWARD

Tension stole the crisp feel from the air when I stepped out of the rental tent. Automatically, my eyes sought out Am. The second I found her, my pace quickened.

She and Robbie were standing close as if they were having some kind of intense conversation. Not the kind I would expect them to be having in the center of a paintball field.

Golden strands of her short hair floated back away from her face, waving to me as I moved closer. Robbie's eyes lifted, saw me coming, causing them to widen. He looked like a deer caught in headlights, blindsided by whatever Am was saying.

That's why he was single. He talked a good game, but he couldn't even handle Am for ten minutes while I returned all our gear.

I would have laughed if his stare didn't appear so dire.

"Eddie," he called, a little relief in his voice.

Amnesia turned abruptly. Briefly, our stares connected, and then she turned back to Robbie. "I guess that explains why I haven't seen you until today," she told him.

"What?" I asked, looking curiously between the two.

"Robbie's the one who dared you that night."

My eyes flew to his. "What the hell, man?"

Robbie looked horrified. "She's relentless!"

"Hardly." She scoffed.

Robbie nodded emphatically. "It was like the Spanish Inquisition up in here!"

Amnesia laughed. "I've never met anyone so dramatic. You should be on reality TV."

Robbie drew back as though she'd insulted him.

I reached out and patted his shoulder. "Relax. Reality TV is her favorite shit to watch."

His expression smoothed, a cocky glint coming into his eyes. "Yeah?"

"Definitely." Am nodded. Since Robbie was suddenly proud of himself, she turned to me. "You didn't say anything."

"We're supposed to be taking it slow, remember? I'm not supposed to overload you with too much information too soon."

Robbie leaned close to her. "Told ya."

"So you all were friends?" Am asked. "You two and Sadie?"

They nodded.

"And you made the dare."

Robbie nodded. "Biggest regret of my life."

"Mine, too." I cleared my throat. "Doing it, I mean."

Amnesia turned toward Robbie. "So that was the stuff you said you guys had been through?"

"Jesus, Rob, did you tell her our entire life story in the five minutes I was gone?" I groaned.

"It was like ten, and I'm telling you she's intense."

Amnesia laughed.

Or maybe Robbie carried around a shit ton of guilt just like me and was too drawn to the chance to clear his conscience with the girl who might have been the victim of our dumb games that night.

I felt her curious eyes, the questions she asked without even saying a word. I couldn't *not* explain; it was too late for that now. Sidling up closer to her side, my palm hooked around her hip. Her body angled into mine, though she was still between Robbie and me.

"I hated him for a long time," I said, recalling how angry I'd been those first few months after Sadie vanished. "I was mad at everyone, but Robbie… I was mad at him the most."

Robbie nodded. I saw the memory in his eyes. It couldn't have been easy to be so young and the target of so much malice.

"I didn't mean it." Robbie's voice was hoarse. "We were just dumb kids. I thought we were just being harmless."

Am reached out to him. "You were."

He looked down at where she touched him, so innocent in the way she tried to make him feel better.

The worst victim of all, more concerned with others than herself.

"I ruined lives that night. Maybe even cost one."

I paused, fully expecting Amnesia to tell him he hadn't, that she was right there, her life still intact.

She said nothing.

Instead, her eyes turned down, her voice remained silent.

"The town was really divided after Sadie… Some hated me; some hated Robbie… and some hated both of us," I told her.

"My parents almost moved us out of here," Robbie added.

"But they didn't?" Amnesia asked.

He rubbed his palm over the short buzz cut on his head. "No. This place was home. And I had to face what I did."

"We started getting in fights at school. The teachers would have to break us up."

Robbie's face held a ghost of a grin. "We spent a lot of time in the principal's office that first year."

I chuckled. "Sure did."

"But you're friends now," Amnesia said, trying to understand how we got here.

"The day of our last fight, our dads were called in to pick us up. The principal had suspension papers in her hands, but our dads had a different idea."

Robbie grinned and picked up the story. "They brought us out here to the annual fall paintball course, bought us a shit ton of paintballs, and told us to hammer each other."

"What?" Amnesia gasped.

Robbie and I grinned at the memory. "Two scrawny, pissed-off teenagers mad at everyone and especially each other…"

"We went at it," Robbie mused. "I had bruises for a month."

"Me, too." I reminisced.

"So you became friends again by shooting each other a million times with paintballs?" Amnesia wondered as though she were walking through the twilight zone.

"It was a start." Robbie nodded.

"Halfway through our war, these guys came into the field and came at us. We had no choice but to work together—either that or get our asses handed to us."

Robbie chuckled.

"What happened?" Amnesia asked.

"We held them off, and by the time we were done, we realized we made a better team than enemies."

"And we weren't so different after all. Both of us felt hella guilty for what happened that night. We both wished we could change what happened."

"So now you come play paintball every fall… to remember." Amnesia surmised, understanding in her tone.

I showed my teeth. "That and to hammer each other. Our dads were pretty smart," I said.

"Amnesia." Robbie spoke, drawing all her attention. She stepped forward, away from me, fully focusing on my friend. "I, uh… I just want to say I'm sorry. It's not enough, but…" He laid a hand over his chest, and I swallowed. I felt what he was feeling. So many times. That tightness in the chest was one of the most crippling feelings I'd ever known. "I have to say it. I regret that night so much. I know I said I wasn't sure if you're her or not, but on the chance you might be… please know I never meant for anything bad to happen."

Amnesia made a sound, as though his apology really meant something to her, and she pushed forward and wrapped her arms around him.

Robbie looked surprised at first, his eyes firing up to mine. I nodded, and he hugged her back.

"It's not your fault," she said, stepping back. Her arm stretched out behind her, her fingers seeking mine. I tangled ours together, and she smiled. "I don't think it's either of your fault what happened that night. And I honestly think Sadie believes the same."

After a beat of silence, Robbie announced, "Paintball is some damn therapeutic shit."

Am looked up at me, and I smiled. I kissed her forehead. I didn't think she understood exactly what she'd given both Robbie and me just then, but it was monumental.

CHAPTER FIVE

AMNESIA

Dr. Kline's office was basically a box of four walls and no windows. The lighting was always dim, and I always wondered if she did it because she thought it was relaxing or if it was so if she accidentally made a face over something one of her patients said, it would give her some cover.

There was a wire basket filled with glowing rocks sitting atop a wooden bookshelf near the door. They were salt rocks or something. She told me once they made for a calm environment and "cleansed" the energy in the room.

I thought they were ugly.

Of course, I didn't tell her that. That would just be mean. But as I sat on the leather loveseat that faced her desk during our many sessions, sometimes my mind would drift and I would wonder how something so ugly could make the room look and feel more pleasant.

I guess me not knowing was the reason I was the patient and she was the doctor.

I'd been talking to her since almost the day I woke from my coma. Dr. Kline knew just as much about me as I did—something I often thought of as disconcerting because we weren't even friends. She was nice enough. Kind and caring toward me.

I was her job. That really should have been a good thing, right? Because she could remain objective. But sometimes objectivity wasn't personal enough. Sometimes objectivity felt cold.

I looked at her now and realized she didn't care if I was Sadie or not. It wouldn't matter one way or the other to her. Either way, her job was to help me deal with it. And if I never found out…?

Wouldn't matter either.

I couldn't accept that. More and more, I felt as though I was going to crawl right out of my skin. The need to know occupied so much of my thoughts.

"You're very quiet today," Dr. Kline prompted.

"I have a lot on my mind."

"Such as?"

"Have you ever gone shopping and stepped out of the store and felt like you left something behind? Or on the way in to work suddenly wondered if you forgot to turn off the curling iron or stove? Or went to the office of another colleague and then, when you arrived, wondered why you'd come in there in the first place?"

Dr. Kline accepted my rambling and went with it. "Of course. That sort of thing happens a lot."

"It's maddening, isn't it? Trying remember what you might have left back in the store or if your curling iron was overheating or knowing you needed something from a co-worker, but not recalling exactly what."

"Yes, it can be quite maddening."

"That's how I feel. Every second of every day," I deadpanned.

She was silent a moment, then began her typical head-shrinker spiel. "I know it's quite frustrating,"

"Don't placate me," I snapped. "You have no idea what it's like to not know! To want to move on with your life—to actually *begin building* a life—but having to sit in a holding pattern because the life you want might not be yours to take."

"You feel like you're taking someone else's life?"

I tossed my hands up in the air. "I have no idea!"

"Because you don't know your true identity. You don't know if you're Sadie." Dr. Kline went on.

I nodded. "Yes."

Leaning back a little in the giant leather office chair behind her desk, the woman studied me. In front of her, the desktop computer was on, the blue light from the screen cast over her features, making her look somewhat garish.

"Does it really matter if you are? Who you were before your coma, that person isn't here anymore. You're just you now. You seemed excited before for a fresh start, a clean slate. What's changed? Why do you think it suddenly seems so crippling to not know?"

I bit down on the inside of my lip. I didn't want to say it.

"Wouldn't it be true that no matter who you were in the past, the life you are creating now and have been for the past few months would still be yours because you've been living it?"

Yes. Yes, to all that.

But also no.

"He won't want me," I whispered. I spoke so low it was practically just a tortured thought.

"What?" Dr. Kline asked, sitting forward, trying to hear.

I reworded my thoughts, speaking up. "If I'm not her, everything will change."

"You mean Eddie." She surmised, understanding.

I nodded. "He says it doesn't matter… but I think it does. If I'm not her, then I'm not the girl he's been waiting for the last twelve years."

"You think he only loves you because of who you may be?"

"I don't know," I said openly. It seemed awfully unfair to think such a thing about Eddie. I knew him. I knew he cared about me… so much.

But I also couldn't shake the way I felt. The way Widow West's words haunted me. *He doesn't love you.*

"Do you think the only thing about you that's worth loving is your name?"

"No," I said. I saw what she was doing. "But it's complicated."

"Yes. This is a very unique situation."

"Didn't you tell me a few weeks ago that Eddie decided you weren't Sadie? That the allergy to shellfish was proof you weren't her, and he didn't care. In fact…"

She went on. "I was here the night you both were brought in over a week ago. I heard him tell you he didn't care if you were Sadie or not."

I nodded. "I thought it was settled. But it's not."

"Do you think perhaps you're projecting your worries about being Sadie onto Eddie instead of turning them toward yourself?"

"That's a lot of shrink talk, Dr. Kline. Dumb it down for me."

She smothered a smile. "Maybe you worry what Eddie will think because it's easier than worrying about how *you* will feel if you aren't Sadie."

"If I'm not Sadie, then who am I?" I whispered.

"Do you want to be Sadie?"

I shrugged. "At least if I was, I would know where I came from."

"No other memories that might give you a clue?"

I shook my head adamantly and then thought about the brief, traumatizing memory I had at the paintball field. "No. I don't want to remember."

"But you want to know."

"Exactly."

"It's normal to feel as if you're being held back by things you can't remember."

"How do you know?" I challenged.

She blinked. "I guess I don't."

It was wrong of me, made me feel guilty, but I felt an inkling of satisfaction when she admitted that.

"What will change if you find out your past identity? Will your future change? Will who you are now change?"

My head was going to explode. I swore it was as though she wanted me to tell her the meaning of life.

"Finding out who I am..." I began and paused. "Will get rid of the nagging thoughts in my head. It will give me some peace."

"But will it change anything?"

It felt like it would, but in actuality? "Probably not." Then I changed my mind. "Unless Eddie still wants to search for answers about his long-lost love."

"I've been your doctor for many months now. I do my best to always stay objective and professional."

"Yes." I nearly groaned. "I know."

She sat forward. The light of the computer shifted behind her, changing the garish appearance into one more human. Softer. "But I am going to share something with you, an opinion, if you will."

"This is better than reality TV," I said, leaning forward.

She smiled. A genuine smile that lit up her eyes. "We really should talk about your reality TV addiction."

"I'm waiting." I reminded her.

"I have cautioned you about your relationship with Eddie."

"We haven't listened," I told her, flat. If she was about to give me her opinion of my relationship with him, I wasn't interested.

"I'm well aware," she mused. "However, I see the way he looks at you. I read body language and people for a living. He's in love with you, and I truly believe it won't matter to him if you're Sadie or not."

I sat back. The weight of her words anchored me in the chair. It felt good to hear her say that. It gave me some relief.

"Eddie was stuck for many years, wondering what-if. Thinking his chance at love was taken from him. Then you came along, and regardless of who you are, you showed him love was possible. In many ways, you gave him back his life."

I nodded. He'd pretty much told me the same.

"I still think you are entirely too dependent on each other," Dr. Kline said, slipping right back into shmucky doctor mode. I guessed that meant our "personal" moment was over.

"I still want to know." I admitted. "Maybe not because of Eddie... because of me." Because of Sadie. For Sadie.

"I just don't feel I'll ever really be able to move on until I know if I'm her... until I know what truly happened to me."

Dr. Kline was quiet a few moments. "I think I may have a way to find out." She moved forward, lifted the black receiver off the base on her desk, and punched in a phone number. A few seconds later, she spoke into it. "This is Dr. Kline. Could I speak to Don, please?"

Who the hell was Don?

"Don," she said warmly after what felt like an eternity of waiting. "How have you been?"

She chuckled at whatever he said, then cleared her throat. "I'm calling on behalf of a patient of mine. Amnesia. She—" Her voice cut off, and her eyes lifted to where I sat. "Yes. Yes, that's her."

"I was wondering if you still had records from twelve years ago?

"Ah, wonderful. Could I send her over, get your professional opinion after an exam? We'd like to get a definitive answer, as you can imagine it's been a difficult time."

My heart was beating hard, thudding against my chest so forcefully it made me short of breath. There was a way to find out if I was Sadie? Like for real? Why had no one said anything?

I could find out. Today. Nerves crackled beneath my skin and vibrated my tummy.

"Ah, I see. Yes, that's understandable," the doctor replied. "How long?"

Some of my excitement deflated. What was she saying? I wanted to jump up, snatch the phone from her hand, and demand answers from someone named Don.

"Okay, yes, that would be great. I'll be expecting your call." After a few more moments, she said her good-byes and hung up the phone.

"What's going on?" I demanded.

"That was Dr. Don Shaw, the local dentist here in Lake Lochlain."

"A dentist?" I scoffed. "You called a dentist for an opinion on who I am?"

Oh my God, if she was playing games with me.

"Let me explain," she said serenely. "Try to calm down."

I laughed.

"Dr. Shaw has been a dentist here for many, many years." She began. "He was Sadie's dentist."

"Okay," I said, still not following.

"He would have dental records on her, and even though Sadie is much older than the last time he saw her, the dental records would still be able to identify her."

I sat straight up. "Really?"

Dr. Kline nodded. "Dental records are used quite often in identifying bodies of people who pass and are… unrecognizable."

"All this time," I said, feeling anger bubble up over the hope. "All these months, all I had to do was go over to the dentist! Why didn't anyone say anything?" I raged.

"Because you weren't ready."

I laughed. "Who are you to judge?"

Her voice was indignant. "I'm your doctor."

I shook my head. All this time…

"There are some things you just need to come to terms with on your own, Amnesia. Finding out if you were the girl who went missing twelve years ago isn't going to solve all your problems. This is still your reality."

"I know," I said, some of my anger deflating.

"Given your progress lately, the recent information that has come to light, and the way you feel stuck, I feel you are ready to know."

Gee, thanks. Glad to have *her* permission to find out about myself. I pushed out of the chair. "So I just go over to this Dr. Shaw's office and let him look in my mouth?"

"Basically, but unfortunately, it won't be for several days."

"Why not?"

"Because the records are twelve years old. They're packed away among many boxes in a storage unit. He has to find them."

Tears sprang to my eyes. She gave me hope then ripped it away.

"He said he'll get over there as soon as possible to begin searching."

An idea popped into my head. "I'll go," I volunteered. "I'll find them!"

"You can't do that." She burst my bubble.

"Why not?" I yelled again. I was beginning to sound like a petulant two-year-old.

"Because those records are confidential. Doctor-patient rules apply. Even twelve years later."

Dejected, I sat back down. "How long do I have to wait?"

"Not long. A few days at most."

"What's a few more days?" I murmured. "It's already been a lifetime."

"Please remember our earlier words, Amnesia. Finding out will give you what you need to move on, but in reality, your life, the one you have now, is still yours."

I went to the door, passing by the ugly salt rocks. "Are we finished for today?"

"Yes."

I started to leave.

"Amnesia?" she called. I turned back. "I'll call you the second Dr. Shaw calls me and lets me know he has the records."

"Thank you." I left the windowless, dim office and walked down the bright corridor. *Just a few more days,* I told myself.

A few more days. Then all this would be over.

CHAPTER SIX

EDWARD

There was a difference between quiet and quiet.

Know what I mean?

Quiet was when the mind was preoccupied or busy with the task before you. Then there was *quiet*. As in lost in your own head, bogged down by thoughts that threatened to overwhelm you, drown you… take you away from the people that loved you.

Am was a quiet person—something I expected. After all, her mind had a lot to process. But today, her quiet was of the second variety.

It was eerie… more and more so lately.

I didn't like it. Again, I felt my patience being pulled so thin it was nearly see-through.

I didn't want to pressure her, but maybe a little bit of pressure was required. If it was between that and letting her slip away, then I knew the choice I had to make.

After her appointment with Dr. Kline, we worked together at Loch Gen. The hours seemed to drag once more, something that seemed more excruciating than before because now I was used to the time speeding by.

Something was wrong. I was merely biding my time to find out what it was.

Once closing time came, I was quick to turn over the closed sign and lock the front door. Amnesia was at the register, cashing out the drawer and closing down the system. I shut off a few lights as I went, my eyes solely focused on her.

She was utterly beautiful, nearly breathtaking every time I glanced her way. It didn't matter if she was standing in the sunshine or rising up over me in the middle of the night. Even comatose in a hospital bed before she ever spoke a word, I was inexplicably drawn to her in ways I never experienced before.

I didn't know there was emotion in the universe powerful enough to invisibly tether me to someone else, not so wholly and completely.

But there was.

And she embodied it.

So when she was this kind of quiet, that unsettled me more than the loudest noise. Nothing would feel right until she was better.

Coming up behind her, my arms wound around her waist, tugging her body into mine. Her face turned toward me, and I nuzzled the smooth skin on her cheek, then peppered it with countless kisses.

"You're my favorite," I whispered, then kissed her some more.

She giggled, the sound lightening the worst of the heaviness that settled into my chest. "You're my favorite," she replied, spinning in my arms so we were facing each other.

My lips dropped to the tip of her nose. With a soft sigh, she tilted up, and our mouths merged. Everything in the moment, spoken and not, fell away. All that was left was the emotion that always pulsed between us. The slightly rough quality to her tongue sent shivers down my spine as it dragged across mine. Sucking her lower lip between mine, I tugged the fullness deep into my mouth and curved my body more closely around hers.

Her fingers grappled with the front of my T-shirt, fisting the fabric tight. Releasing her lip, I went deep, diving into her mouth and stroking everything within reach with my tongue. She moved restlessly, so I pushed my thigh between her legs, the muscle rubbing at her center, and she shivered.

Rocking a little across my jeans, Amnesia ripped her mouth away from mine and kissed across my jaw and toward my ear. The sharp edge of her teeth scraped over the delicate flesh, and I groaned. Lifting my leg, her feet left the floor, and she was completely balanced on my thigh.

Her face dropped into my neck, her breathing turning into short gasps.

As I picked her up, her ass hit the counter where I usually bagged groceries. Instantly, her legs fell open, and I stepped between them and attacked her mouth again. I made out with her until my lungs felt ready to explode, and I was forced to pull back enough to get some air.

The sound of us both gulping in oxygen filled my ears. In my pants, my cock urged me on, demanding I kiss her again. I wanted to. I wanted to strip her down right there and do wicked, wicked things to her body. Things I would secretly laugh at when I was bagging groceries tomorrow.

Just as I was centimeters from her mouth, I groaned and pulled away.

"Eddie?"

"You have the power to tempt a saint."

"Are you a saint?" she asked, raising an eyebrow.

"Oh, baby. Far from it."

"So…" She picked at the hem of my shirt.

I groaned. My knees actually trembled with need. "So the windows in here need some blinds."

"Think anyone's out there?" she whispered, still playing with the hem.

"I really don't fucking care," I spat. "Fuck," I muttered. "But I sure as hell would tomorrow if someone was talking about how they saw you sprawled across the counter while I made you my dinner."

"That's quite a picture you paint," she said, enticing me with her conspiratorial smile.

"You're testing my patience." I warned.

She leaned forward. "Good."

I dropped my forehead onto hers and groaned. Cupping her face in my palms, I focused on getting her alone. "How about we take this somewhere with less windows?"

She nodded.

Grasping her by the waist, I helped her onto the floor. "Go lock up the drawer. I'll be right there." I fished the keys out of my jeans and handed them over.

She went one way and I went the other, practically jogging back to the coolers. I went to the section I wanted, yanked open the door, and plucked out a bottle of white wine. Carrying it by the neck, I backtracked to the aisle with plastic cups and grabbed a sleeve, tucking them beneath my arm.

Am was just finishing up in the back room when I stepped through the door. She saw the wine and cups, a smile transforming her face.

"You're mine tonight, Am," I growled.

"I'm yours every night."

Well, that made me feel pretty cocky. I liked the feeling.

"C'mon." I urged, wrapping my free hand around hers and pulling her along, out the back door. My truck was parked out back tonight, and the second I stepped outside, the large spotlight flicked on, flooding the entire area with artificial light.

"Walk by the water?" I asked, noting the way her gaze went straight toward the shoreline.

She nodded, smiling because I'd read her mind.

Instead of heading down toward the water, I yanked open the passenger door on the truck. "At home. It's more private there."

Instead of parking in my usual spot beside the house, I kept going, driving right past the place, across the yard, and down toward the water.

Amnesia laughed. "What are you doing?"

"What's the good in having a truck if you can't use it?" I grinned.

I parked so the bed faced the shoreline and the front end pointed to the house. Once the engine shut off and the headlights darkened, no longer illuminating the grass, I grabbed the wine and the cups, motioning for Am to follow.

We met at the back of the truck. The tailgate made a groaning sound as I lowered it. Using my teeth to rip open the pack of cups, I pulled out two and threw the rest into the back, where they disappeared in the dark.

Amnesia giggled, making the cups bounce around in her hand as I tried to pour the cheap wine.

"Hold still, baby," I said, nearly dumping it on her fingers.

"Sorry!" she said, going still.

Feeling feisty, I jerked my hand and sloshed the alcohol over the rim and spilled it over her hand.

"Oh!" she said, jerking back. "I'm sorry."

I set aside the wine, same with the cups, then lifted her hand, the entire time holding her eyes. "I told you, you don't ever have to apologize to me."

I brought her hand up and licked it, lapping up the wine I purposely dumped across her skin. Her eyes closed a little, the expression turning fuzzy.

One by one, I slipped her fingers between my lips, dragging up to suck off all the wine. Her body swayed near mine, but I acted as if I didn't notice. Instead, I just ate up all her fingers, then licked over the back of her hand once more. When all traces of the wine were gone, I kissed the center of her palm.

"Wine?" I asked, abruptly turning away, picking up the cup and extending it to her.

"Uh... yeah," she murmured.

I suppressed a chuckle.

Watching her over the rim of the cup as I swallowed, I enjoyed her struggling to come back to reality after I'd teased her.

"Let's walk," I said, carrying my cup, taking her hand.

The air was pretty cold. October in Maine was fall, but sometimes it felt more like winter. Especially down here on the pebbly shores of Lake Loch, where the breeze off the water was always several degrees cooler than the rest of town.

The water lapped against the shore tonight, not roughly, but not what I would call gently either. Its presence was definitely noted, the sound not unpleasant. I enjoyed the ever-moving being of the lake, the way it changed almost based on a whim, like a moody woman or a pissed-off man.

The moon wasn't full tonight, but it floated high in the dark sky. Stars sparkled on the horizon and made me think of a summer night instead of a nearly winter one.

"I bet the shoreline is beautiful when it snows," Amnesia murmured, gazing out ahead of us.

"It is," I said simply. "We'll walk down here after the first snow so you can see."

"When is the first snow usually?" she asked.

I glanced at her out of the corner of my eye. An innocent question, but I didn't like it. "Actually, anytime now. We've been buried under snow on some Halloweens!"

"I don't remember if I've ever seen snow," she told me. "It'll be like seeing it for the first time all over again."

Some of the chilled wine slid down my throat. *Screw this.* Tiptoeing around my girl wasn't how I wanted to spend the night. Or any other day for that matter. "Why does it sound like you're wondering if you've seen the first snowfall, Am?"

The wind off the water blew her hair back, revealing all her features as we strolled along the shoreline. We weren't close enough to get our feet wet, but the pebbles were uneven beneath our shoes. I loved that she looked "undone." Her beauty was natural, the kind she didn't work at or fuss with.

"She told me I wasn't Sadie." The words blew back at me like her hair in the wind. The plastic cup dented in a little, making a sound, when my hand squeezed around it.

"That's what she said," I echoed. I'd been wondering, even guessing what Widow West said to Amnesia that night in the hospital, and of all my ponderings, that was never it.

Amnesia kept walking, her eyes roaming the water and landscape ahead of us. After taking a small sip from her cup, she nodded. "I practically begged—demanded she stop playing games and tell everyone I was Sadie."

"I know, sweetheart." I agreed, reaching for her hand. The second I had hers tucked into mine, I felt slightly better, more grounded.

"But then in that room, that's what she said."

"And that's all?" I asked. "Just that you aren't Sadie?"

I felt her glance from the side of her eye. I didn't acknowledge it or the turbulence that radiated from her. Close by, a wave crashed on shore.

"She said you don't love me."

My reaction was physical. The idea was so preposterous I actually stopped walking and tugged Am around. "Are you kidding me?"

She shook her head, staring down into her cup. "She said it. Said you loved Sadie, not me."

I laughed, but it was a cold, humorless sound. The anger those stupid words incited in me was white hot and piercing. So much it burned my chest. On impulse, I tipped the cup back and downed the rest of the weak wine, hoping the chilled liquid would dilute the heat in me.

It didn't work.

"And you believed her," I said, monotone. I wasn't sure what was worse—the words the bitch muttered or the fact that Amnesia considered them.

"No," she said quickly. Then I felt her relent. "I didn't want to. I'm just so confused."

Unable to be mad at her, I pulled her in, enclosing her against my chest, using my arms to block the wind. Am pressed close, so close I felt the rise and fall of her chest with every breath, the steady beat of her heart.

"I know you are," I said. "That's why I didn't want to push. But dammit, Am. If I had known this was the shit that woman said to you, I would have put a stop to it that very second."

Her face lifted. The tip of her nose was pink from the wind. "You can't put a stop to my own thoughts, Eddie."

"The hell I can't," I growled and claimed her mouth fiercely.

I kissed her with possession I always tried to hold back. I went at her full throttle, wanting her to feel the intensity with which I loved her, the obsession she made me feel. It was scary to feel with so much force, to love with more than I was.

I'd always held some of that back, not because I thought it would scare her, but because it was a fucking lot to process. I didn't want her to feel responsible for any of my feelings. They were mine and mine alone. It wasn't her job to look after them or me, but it sure as hell was my job to make sure she knew I loved her.

The way her body drooped in my arms made satisfaction hum in the back of my throat. It vibrated my tongue as I rubbed it against hers, making her fingertips dig into my biceps. Her head fell back. I used my palm to cradle it, keeping it at the perfect angle so I could possess all of her mouth. I kissed hungrily, no tease, no play… just full-on desire.

A flush built in my toes and slowly moved up my legs, past my stomach, and into my chest. My stomach felt jittery, my brain thick with fog.

At last when I lifted my head, my lips felt damp and swollen. It took several seconds for my vision to adjust.

"Eddie," Am whispered, breathless.

In response, I lifted an eyebrow, gazing down at her equally puffy mouth.

"Well, maybe… you can," she said, still partly winded.

Feeling pretty full of myself, I smirked. Putting my fingers beneath her chin, I made sure she was looking at me. "What she said was a lie. Something meant to hurt you because it was all she had left."

"You said yourself you think I'm not Sadie."

"You're missing the point, baby," I said.

She frowned.

I picked her up, her legs automatically wrapping around my waist. When her ankles hooked together at my back, deep possession unleashed within me. Locking my arms around her torso, I stared her straight in the eyes.

"I love you. I love you so much I wonder how I breathed before I fished you out of this lake. So much you occupy about eighty percent of my thoughts and all of my dreams. I don't give a flying fuck if you're Sadie. I don't care if you're the queen of fucking England. It doesn't matter where you came from or what your name used to be. Please understand that, Amnesia." I leaned my forehead against hers, felt her indrawn breath. "Understand that you're mine."

"You really don't care?" There was a bright sheen to her eyes, tears she held from spilling over.

"I care because you do, but not because it will change anything between us."

One of the tears finally fell. I watched it glisten a path down her freckled cheek and curve under her jawline. Leaning forward, I licked the moisture, trailing up to gently kiss the corner of her eye.

"I love you, Eddie. I don't even need every memory I ever had to know I've never loved anyone like this before."

"That's my girl," I said and kissed her.

Still keeping her in my arms, I backed up a little and sat, keeping her firmly in my lap. Our faces were parallel, our eyes level. "I wish you would have told me sooner." I admitted.

"I wanted to. I've just been scared."

I frowned. "You were that worried about the way I would react?"

"At first, but then I realized I was more scared for me."

I scratched the back of my head and tried to keep up. "Help me out here, Am."

"If I'm not Sadie, like she says, then who am I? I'm exactly where I started—nowhere."

"Yeah." I agreed. "You need to know." If she didn't, she'd always wonder. There would always be that looming question.

A strong wind blew off the water, pushing her hair around her face. I tucked it back behind her ears. "You know she was probably lying," I said.

"I know." She agreed. "It's more likely she lied than actually told the truth, but it's enough to make me doubt. Between her and the allergy…" Her voice faded away.

I coaxed her against my chest, resting my chin on top of her head, hugging her close. She lay against me for long moments, neither of us saying a word. Instead, I stared out across the inky water, thinking how much like a living being the lake was.

Funny, since Amnesia came, the pull I always felt to wander the shore wasn't as demanding. I was still oddly drawn there; I knew I always would be. My eyes still scanned the ever-bobbing surface. My stare ultimately always landed in the direction of Rumor Island.

Tonight, it was a looming shape in the distance, with jagged edges from the mature trees that jutted out across the small area. It seemed darker than usual, like a shadow within a shadow. I studied the shape of it, though, as I had a million times before.

I wondered what would have happened if I hadn't found Am on the lake that night. Would she really be over there, just a mile away, somehow hidden on that island? Hidden in plain sight. Had she been there all this time, right there in front of me—a giant joke the universe had at my expense?

As I stared, sounds of water lapping over rocks and cold air with a hint of winter blowing, something caught my eye. Something out of place among the dark. It was faint, enough that I blinked several times, thinking my mind was playing tricks on me. That perhaps all the morbid thoughts marauding around in my head were making me imagine things.

Out there in the center of the darkest night, on Rumor Island, a pale light glowed. It was nearly indistinct. If the island wasn't so dark tonight, it likely wouldn't even have been noticeable.

But it was. And it was there. I stared, curious, as the pale-yellow color floated through the night. It traveled in a straight line, or so it appeared, and just as I was about to call attention to it, the light seemed to turn and blink out. It faded away, leaving me sitting there staring, wondering if I'd really seen it at all.

Amnesia shifted, lifting her head off my chest. From this close, I could tell her cheeks were pink now, matching her chilled nose.

"Let's get you back to the truck."

I didn't wait for her to reply. Instead, I stood, making sure she was steady on her feet before reaching down and gathering our cups. With the trash in one hand and her hand in my other, we headed the short distance back to my pickup.

"Dr. Kline knows of a way for me to find out if I'm Sadie," she told me, glancing through the curtain of her short hair.

I glanced over swiftly. "What?"

She nodded. "She just told me today. I can't get it out of my mind."

"How?" I said, my mind racing. "And why is she just now saying something?"

Amnesia made an indelicate sound that made me smile. "She said I wasn't ready to know for sure until now." She made a scoffing sound. "Can you believe her?"

"No," I replied. "She has a total god complex."

"Right!" she said, practically leaping at me in agreement.

The water rushed forward, coming closer, making Am squeal. With one arm, I lifted her off her feet just before the murky liquid splashed over her Adidas.

The Adidas I bought for her. They matched mine, a detail that gave me immense pleasure.

"So what is this foolproof method the good doctor has?" I asked, sitting her back on her feet.

"Apparently, dental records can identify a person," Amnesia said, slightly puzzled.

"Why the hell didn't I think of that?" I swore. "Damn."

I felt her wide stare. "So it's true?"

I nodded. "Yeah, they do it a lot."

"She called the town dentist," Am said, and I butted in. "Dr. Shaw."

"Yeah, him." She agreed. "He has to dig through twelve years of records in some storage unit to find Sadie's so he can compare them to me."

"How long is that gonna take?" I asked, impatient.

"A few days."

"Promise you'll tell me when you go. I want to be there," I said seriously. "And not because I care what your old name used to be, but because I want to be there for you."

"Cross your heart?" she asked.

I smiled. "Hope to die."

She whispered the rest. "You will be forever mine."

"Forever," I echoed. At the truck, I tugged her around to face me.

"It's going to feel like forever waiting for that dentist to find those records." She frowned. "Waiting sucks."

Wanting to see her smile, I wagged my eyebrows. "I can think of a few things to do to pass the time."

"I'm sure you can." Amnesia laughed.

Surging forward I scooped her up, tossing her body over my shoulder as though she weighed nothing more than a huge sack of potatoes at the store. Amnesia's squeal carried on the wind, and I smacked her ass, which was right beside my face.

"Hey!" She squealed again, then smacked my ass.

"Get it, woman!" I said, sticking my butt out so she could whack me again.

Her laughter was a beautiful sound, but as fun as this was, I was ready to take her inside. The up-close view of her ass was turning me on.

"Put me down, Eddie," she demanded, even though she wanted nothing of the sort. The view of my ass was too pleasant for her to want free.

"I'm going to." I agreed readily. "Soon as I get into the bedroom."

Starting toward the house, I figured I'd just leave the truck where it was for the night. It was my yard. I could park anywhere I wanted. I was too anxious to get inside with Am. I felt like a weight had been lifted that had been pressing in on us both.

Thank fuck she finally opened up.

"Wait!" she called out, sudden alarm in her voice.

I stopped immediately. "Did I hurt you?"

"No," she hurried to say, then scrambled around me, staring out toward the water. "But look!"

Her pale hand was like a neon sign in the dark, pointing out to Rumor Island. The light was back. It bounced around, almost in slow motion, the light so far out it was nearly faded.

"You see that, right?" Her voice was hushed.

"Yeah, I see it."

"I saw it the other night, when I came outside after my nightmare. I thought I might have imagined it."

"That's what I thought when I saw it a few minutes ago." I agreed.

"It looks like a light, maybe a flashlight... No." She frowned, but never tore her eyes off the illumination. "Like a lantern, you know, the kind from back in the day."

"Back in the day?" I teased.

She shrugged. "Do people still use those things?"

"I don't think so."

"Then, yeah. Back in the day." Her voice was exasperated but teasing.

"It does have that kind of glow," I murmured, realizing she was right.

Her hand reached for mine, our fingers entwining. We didn't look at each other, though. Our focus was on that light.

"I thought the island was empty," Am whispered. "The widow is still in the hospital."

I made a sound of agreement.

"Didn't you say she lived out there alone?" she questioned.

I nodded. "Yeah, ever since her husband died years and years ago."

"You're sure?"

"I've never seen anyone with her. No one has."

Just as I spoke, the light went out, almost like a flame on a candle met with too much wind.

"It's gone," Amnesia whispered, still staring, waiting for it to reappear.

"C'mon, baby. It's cold. Time to go in."

She allowed me to lead her away, but the entire way to the house, she kept glancing back.

CHAPTER SEVEN

AMNESIA

Sadie. A nearly silent voice echoed through the stillness of the midnight hour.

Goose bumps broke out over my skin, spider-crawling over my bare arms and legs, leaving behind an itchy, creepy feeling in their wake. The voice was low, sort of scratchy. Ominous.

Wake up, Sadie. Get ready.

The hair on the back of my neck stood on end. Despite the goose bumps and the cold feel to my skin, a fine sheen of sweat broke out over my entire body.

He's coming for you, Sadie.

My stomach turned violently as if I were in a boat that made a sudden dip over a giant wave.

He's tired of waiting for what's his.

I gasped so deep my body flew up off the mattress. Pressing a hand to my frantically beating heart, I told myself everything was okay. It was just a dream. An eerie dream filled with nothing but a voice, a voice nightmares were made of.

I wasn't sure what was worse—the voice or the warning it gave.

The urge to get up and dust away the sudden icky feeling clinging to my body was strong. After a quick glance at Eddie, I slipped from beneath the covers and padded over to the window.

I was completely naked, but I didn't bother to cover up. It was just me, and the cool night air was relief against my flushed skin.

The windows were covered with curtains, and even though I was scared to pull back the fabric (even just a little) because of what might be there looking back, I reached for it anyway.

Without realizing, I held my breath and peeled back the curtain at an embarrassingly slow rate. Squeezing one of my eyes closed and looking with the other, I peeked out.

Of course nothing was there, just the yard, the moon, and the lake. Telling myself I was beyond dramatic, I opened both eyes up and pulled the curtain back to stare down to the water.

The waves shimmered beneath the moon, glittering like diamonds.

I let out a cleansing breath, trying to exhale the horrible dream. I was so lost in thought I didn't hear Eddie behind me until his body heat announced him and his own nakedness pressed against mine.

"What are you doing over here?" he whispered, groggy, into my ear.

Desire stirred in my lower belly. His voice in my ear and the feel of him against me was intoxicating.

"Couldn't sleep," I whispered, sliding my hands along his arms and hugging him closer.

His voice was still sleepy when he softly spoke again. "You're drawn to the water just as I am."

"It definitely has a pull." I agreed.

I felt restless, as though something were niggling at the back of my mind, but I didn't know what. Even though I opened up to Eddie, things still felt unsettled. Maybe they would always feel that way. Until I knew. Where I'd come from, what brought me to the shore of Lake Loch months ago.

Was I Sadie? What was my connection to Widow West.

Leaning my head back against Eddie, I stared out the window, letting the questions consume me.

Way out in the distance, a light caught my eye. So small I probably shouldn't have noticed it. But I did, and once in my line of sight, it was all I saw.

Gasping, I moved forward, laid my palm flat against the cold glass of the window, and stared out.

"Do you see it?" I asked.

"Yeah."

"There's someone out there," I murmured, almost an afterthought. Like an idea that didn't occur to me until it was already out of my mouth. The words didn't sink in until *after* I spoke them.

My breath caught, the pads of my fingers pressing harder against the glass. "That's it," I told myself.

"What is?" Eddie asked, moving forward to keep us pressed together. His chin settled on my shoulder, the unshaven roughness of his jaw slightly prickly against my skin.

I turned my face just slightly, angling toward him a bit more. My eyes slid back out toward the island, searching for the mellow light captivating me.

"What if Widow West really was taking me back to Rumor Island? What if there really is someone else out there, *him*?"

The sleepy quality to his voice vanished, and a fine, humming tension coiled beneath his skin. "Him who?"

"The man I keep remembering, but never actually seeing. The one who kidnapped me. The one who wants me back."

"The police searched that island, Am. So many times."

"Yeah, nearly twelve years ago. What if he left, went into hiding until the search ended, and I—Sadie—was presumed dead? Have they been there since?"

Eddie fell quiet.

The words tumbled out of me, the tone of my voice hollow, almost haunted. "What if he's there now? Wandering the island at night, waiting for the widow to come home. Waiting for her to bring me back."

"There's no way a man could live out there all this time and no one know."

"There's also no way a girl could disappear in the lake and then wash up eleven years later."

His arms pulled me snug against him. I knew he didn't like the path my thoughts were taking me, but I couldn't stop. I wouldn't. I felt this sense of… truth.

"That man out there," I whispered. "He may know who I am, Eddie."

"If that man out there knows who you are, I'll kill him."

I craned around, my eyes searching his face. The azure of his stare was deadly. It was the same look he'd had at the paintball field when that guy shot me.

"If that light out there is the man who kidnapped you all those years ago… held you captive and abused you, it won't matter if he knows your name, Am. I'll kill him, and no one will be able to stop me."

There was no bravado in his voice. Not even passionate anger. This was a vow. A vow from a calm, collected man. The promise of someone who also had been held captive by questions with no answers, by guilt and by… love.

I laid my hand against his cheek. His eyes lowered to half-mast. "If you kill him, he'll win. We'll be separated. Something I honestly don't think I could bear."

Deadly calm, almost methodical, he replied, "Not if no one knows."

"You won't kill him," I said.

"How do you know that?"

"Because I'm asking you not to. I need answers, and I can't get them from a corpse."

His eyes shut briefly. I felt the rise of his chest with his inhale. Moonlight streamed in the window, hitting the expanse of his torso. I shifted around totally, putting my back to the window to focus fully on him. After smoothing my palms over his chest, I leaned down and kissed him there.

"I'll never do anything to hurt you, sweetheart." His hands splayed out over my hips.

I lifted my head, answering definitively, "I know."

The warmth of his lips brushed my hairline, and I smiled.

"We talk like we know someone is out there. Truth is that light could be anything… or nothing at all."

"Have you ever seen it out there before?" I asked.

He was silent a while. His body shifted, gathering me close. "No."

"It's something," I whispered. "Someone."

"We don't know that, Am."

"I need to know. I have to find out."

"What are you saying?" he asked, pulling back to look down.

"I'm saying I want to go out there. I want to go to where the widow was trying to take me that night… I want to go to Rumor Island."

CHAPTER EIGHT

EDWARD

"No," I said, final.

She straightened away, pulling out of my hold. Her chin lifted defiantly. "I didn't ask permission."

"The last time I went to Rumor Island, someone disappeared and I spent the rest of my life feeling guilty."

"You don't have to come."

I laughed. Then I laughed some more. "You can't be serious."

She stared at me with a straight face.

Well, wasn't she a piece of work?

"Get one thing through that gorgeous head of yours right now," I intoned, leaning down so we were eye to eye. "Under no circumstance would I ever, *ever* let the woman I love, the woman who is literally a piece of me, get in a boat and row herself over to an island where she might or might not have been held captive and abused. I would rather eat glass and shower with a rusty metal sponge. I will protect you this time. I will."

Her eyes softened, but her nose wrinkled. "I love that you love me that much. I mean, taking a shower with a rusty sponge… that's nasty. And oddly sweet."

"I'm being serious," I growled. This was a convoluted conversation.

"Your posturing is beside the point," she announced.

Who the fuck was posturing?

"You can't protect me, Eddie. Not from my own mind, from the memories that will continue to unlock themselves if I don't find out what the hell happened to me."

I felt my brow furrow. Her words were like an arrow right into the depths of my heart. "You think going there will keep the memories at bay?"

"Maybe." She shrugged. "It's worth a try. Every night when I close my eyes, I worry some new horror is waiting to reveal itself to me. That day at the paintball field…" Amnesia swallowed, voice faltering.

"What?" I insisted. Panic rose up inside me.

"When I stumbled, I had a sharp, piercing memory… It was rotten."

"You didn't tell me," I said, curling a hand around her elbow.

"I didn't want to ruin our fun day."

A frustrated sound ripped from my throat. "What was the memory, Am?"

She shook her head as if just thinking about it made her queasy.

"Amnesia."

"When the paintball hit me, it stung… just like you said it would. But apparently, it reminded my body of something else." She stopped speaking, glancing away. "Of being whipped."

I groaned. I couldn't help it. The thought of her being tortured that way made me feel tortured as well. It made my heart ache. Without saying anything, I cupped her shoulders and turned her around so she was facing out the window, her bare back to me.

In the reflection of the window, I saw her eyes squeeze shut. She knew. She knew exactly what I was doing.

I glanced down, gazing over the marks I'd seen a thousand times, but never brought up. "Now I know what these are from," I whispered, grazing the tips of my fingers over the thin silvery scars that marred her smooth back.

"Now I do, too," she answered self-consciously.

I knew she worried about them at first, whenever we would undress in front of each other or I would strip her shirt off her body to make love. The scars went unspoken between us. No one ever called attention to them.

A little shiver worked down her back. "I always worried you would think of me as freakish or less beautiful. But time and again, we made love. You washed my back in the shower and rubbed over them at night. But you never brought them up."

She lifted her head, caught my reflection in the window, and met my stare.

"Until now."

"I don't see them when I look at you, Amnesia. Obviously, I know they're there. My fingers have felt them, and so have my lips. But they aren't you. I don't see these scars when you're naked before me. All I see is the woman I love, and to me, you're perfect."

"I'm sorry," she whispered. "Your words are beautiful. It makes me almost sad I told you what the scars are from. I feel like they dirty me."

"I'm the one who's sorry." I traced over one that slashed across her back. "So fucking sorry you had to endure something so vile."

"I don't remember, not much. Only that brief moment at the field. It was enough. I want to keep it that way. I don't want to know, Eddie. It scares me... so much."

"I know." I sympathized, folding my arms around her. "It scares me, too, baby."

"Maybe if I get some answers to my most nagging thoughts, the subconscious way I push my brain to remember will ease off. Maybe I'll be able to accept not knowing everything if I know *something*. I feel knowing protects me from feeling. Can you understand that, even a little?"

I didn't think I'd ever understand the full extent of what it was like to be inside her mind. When I tried to think about it, red tinged my vision, and I seriously understood crime of passion. I had to push past that, though. I had to be stronger than even her greatest demon. My hands slid down over her shoulders, across her waist, and dragged up her back. Without thinking about it, my fingers softly probed the lifted scars there, tracing them as I tried to weigh what I wanted to do against what she needed me to do.

I waited until I truly meant the words, then spoke. "If this is what you need, then it's what we'll do."

I saw hope surge in her eyes, which in turn lifted it out of the heaviest of emotion whirling inside me. "Really?" she asked, slight awe in her voice.

"I won't ever deny you anything," I vowed.

"Other than a trip to Rumor island alone." She teased.

I glared. Now was not the time to jest. I was trying to be strong and romantic and shit. Besides, charm was *my* thing… not hers.

"Too soon?" she asked, a sparkle in her eyes.

Well, shit. Maybe charm was her thing, too.

I wanted to smile, but then I remembered what we were discussing. "If I'd known that paintball hit made you remember being whipped…" I felt my teeth bare. "That asshole wouldn't have been able to walk out of there."

"Another reason I didn't say anything," she quipped.

My eyes settled on her face. I needed her to understand. "I'm very serious when it comes to protecting you. Shielding you from any more pain."

"I noticed."

"I couldn't stop what happened all those years ago, and I… I didn't find you." I swallowed. Knowing Am might have been so close ripped me apart. I hadn't done anything. "But I swear to heaven and to hell, if anyone wants to hurt you now, they will go through me."

"You're pretty sexy when you're all growly and intense." Her arms wound around my torso.

I raised an eyebrow. "Growly?"

"It's a thing."

"A thing you just made up," I deadpanned.

"But I like it. It turns me on."

Well then. "I'll allow it."

"You really never see my scars when you look at me?"

Something inside me softened. "No, baby, I really don't. And they don't make you dirty. They make you more beautiful."

Suddenly, fear crept into her tone. "I don't know what I'd do if I ever lost you."

"Hey," I purred. "You will never have to find out."

She launched across the short distance between us, wrapping her body around mine. Want hammered inside me; the skin-on-skin contact we had was making me crave her.

Just as I thought about twirling around and tossing her down on the bed, she glanced up, eyes wide, full of energy. "Let's go."

"Go?"

"To Rumor Island."

"Hell no!" I said, incredulous.

"But you said…"

"I said I understood. I did not agree to taking you across the lake in the middle of the night to an island I am unfamiliar with. Woman, you are out of your ever-loving mind."

"We can't call the police. Search parties take too long to organize. They're loud. They'll scare him away."

If he's even there. This is such a long shot. But even I couldn't help realizing she had a point. That light was some kind of sign. Of what, I wasn't sure.

"We'll go when it's light out." I compromised. "At least then we can see what we're dealing with."

She thought it over a moment. Briefly, I worried she was going to argue. I didn't want to quarrel with her. I wanted to bury myself inside her.

"We'll go tomorrow?" she asked.

"I'll call Dad and have him handle the store."

"What will you tell him?" She worried.

The truth. Well, a partial truth. "That I need a day with my girl."

An invisible weight lifted off her. I felt it leave the room.

"Thank you," she said sincerely.

"That island may not have the answers you're looking for." I felt the need to caution her again.

"It may," she rebutted.

She was right. The more and more I thought about it, I realized Rumor Island might hold a hell of a lot more than just rumors.

CHAPTER NINE

AMNESIA

I felt like a wind-up toy that had been wound so tight and was desperately waiting to be set down so I could spin off uncontrollably.

I admit the idea of going to Rumor Island was kind of crazy. Sort of like walking into a room with a bunch of potential hidden traps. Scenarios like that only worked out for people like Indiana Jones (we liked movies, too) and others who had mad survival skills.

But you know, I think I had some mad skills in that department. The scars on my body said so. The few memories that haunted me proved it.

I even survived myself. As in I tried to commit suicide and lived.

My thoughts, which had started out sort of lighthearted, even excited, turned dark. Reminding me everything I'd been through was nearly depressing, especially the part where I realized I'd be going back to a place that literally made me so miserable I thought death was my only option. Suicide was no joking matter. In fact, it was quite impossible to even wrap my head around.

I was so far from that mental place. I couldn't even imagine wanting to end it all. I had way too much to live for right now, and I was able to say that with barely any of my memories.

It made me wonder just how drastically changed I was from before. Was I a completely different person, or was it just because wherever I'd been was such a nightmare?

I wasn't sure.

Did it even matter?

I guess in some ways it did, but in others? Not so much. I loved where I was right now. Who I was. Eddie. I didn't want to give it up. I loved this little town with its foggy brick street, small mom-and-pop shops, and views of the elusive lake. I even loved the mystery here, and yeah, I caught myself more than once scanning the water for signs of the legendary Loch Ness.

Hey, it could totally be out there.

Still, as I told Eddie just hours before I needed some answers. Was it strange I just wanted to know things without actually remembering them? Did that mean the information I got would be less reliable? Because it was seen and not felt?

Did not remembering something make it any less significant?

I didn't think it did, but again, I didn't really know. Maybe I would revisit that question after our trip across the lake.

The second the sun rose over the water, shooting its orangey-sapphire streaks across the horizon, I got out of bed, unable to wait another moment. Eddie was less than thrilled over my excitement. I knew he was worried about this and about me.

I couldn't contain it, though. I suddenly felt I had some kind of lead. Like there was something out there that would tell me something. I knew going back there was risky, but I had to do it.

After putting on a pot of coffee, I retreated down the hallway and crawled onto Eddie. "I need to go home for a bit," I whispered.

He made a sound. "You are home."

I smiled. I liked when he said that. "I mean Maggie's. I need some clothes."

His eyes weren't even open yet, but he replied, "If you'd move in here, you wouldn't need clothes."

With a sigh, I laid my cheek against his back (he was lying on his stomach). His skin was warm to the touch. I wanted to move in. I did. But I couldn't. I was held back by unknowns, by what the widow said. Eddie told me time and again it didn't matter if I was Sadie or not. I believed him. I did.

But feelings were subject to change.

If I found out for certain I wasn't the girl he lost, how could he not react?

I didn't want to make this any harder on him than it already was. After all, I wasn't the only victim here. Eddie was just as much as I. Even his friend Robbie was left scarred.

"Soon," I whispered, hoping it was a promise I could keep. Maybe after today, I would have what I needed to take that step.

Eddie rolled onto his side, and I fell over onto the mattress in front of him. His arm came down, anchoring me in place. His eyes were still closed.

I poked him in the nose. "It's light outside."

He groaned.

I poked him again. "I made you some coffee."

One eye cracked open.

"I love you."

Both eyes opened, and I got a smile. "All right." He caved. "I'm up."

I pulled on the clothes I had on the day before, shoved my feet in my sneakers, and poured him a large travel mug of the hot brew. I wasn't a coffee person. I'd drink it, but I'd much rather have hot chocolate.

The morning was cold and the grass was damp with dew that sparkled a bit beneath the bright morning sun. The sound of the waves was calming this morning, and from the look of the sky, I knew it would be a beautiful autumn day.

The second we parked in the driveway at Maggie's, the front door opened and she poked her head out. "Don't you try and sneak in the back door," she told us. "Get in here! I'm making breakfast."

"I like food," Eddie called out.

"I'll be up in a few. I'm going to change and stuff," I told him once we were inside on the landing. He went up and I went down, the scent of pancakes following me into my room.

I still didn't have a lot of clothes, something I planned to remedy once I got my first check from Loch Gen. I didn't intend to go ham (ham = crazy; they said it on TV. I didn't really know why ham and crazy were similar, but whatever) with the shopping, but picking out a few items I really loved for myself seemed like such a treat. I was pretty low maintenance now, something I really didn't think would change, but it might be nice to be a little more feminine sometimes.

Not thinking too much about it, I pulled out a pair of faded jeans, a long-sleeved T-shirt, and some socks. Tossing them on the bed, I went to the bathroom to get ready for the day, then came back and dressed. Before heading upstairs, I glanced at the small Loch Ness Eddie had given me from the store. I kept it on my bed.

The entire upstairs smelled like butter and tension. It wasn't a very good combo, even though a lot of cooks would tell you butter went with everything.

"What's going on?" I asked.

Eddie was standing in the doorway between the kitchen and the breakfast room with a mug in his hand. Maggie was at the stove, dressed in black leggings and an oversized kimono-style pullover with a colorful design.

She turned, pointing the spatula at me in accusation. "Rumor Island, Amnesia." Her tone was intensely disapproving. "No way in hell, young lady."

I blinked. Defying Eddie was one thing… but Maggie? That was a different beast entirely.

"Maggie—" I began, and she started shaking her head.

"Why in heaven's name would you want to go there? After everything?"

"Because it's not *after* everything. It's still very much present in my life," I explained.

Maggie spun back to the stove and flipped a few pancakes. "I still don't like it."

"I have to do it," I said, going to her side and touching her arm. "Please understand."

She was silent while moving the flapjacks onto a platter. When it was done, she flipped off the burner and set aside the spatula.

I glanced at Eddie. He winked.

Clearly, he wasn't as bothered by this as I was.

"Take these to the table," she said, handing me the platter loaded down with pancakes.

"This could feed an army," I told her.

She shrugged. "Eddie's here."

We loaded our plates in silence, and I gazed out through the room made of windows into the trees, which were rapidly offering their foliage to the grass around them. Everything was in beautiful tones of brown, orange, and yellow. There were pops of vibrant red and even a few plum-colored explosions among it all. A fall breeze ruffled the branches, and I watched leaves drift down lazily.

It was beautiful and peaceful.

Maggie cleared her throat. "You really feel like you have to do this."

Yanking my eyes from the view, I turned to her. "I truly do. Me. Not anyone else either. I have to see that place. I have to feel it." That part scared me most. The feeling.

"You'll take your phones? Call for help the second you see anything remotely dangerous?"

"I swear it," Eddie put in. At the rate he was consuming carbs, I honestly was shocked he'd been listening.

Maggie's eyes were still concerned, but she nodded. "Do you have a boat?"

Well, crap. Why didn't I think of that? Had I planned on swimming?

"Figured I'd borrow Tom's," Eddie answered.

Well, at least he'd thought it through.

Maggie got up and left the room. I took the opportunity to slip some bacon under the table to Elmo. A moment later, she returned with a simple silver ring with a key attached.

"No more bacon," she said, giving me the evil eye.

Eddie laughed. "She totally caught you."

"What's that?" I asked, adeptly changing the subject.

"It's the key to Chris's boat."

Eddie looked up from his plate. "You still have Chris's boat?"

She nodded. "He loved that thing, and I've never been able to part with it."

"It was a great boat." Eddie agreed.

"You're welcome to use it today. It's a bit larger, maybe a bit nicer than Tom's old fishing boat."

Eddie made a soft sound. "It definitely is."

"But are you sure you want us to use it? It must mean so much to you," I asked.

"Oh yes. It hasn't been run in months. I usually have someone give it a few tune-ups each year, and once in a while, the mechanic takes it out on the water. But it just sits there. Chris would love to know someone is enjoying it."

"I don't know how enjoyable this trip will be," Eddie intoned.

"Yes, well…" Maggie agreed. "Exactly why you should take the boat."

"Thank you," I said sincerely. Eddie echoed my sentiments.

"Of course. If you are hell bent on doing this, then at least I can be supportive."

My chair made a sound when it scraped back from the table. I rushed over and threw my arms around Maggie.

She hugged me back with a chuckle. "Don't hug me yet. I have a condition."

"What is it?" I asked, pulling back.

"I want to see you both here for dinner. I will want details and to see with my own two eyes you're okay."

"Deal," Eddie said, punctuating it with a huge bite.

I didn't bother to sit back down. I was too nervous, too jittery. Instead, I paced in front of the windows, barely able to admire the view.

A second later, Eddie stood from the table. "I think if we don't go soon, her head may combust."

I laughed nervously. "I can't help it."

"Please be careful." Maggie cautioned.

"I'll take care of her," Eddie vowed as he pocketed the boat keys.

"Do you remember where our dock is?" she asked.

"I remember." Eddie held out his hand for me, and I went to his side.

Finally, *finally,* we were on our way.

CHAPTER TEN

EDWARD

I understood why Amnesia wanted to go to Rumor Island. Hell, even I was curious about the place. Staring at it from shore my entire life, and more specifically the past eleven years, only built it up in my mind.

But fuck. This was stupid.

I was doing it, though. *We* were doing it.

Closure. To me, that's what this was about. For her. Not for me. Seemed the closure I sought all these years wasn't really needed anymore.

That made me feel guilty. But also, it made me feel relieved.

I didn't know what that light we saw out there was, but honestly, it seemed like a long shot it was the man who kidnapped her. Who would be stupid enough to hang around? It was like asking for a prison sentence.

Or a grave.

I was a fan of the second option. Rotting away with the worms almost seemed too good for that motherfucker, but hey, I'd take it.

The water was calm today, moving gently with the current, no sign of a storm or even a disturbance in the near future. It was the kind of day fishermen loved, and there were quite a few out on the water.

Chris's boat was docked at a local boat slip, where a lot of people here at Lake Loch kept their boats. There were also rentals available for those here on vacation. Maggie's late husband had a nice slip. It was covered, a luxury very few here had. The "boat garage" looked like a little wooden shack on the end of a dock. The wooden shingles on the sides went down until they nearly skimmed the surface of the lake.

When Maggie said she had the boat maintained with tune-ups, I figured I would find it in usable shape.

Maggie lied.

It wasn't just maintained. It was perfection. Far beyond just "usable" shape.

It was clear how much she loved her husband, because his boat still looked brand new. Knowing Maggie, it was one last thing she could do for him even in death.

"I don't know much about boats," Amnesia mused, "but I'm pretty sure this is a nice one."

She was right. It looked good as new, and it started right up like it, too.

As the craft cut through the water, I hoped it didn't look "too nice," as in drew attention to our approach.

That was the thing about boating to an island. Not much surprise or secrecy.

The way the house perched on the top, if anyone was inside, all they'd have to do was look out a window to see us coming.

I kept my eyes peeled, staying hyperaware of my surroundings for anything out of the ordinary... or anything at all.

I had no idea what to expect, and that meant I couldn't trust anything.

I wanted Amnesia to get the answers she wanted, but deep down, I hoped nothing was over there, that the island appeared abandoned and we found nothing at all. Waiting for the dental records seemed like a hell of a lot better of a bet than what we were doing. Am couldn't wait, though, and I couldn't stand watching her suffer while she did.

Pulling my eyes away from our surroundings, I glanced at Am sitting behind me. She wanted to sit out front, but I wasn't about to have her in front of me. If something happened and I needed to shield her, this would make it a lot easier.

She was staring straight ahead, eyes fixated on the looming island. It seemed a lot less intimidating from shore. Out here, as we drew closer, the size, shape, and almost wild appearance grew tenfold.

Tall trees jutted up from the rocky earth, towering into the blue sky like dark swords. The house took on a ragged appearance, as if over the years, the elements had not been kind and the owner even less so. There didn't appear to be much maintenance to the residence; instead, it was almost falling into disrepair, in need of a serious paint job, some patching, and a brand-new roof.

I knew from talk there was a dock on the other side of the island, so I made a wide arch around it, taking care to study as much of it as I could.

So far, nothing seemed wrong.

But Rumor Island always appeared that way.

It was a deceitful place.

Leaving one hand on the steering wheel, I reached out behind me with the other, wiggling my fingers in the air. Seconds later, Amnesia slid hers against it, and I grasped, noting the cold feel of her skin and the way her fingers shook.

She was brave, far braver than she had to be.

Pulling her into my side, I leaned close to her ear so I didn't have to yell. "You sure you want to do this?"

She nodded.

"I'm gonna pull up to the dock," I told her, preparing to cut the engine and coast in. There were no boats here. I didn't know what that meant, though. Maybe Widow West only had one, or maybe there were more and whoever else was here was already gone.

With the motor silenced, I listened intently as I secured the boat to the dock (which had seen better days). The only sounds I heard came from nature, which oddly made this eerier.

"It's quiet here," Amnesia whispered, as if she too felt the weird vibes in the air. "And is it just me, or does it feel colder?"

"Stay with me at all times. Don't ever wander off. No matter what." I was also whispering. As I laid down the rules, I tugged the ends of the green Loch Gen hoodie closer around her and zipped it all the way up.

God, I fucking loved her. *Please, let me keep her safe today.*

"What if we find him?" Her eyes rounded, and genuine fear flooded in.

Her terror made me feel fiercer, more prepared to fight. A surge of adrenaline pulsed through me.

"We'll call the cops," I said, patting the right front pocket of my Loch Gen hoodie where I put my phone.

They can come and collect his dead body. I didn't bother saying that out loud. She was already frightened enough.

"I'm going to make him answer my questions." Determination filled her voice.

"I promise."

There was no more stalling. No more waiting and listening. I was first off the boat, reaching down to help her up onto the wooden planks that I didn't trust at all. Instead of holding her hand, I wrapped an arm around her torso as we walked, just in case one of the boards fell out from beneath her and I needed to move fast.

The dock wasn't very long. It went right up to the shoreline, which was rocky with no beach whatsoever. This side of the land was denser with trees and nature, not utilized at all. From the dock, there was a path that cut right between two tall trees, an entrance to what felt like a dark forest. Yes, that sounded a little dramatic. It wasn't.

"This place is creepy," Am murmured as we walked over the path toward the trees.

"Definitely not on my bucket list of places to visit again," I quipped.

There weren't many sounds of birds as we walked on the path. Or of small animals scurrying through the leaves and grass. Everything was still here, almost dead.

Or scared.

Up ahead, I saw the tree line thin out; just beyond it, everything seemed a little brighter.

"The house must be through there," I told her, even though she probably already figured it out on her own.

Sure enough, the second we made it to the line of trees, the house came into view.

"How old do you think that place is?" she asked, voice still hushed as we teetered at the tree line.

"Older than me at least. It was here before I was born," I replied. And by the looks of the white clapboard building, it definitely didn't get any updates over the past twenty-five years.

"C'mon," Am said, tugging my hand. She started walking, but I moved ahead, angling myself in front of her as we went.

Wind carried through the trees, pulling at my hair and clothes. It did feel colder here; my cheeks stung a little from the bite of the air.

There was no way... *no way* she'd spent the last eleven years here on this island, so close yet so far away. This was a hideous place. I'd only been here a few minutes and already I couldn't imagine staying for any length of time.

"Anytime you want to leave," I told her, "just say the word."

The ground was uneven, the grass grew in patches, and in between, the ground was rocky. I would judge the island to be maybe one and a half to two miles wide. The only building I knew of was the house, where we were heading first.

"The front must be on the other side," she said, tugging me off to the side where a worn dirt path led us around.

There was an old-school laundry line not far from the house. Tall grass grew around the poles that held it up. Two thin lines stretched between them, bobbing in the wind. On one end, forgotten laundry blew around. The ends of the white sheet were tattered as if it had been left in the weather for a while. There was also a towel and a long white nightgown.

"There's a garden," Am said, pointing to a fairly large plot of land boxed in with wood and protected by a short row of metal fencing. "She must grow her own food."

"Makes sense," I said. "She didn't come to town very often."

"Are there any other towns nearby? Accessible to the lake?"

I thought about it and nodded. "Yeah, but it's farther away. A longer boat ride."

"There's the door," she said.

We stopped around the "front" of the house. It was only distinguishable as the front because of the faded red door in the center. Otherwise, it looked exactly the same as the other sides we walked around.

It was ominous the way it just sat there, towering above us as if it owned the land.

Amnesia's fingers shook in mine, but her feet started forward. We walked up some crude stone steps that led to the front door.

"Should we knock?" She wondered.

This wasn't a polite social call. I wasn't about to announce my presence with a neighborly knock. Instead, I reached out and turned the handle. The door gave way, a loud creaking sound filling the air as it swung in.

We stood there for long seconds, both of us kind of surprised the place was just unlocked. Of course, when you lived on a private, creepy island, there probably wasn't much reason to lock up.

We stood there long enough that a great gust of wind pushed behind us and a few brown, crumpled leaves blew inside, scattering across the wooden floor.

I went first, using my arm to shield Am, keeping her behind me. My free hand hovered over my lowered back.

No one knew it, but I'd brought some heat. The cool metal of the gun was actually reassuring against the small of my back, tucked into my jeans as a promise of safety.

I'd use it. I wouldn't regret it either.

The floorboards creaked under foot. The house smelled slightly stale but also of a hint of lemon. The chemical kind, the kind in cleaning supplies.

The house wasn't very large, but it wasn't cramped either.

The living room was off to our left. The hallway extended past, heading toward the back of the house, where I could see a partial view of a white refrigerator and the metal legs of a chair pushed up to a kitchen table.

"Hello?" Amnesia called out. Her voice made my shoulders stiffen. "Is anyone here?"

The sound of silence echoed back, that and the blowing wind that made the house groan.

"This place needs a serious makeover," Amnesia said, gazing around at the old furnishings. Everything was wooden, the couch had flowers on it, and the TV actually had an antenna. I wondered if it even worked.

"This place would make a good set for a horror movie." I noted.

"It's clean, though," Amnesia said, moving through the living room and passing beneath the archway that led into the kitchen. "Like the widow cared about keeping it tidy."

"Maybe she was bored in between kidnapping," I deadpanned.

"That would be funny if it wasn't likely true."

The kitchen had a white farmhouse sink, old wooden cabinetry, and ugly green countertops.

"Look at this," Amnesia said, letting go of my hand and going to the old-school fridge. "There are pictures."

The front of the appliance looked a lot like everyone else's. Littered with photographs and magnets displaying vacation spots. There was one for Boston, one for Lake Loch, and even one for California.

There was also a bottle opener magnet and a memo notepad with one single word scrawled across it.

"Looks like she's out of milk." I noted, pointing to the paper.

Amnesia didn't care about the magnets or even the grocery list. She stared intently at the old, almost yellowing photographs taped to the front.

"Do you think this was her husband?" she asked, fingering the edge of one of the Polaroids.

My chest grazed her shoulders and back when I peered over her at the picture. It was of a man and woman. They were posing for the camera, large smiles on their faces. The man was about a head taller than the woman, dressed in a red flannel shirt and khaki pants with boots. He was holding up a huge fish on a line, clearly proud of his catch.

He had dark, short hair, was clean shaven, and was wide with broad shoulders.

"I heard he spent some time in the army before they moved here," I said.

"She was pretty," Amnesia noted, pointing at a young Widow West.

I made a sound. Maybe she was. I couldn't see past the shitty things she'd done, though. Her hair was long just like it was now, but instead of gray, it was a light-brown shade. She was thin, but not as thin as she was now. Her eyes were the most different. In this picture, she had the eyes of a woman in love. A happy woman, a woman that still had her sanity.

Her eyes didn't look like that today.

There was another image of the couple standing in front of a Christmas tree, the man wearing a Santa hat and red pants. And another of them dressed up, her in a white lace dress and him in a suit.

"This must be their wedding day," Amnesia murmured.

"Look at this one," I said, leaning down to the photograph that was stuck toward the bottom of the fridge, almost as if it had slid down, but no one bothered to fix it.

I pulled it off the fridge completely, straightened, and held it out in front of Am, leaning over her shoulder to look at it with her.

"They had a baby?" Amnesia asked, surprise making her voice rise.

"I never heard that," I said, puzzled.

It was the widow and her husband standing in front of this house (which looked a hell of a lot nicer). Flowers bloomed around their feet, and both were beaming with pride. In her arms was a bundle, unmistakably a baby, wrapped up in a white blanket.

The very top of the baby's head was the only thing visible, and it had very little hair.

I flipped the photo over, but there was nothing written on it. No name. No date. Nothing.

"If they had a baby, where is it?" Amnesia asked.

"Could be a niece or nephew. The child of whoever took this picture."

"Maybe," Amnesia amended. "It's odd…"

"Everything here is odd, sweetheart."

She stuck the picture back on the fridge, and we explored the rest of the house.

It was empty. Each room looked the same as the last, tidy, outdated, and tinged with the scent of eccentricity.

I didn't bother locking up on the way out. Clearly, they weren't concerned about that kind of thing.

"No one is here," I told Am. "We should just go back home."

She wasn't listening, though. She'd moved to the top step and was staring out over the island.

"Amnesia?"

"This way," she said, the sound of her voice slightly hollow. She took off, and I scurried to keep up. At the bottom of the stairs, I caught her hand and gave it a squeeze.

She barely glanced back before forging on, away from the house, across the yard. The ground sloped down slightly before leveling off. The sound of the waves hitting against the rocks carried on the wind, the sun shining brightly.

We walked under trees, through tall grass, and even across bare rocks.

"Where are we going?" I asked.

"I'm not sure," she replied and kept walking.

From this side, I didn't see many boaters, maybe one in the distance. This place felt truly isolated, more than I thought it could. It was like stepping back in time, like this island was a portal to thirty years ago, old and backward even compared to the slow-evolving town of Lake Loch.

"Look." Amnesia practically wheezed the word, halting so fast I collided into her, grasping her shoulders to keep us both steady.

My eyes followed hers. "Is that a grave?" I asked.

What the hell? This place was fucking weird.

"I think so," she whispered and started forward.

I sighed insufferably. My girl, ladies and gentlemen. Heading toward a grave instead of running away. We walked up a slight hill. It was covered in trimmed grass and patches of dry dirt.

In the center of a pounded-down mound was a crudely made wooden cross. It had been there a long time; the wood was faded and weathered. It was anchored very well, though, placed there with care.

Just below the cross was a small rectangular concrete slab. It was polished a dark gray and there were a name and dates carved in the top.

John West III
Husband and Best Friend
1959 – 1990

"It must be her husband." Amnesia noted.

"Yeah." I agreed. I remembered hearing his name whispered through town.

"Look," she said, reaching around, grabbing the front of my hoodie and pointing. "There's another grave marker."

There was. This one much sadder than the one above it.

Beloved Child

Amnesia covered her mouth with her hand. Her shoulders shook. "She lost her husband and her baby."

"No wonder she's insane," I murmured. I actually felt sorry for the old bat.

"I can't imagine losing my husband and my child." Amnesia's voice was overcome with emotion. Instantly, she turned and buried her face in my chest.

I held her close, rubbing my palm over her back as I stared down at the graves. It made sense why she never left this island. If her husband and child were buried here, if this was the place that held all the memories of the life she lived with them…

I wouldn't have left either.

"It feels like an invasion to be here right now," Amnesia confided, looking up at me with sorrowful eyes.

"Come on. Let's go home." I urged, tucking her beneath my arm and leading her away from the headstones.

"I was so sure we'd find him. Find something."

"We still have the dental records." I reminded her.

"I wanted more," she whispered.

I knew she was let down, but I couldn't help thinking maybe this was for the best.

Reaching the crude path, my feet turned toward the house and beyond it where the boat was docked. But Amnesia faltered, her steps hesitant.

"Am?" I asked, turning back.

The look on her face was faraway, haunted.

Stepping close, I hunched around her. "Hey, what's wrong?"

She blinked, clarity coming into her eyes. "This way," she said, tugging me in the opposite direction.

"I think we've seen enough," I argued.

She let go of my hand and went anyway, as though she were spurred on by something only she could see. Nervous energy crackled along my nerve endings as I followed along.

She said nothing, and neither did I.

She walked for what felt like forever, winding around the edge of the island, where the land nearly dropped off into the lake.

The trees grew thicker, the sunlight dimmed by the cover overhead. I watched Am let the hoodie fall down over her hands, tucking her fingers in the fabric to shield them from the cold.

My eyes stayed peeled, my body on high alert. Everything inside me was coiled, anticipating something… I just didn't know what.

"They searched the entire island?" she said suddenly, her voice quiet.

"Yes, they searched this place more than once. Nothing was ever found."

A few steps later, she stopped abruptly, looking up. "There it is," she told me, terrifyingly void of emotion.

I followed her eyes, looking up into the trees.

There was a deer stand over us, up in the branches. Leaves fell over it, covering the old, unreliable wood with foliage.

"That's what I jumped from that night, the night you found me."

My stomach twisted. Stepping closer to the line of trees, I peered over the edge, glancing down at the water. It was rocky down there. A few feet out, the water was clearer, less dangerous. She must have jumped outward, away from the rocks.

"I guess that proves the memory I have of jumping off it. Of running from him here, on this island."

I lunged forward, grabbing her, roughly pulling her against me. I wasn't sure if I was holding her so tight for her or for me. Maybe it was both.

"He's not here," I told her. "He can't hurt you today."

"The memories will always hurt me. They threaten to appear any moment."

My heart squeezed. She was right, and I hated it.

Amnesia pulled away and continued on.

"Where are you going?" I said, rushing to catch up.

She didn't answer, just kept moving, weaving through the trees. Abruptly, she stopped again, staring off in the distance. I could see the way her breathing increased, the way her chest rose and fell rapidly.

Her body began to shake. She chewed her lip nervously.

"Amnesia." I grabbed her arm, trying to pull her close.

"Here," she said, resisting me. "He's here."

Concern darkened my face. "There's nothing here, baby," I said gently. "It's just trees and dirt."

Her eyes flashed up to mine. "He's here." She insisted. "I can feel it."

She was creeping me out. "Okay," I answered patiently. "Where?"

She turned in a circle, so I did, too. "We're missing something," she murmured. "Think, Amnesia. *Think.*"

We stood there for a long time. I watched her pace a small area over and over again. She became increasingly agitated, which was very difficult to stand by and observe.

Veering from her pacing, she wandered over toward the edge of the island. The drop-off toward the water wasn't as sharp. She stood with her back to me, hair blowing wildly around her face, and the giant Loch Ness on the back of the hoodie stared at me, almost mocking.

"Why can't I remember?" she screamed toward the water. "Why?"

I was done with this. Done with watching her suffer.

Rushing forward, I wrapped my arms around her from behind and pulled her tight against me. "That's enough, Am. No more. You're killing me."

She started to cry. Deep, gut-wrenching sobs that wound me up so tight it hurt to even take a breath. "I just want to know," she wailed, her knees buckling.

I supported her weight, keeping her upright as she sobbed. I pressed my face into her neck, wishing I knew how to take this away.

With a hiccup, she turned, wrapped her arms around my waist, and squeezed close. I pressed my hand against the back of her head.

She cried more, then ripped away, stumbling a few feet behind me.

I went after her. Before I caught up, she melted to the ground, sitting cross-legged and bowing her head.

Sniffles floated around her, and my heart broke. I sank down to the ground with her, spread my legs so she was between them, and tugged her close.

Her crying quieted until the only sounds were her heavy breathing. She wiped her face over my sleeve again and again, but I only held her tighter.

I knew I should drag her off this hellhole island, but at the same time, I felt like she needed to sit here and cry.

Her sudden gasp was so violent and unexpected I jerked back, looking down at her, alarmed.

"Amnesia?"

Blindly, she reached out, squeezing my wrist with strength I really didn't know she possessed.

"They searched everything here?" she asked again.

I wanted to groan. "Yes, baby. Everywhere."

"Down there?" she whispered and pointed at the ground.

I frowned. "The ground?"

She shook her head impatiently. "Beneath it."

"What do you mean?" My heart started pounding.

"He's here," she intoned. Her fingers scratched at the dirt we sat on. "Underground. Beneath us."

CHAPTER ELEVEN

AMNESIA

"Help me look," I said, scrambling to my feet and dashing away the wetness on my cheeks.

"For what?" Eddie asked.

"A door!" I exclaimed. "An opening! Something!"

I didn't wait for him, but began searching the ground for signs of something. I knew it was here. I was sure of it.

"Baby," he said, almost as if he felt sorry for me.

Something inside me snapped. I jerked upright, staring him straight in the eye. My body was vibrating it shook so badly.

"Don't you baby me," I half growled. "I'm telling you something is here. Believe me." A lone tear trailed over my cheek, and I quickly brushed it away. Tears would get me nowhere.

He blinked. Nodded firmly. "Of course, I believe you."

We said nothing more after that. Instead, we worked, faces downturned toward the ground.

Flashes of the memories I had before haunted me. The sound of chains rattling, the way everything was always dark. Always cold. The almost crude wall and floor, as if it were made of jagged concrete… or rock.

The feeling that when dim light shone down into the space, it was like heaven looking down upon hell.

Maybe I hadn't been kept on the island.

Maybe I was *in it*. Under it. Hidden somewhere no one would expect.

"Holy fucking shit." Eddie's voice broke into my thoughts. I glanced up.

He was staring down at a patch of grass, body stock still, tension radiating off his every limb.

"Eddie?" I asked.

He glanced up, eyes partially disbelieving, partially angry. He didn't say anything, just held out his hand to me. I went to him quickly, taking his hand, which was much warmer than mine.

"Look," he said, drawing me into his side, putting his arm around my middle.

"What am I looking at?" I asked, slightly confused.

"Notice anything different about this grass?"

I studied it, then looked around at everything nearby. "It just looks a little greener than the rest." The grass here was patchy, but that was just the landscape of the island, not necessarily something odd.

"Exactly," he murmured, then promptly blew my mind.

Eddie leaned down, taking large handfuls of the tall, greener grass, and tugged. It gave way, lifting off the ground like a heavy carpet, folding in on itself as he straightened.

Gasping, I stared down at the wooden platform that was hidden beneath it.

"I was right," I echoed, almost as if I shocked myself.

There was a small metal ring bolted on the top of the hatch door and several large bolts that kept it bolted closed from the outside.

Trapped.

Locked away.

Hidden in the dark.

Hidden in plain sight.

Tears filled my eyes again. Eddie made a sound and yanked me to him. "This is fucking sick," he rasped.

I didn't say anything. My stomach filled rapidly with dread and this panicky, hollow sensation started to take over.

"All the locks are undone," Eddie observed, something that had completely escaped me.

"Do you think h-he's down there?" I quaked. "Hi-hi-hiding?

His arms held me tighter, so tight it almost hurt. "I don't know." Suddenly, he burst into action, practically leaping on top of the door and slamming two of the deadbolts home.

"What are you doing?"

He looked up, his blue eyes wild. "Trapping him inside. Keeping him there until the sheriff arrives."

"You can't!" I cried.

He frowned.

"I need to know, Eddie. Now. I need to ask him if I'm really Sadie. If he kept me down there all these years."

A tortured sound ripped out of him. "You really think he kept you locked in a hole all these years?"

My chin wobbled. "I really do," I whispered. "How else would I have known it was here?"

Eddie's jaw worked, but I was past seeing his anger. Beyond really seeing anything except the past.

"He broke my arm down there," I said, no emotion in my voice. "I chopped my hair down there because he got mad when I braided it…" My voice caught as I remembered the chains. "I was naked, chained… He raped me."

A guttural sound echoed around the entire island. I jumped from the intensity of the sound. Reality came back, my stomach wobbled, and I swallowed, working to hold back the vomit.

"Fuck the cops," Eddie said in a tone I didn't recognize. In a tone that matched the sound I'd thought was an animal. "I'm going down there."

My eyes almost fell out of my head. My mouth dropped open wide. He was standing there, legs wide and planted against the hatch. There was a gun in his hand, drawn and ready, as though he knew exactly what to do with it.

I didn't even know he had a gun.

"Oh my God," I whispered. "Where did you get that?"

He didn't look at me when he answered, but down at the wood. "Did you think I would bring you here without a way to protect you? I didn't think I'd need it… but in my wildest nightmare, I never thought I'd be going down into a hole where the woman I love was tortured."

I didn't even think about the gun or his solid intent to kill. I didn't even notice the killer edge in his eye or the taut way in which he spoke. He was my Eddie, and my Eddie was no threat to me.

I rushed over, my feet thumping over the wood. "You can't use that." I laid a hand on his chest. The pounding of his heart was unmistakable. "You're not a killer."

"No." He agreed, putting his free hand over mine. "I'm not. But I'm also no saint."

"I don't need a saint. But I need you to be here, and if word gets out you killed a man on Rumor Island, they'll take you away."

"No, they won't." He sounded so sure. "No one in town would turn me in for killing this son of a bitch."

"We don't even know if he's down there." I reasoned. "At least put it away until we find out."

"If I put it away, *then* we find out, it will be too late."

He had a point.

"At least take your finger off the trigger."

His eyes met mine. "You know I would never hurt you."

"I know."

He nodded, took his finger off the trigger, but kept the gun in his hand.

"Let's just see if he's down there. Then we'll decide what to do," I said, trying to be sensible. It was clear Eddie might not be capable. His intense anger might prevent him from thinking clearly. Even though I desperately wanted answers and to speak to the man who stole my life, if he was down there, it might be better to let the police haul him away.

It would take longer to get my answers that way.

But it might also keep Eddie out of the jail cell beside the creep.

"Stay back." Eddie warned. "Promise."

"I swear." I nodded, solemn. I pressed a hand to my stomach, trying to calm the way it rolled around.

"Step back," he said, stuffing the gun into the waistband of his jeans.

I moved back several yards, unable to take my eyes off the latch.

Eddie moved in front of me, cupping my jaw with his steady hands. "Look at me."

I did, his blue eyes a wonderful place to rest.

"I love you," he vowed. "No matter what, okay?"

It was tough to swallow. Emotion clogged my throat. Instead of speaking, I gripped the front of his hoodie, filling my hand with the fabric. Standing on the tips of my toes, I leaned up and he met me halfway.

Our kiss nearly sizzled in the air. It certainly sent emotion crackling through my body. He hugged me tight, delving his tongue deep into my mouth. A small sound of comfort echoed in my throat as the kiss went on and on.

How easily he took away reality, even for just a small second. How easily he gave me back some footing, even as we stood here on uneven ground. This was one of the most precarious moments of my entire life (that I could remember), and I was scared to death, about to vomit or cry. I had no idea what would happen next.

But it didn't matter.

He was here. He was mine.

The kiss grew softer, gentler. The warm thickness of his mouth was so desirable I drew back enough to lick across his bottom lip.

He smiled against me, and I cuddled into his chest, dipping my face into him. Our bodies rocked back and forth a little as he held me. The comfort he surrounded me with was unmatched.

The moment we created between us was short lived. Interrupted by a few tentative knocks.

Eddie straightened and spun, tucking me behind him and holding me there with both his arms. "Who's down there!" he called, his voice deep and low.

There was another knock, louder this time.

"Hello!" a muffled voice replied.

"Stay back," Eddie said. "It's probably a trick."

I nodded, wide-eyed, and watched as he stepped closer and drew his gun. After undoing one of the deadbolts, he placed his hand on the other.

"I'm opening this door, and I have a gun. I'll fucking shoot you dead, so don't try shit!" he spat.

I shuddered.

"Please, no!" the voice yelled, still muffled from where I stood.

Eddie's face twisted. It was the oddest expression I'd ever seen him wear. The gun in his hand went slack for a moment.

Then shaking it off, he threw back the lock, grasped the metal ring, and pulled open the door.

CHAPTER TWELVE

EDWARD

The door banged back against the ground when I threw it open. Everything below was dark and still. The scent of earth and must rose and wrapped around my nose.

Lifting the gun, I trained it at the opening because, frankly, I expected something to launch itself out in a planned attack.

"Hello," I called down into the dark hole, puzzling over the fact someone had just been there but was now swallowed up by the dark.

"Who's down there!" I called out again.

Amnesia shifted, and I glanced up, making sure she was okay. She looked nearly haggard. The stress of this island, the feelings it brought up, or maybe the memories—hell, could be a cocktail of all three—were hurting her. Draining her.

It scared me.

"Is it him?" she asked, her voice small.

My teeth gnashed together. How anyone could hurt her shocked the shit out of me.

"Show your face!" I roared, this time with an underlying threat in my tone.

The faint sound of movement below made me stiffen. I raised the gun again, aiming it and holding steady with both my hands.

Slowly, achingly slowly, a figured moved into the light streaming inside.

I caught a flash of white fabric before a face lifted, and my breath caught.

Of all the things I expected to see down in that manmade cave, I saw the very last I ever imagined.

It wasn't a man.

Or an animal.

It was a ghost.

"Eddie," she whispered as though she too couldn't believe her eyes.

I tore my stare away and looked at Amnesia. Then back down into the hole.

She was still there. Both of them.

"What is it, Eddie?" Amnesia asked.

I looked back down, feeling my knees begin to shake.

"Eddie, you came for me," the voice in the hole said, and then she began to cry.

"Sadie," I whispered. "Sadie."

She was looking up at me, a face so familiar, a face that appeared the same, just a little bit older. "You remember me?"

I wanted to groan. *How could I forget?*

"Eddie, who is that?" Amnesia asked, creeping closer.

My body tightened again. "Stay back." I warned. The danger of this situation wasn't erased because I was looking down on a ghost.

"Who else is down there?" I demanded, harsh.

"I'm alone," the girl in the hole replied. Her voice shook. "Is h-he up there?"

"No one's here but us," I told her.

"Does that mean I can go home?" she asked and began to cry again.

My chest squeezed. I did the only thing I could think to do. I jumped down into the hole.

Amnesia's voice was scared and frantic above me. The second I landed, I looked up. She was peering down over the edge. Her small, pale fingers curled around the opening. "Eddie!"

"It's okay," I called back. "I'm fine. I'll be right up."

It took a minute for my eyes to adjust to the barely-there light. I wished I had a flashlight, but since it was daytime, I hadn't thought to bring one.

The sound of a match scratching against something put me on high alert, but then a soft glow filled the darkness.

I looked across the space where she was standing. In her hand she held up a lantern. She was dressed in a white nightgown that was so long it hit the floor. The straps were thin, just like the material, and it needed a good wash.

Her hair was light colored, but not as blond as I remembered. The strands were straight and long, hanging down her back, past her shoulders. She was slim, medium height, with brown eyes.

"You came for me," she finally said, her eyes never once leaving my face. "You still look the same. Only much more handsome."

I groaned. It ripped right out of my soul. "Sadie," I said. "It's really you?"

"It's really me."

I lunged through the darkness, no thought at all in my head. She placed the lantern on a nearby table, and I pulled her into my arms.

She melted against me. The long strands of her hair brushed over my arms as I squeezed her close.

"I thought I would never see you again," she said, emotional. "I thought I was going to die."

"No," I said, adamant, drawing back and taking her by the shoulders. "I won't let that happen."

Her eyes roamed my face. She reached up, fingering my curls. "Still curly after all this time."

I couldn't believe it was her. The girl I lost. The girl I'd been convinced was my future.

"I'm so sorry," I said, unable to keep the distress from my voice. "I'm so sorry I let this happen to you. I…"

She hugged me again, silencing my words. "Thank you for coming. Thank you for saving me."

Her voice was the same. Memories came flooding back to me, all the time we used to spend together.

Behind us there was a bang, and a shadow crossed over the opening in the ceiling. Sadie reacted instantly. Her body went limp. She slid down my body and hit the ground, throwing her arms over her head. I stared in shock and horror as she cowered.

There was another loud sound that echoed around the hole.

"Oh my God! He's coming!" she cried, reaching out and grabbing my foot. "He's coming. Hide!"

CHAPTER THIRTEEN

AMNESIA

He jumped.

Literally leapt right down into a dark, suspicious hole where a killer was squatting.

What the hell was he thinking?

I raced over to stare down, prepared to throw myself down there if needed.

"It's okay," he called out. "I'm fine. I'll be right up."

Is he out of his mind?

Who was he talking to down there, and why did the voice seem familiar? Not at all like a man.

There was no yelling or gunfire (thank God), nothing that made me think something terrible was going on down there.

If nothing terrible, then what?

What the hell is happening?

Standing up, I paced a little, staying very close to the opening. I knew I needed to get down there immediately.

The desire to find out exactly what was hidden in that hole, what made up the space, was intense.

But…

Something was holding me back.

Eddie was down there. He wasn't screaming or fighting. That meant it must sort of be safe. Right?

Probably not.

I was scared. So scared my limbs were shaking and I kinda felt I might pee my pants.

PS: Don't tell anyone about that part. How embarrassing.

What if I went down there and never came back up? What if the door blew shut or the man showed up and locked me down there?

What if I went down and the last eleven years replayed in my head on fast-forward and my life was changed forever?

Eddie made a sound, and I rushed back over. There was a soft glow somewhere down there to one side.

"Eddie?" I called.

He didn't answer.

My tummy twisted. I began chewing my nails.

"Eddie, are you okay?" I called out again.

Still nothing.

I jumped up, pacing away. Then paced back.

I was going down there. To hell with the consequences. If it were me, Eddie would already be down there, ready to fight.

I charged over, determination (or maybe adrenaline) filling my limbs. There was a metal ladder leading down into the hole. It was thin, unsafe, and frankly scary looking. I turned around and dropped my feet on the top rung. The metal vibrated loudly, making my entire lower body quake, but I didn't stop.

I started climbing down, the metal groaning and shifting as I went.

"Oh my God! He's coming! He's coming. Hide!" a woman screeched. My body reacted, turning toward her yell. That voice was familiar to me…

"Hello?"

"It's not him," Eddie said. "It's okay. No one's going to hurt you."

Who was he talking to?

"Amnesia." Eddie appeared out of the dark when I was just about at the bottom. My fingers hurt from gripping the metal so hard. "What are you doing?"

"I called for you. You didn't answer," I replied.

He reached out, completely lifted me off the ladder, and put me gently on my feet. His chin lifted toward the surface where the sunlight streamed in. "We can't all be down here," he said, grim.

"I'm sorry," I whispered, gazing around.

"Don't be sorry," he said, leaning over and kissing my temple. "You were scared."

"I still am," I whispered.

Eddie wrapped an arm around me, and I leaned my cheek into his chest with a sigh. From the safety of his arms, my eyes gazed around the poorly lit space.

The walls were rock, as though this place were carved right into the land. The floor was hard, uneven, and dirty. I had a distinct memory of what it felt like to be dragged across the surface, completely naked, and flinched.

Eddie's other arm came around me, and I gripped his arm.

There was a crude wooden table and chains… lots of thick, rusty-looking chains.

My eyes moved past them, past the empty side of the room, where a wadded-up article of clothing lay, then on toward the light… and the girl who stood within it.

The second our eyes collided, I gasped and straightened away from Eddie.

"Sadie," I murmured without even meaning to.

"You remember," she said, staring at me as intently as I looked back at her.

"You're Sadie," I echoed, shock rippling through me.

She started to say something, but I spun, tears flooding my vision, and looked at Eddie. "I'm not her," I said, voice weak and wobbly. "I'm not Sadie."

He shook his head. "No, baby. You aren't."

I collapsed against him, a sob ripping from my chest. As I cried, my mind raced. I'd come here for answers, thinking I would find my kidnapper. Thinking I would find proof of what everyone already knew.

That I was Sadie. The girl who vanished over eleven years ago.

Turns out everyone was right to doubt it. Even Eddie.

I wasn't Sadie. She was. And I knew her… but I didn't know how.

I didn't know how I knew any of this place, but it was so obvious I did.

I'm not Sadie. Just like Widow West said.

He doesn't love you. The vile echo cracked through my mind, and I flinched.

"Hey," Eddie murmured, brushing at my hair. "It's okay."

It wasn't okay. Nothing I thought I knew was right. Was anything?

"If I'm not her, then who am I?" I pulled back and looked up at Eddie.

He cupped my cheek, and I pushed my face into his palm. "Amnesia," he answered. "My Amnesia."

Across the room, Sadie made a sound. Eddie jerked away from me, going to her immediately. She started crying before he reached her, and I watched him wrap his arms around her.

I stared at them for long moments, trying to wrap my head around even just an ounce of this.

I heard her voice, tried to listen to what she said, but I was lost in my own head, in my own world.

Again, I looked around the room, seeing things that were familiar to me, and succumbed to a sudden entourage of emotion that drained me instantly.

This place was so vile. *So* horrible.

I'd prayed to die down here more than I prayed for escape. Pain echoed through my body, especially where my arm was snapped and on my back where I'd been whipped.

Suddenly, a loud cry broke out over the room. Someone started yelling, *Stop, please stop! She's going to die!*

This is all your fault, Sadie.

All. Your. Fault.

The whistle of leather cutting through air and then the sharp slap it made against skin was distinct. I fell to my knees as pain unlike any other befell me.

Someone was screaming, writhing in pain, but the beating just went on.

You're next, Sadie, he intoned. *You're next if you don't shut up.*

Vomit burned the back of my throat. I felt it hurl up through my body and eject from my mouth. My knees felt scraped and raw, but the pain was subdued compared to the pain in my back.

I heaved again, reality clashing with memory. I didn't know what was real and what wasn't. I didn't even know who I was.

"Who am I?" I asked and then heaved again, the vomit burning as it came up. It hurt so bad my lungs felt even they might collapse.

You're mine, a deep voice intoned. *You're no one's but mine.*

"Amnesia!" Eddie pleaded. "Jesus, please."

"Eddie?" I asked, lifting my head. It felt I was coming out of my coma all over again. Confusion and light warred within me. I coughed.

"Am, baby, it's okay. You're out now. You're out of that twisted cave."

"What?" I moaned.

"You're here with me. No one's going to hurt you. Cross my heart."

"Hope to die," I whispered. "You will be forever mine." The words, though I spoke them, calmed me. Probably because those were Eddie's original words.

I felt his hands in my hair. Everything seemed to come back, realign. I no longer felt I was on the world's best (or worst) tilt-a-whirl. Opening my eyes, I saw Eddie above me, the sun at his back, black curls glistening and ruffled in the wind.

I felt myself smile up at him. "What happened?" I asked, sitting up.

"You had some kind of panic attack," he said, concern darkening his face. "Being down there was too much."

It all came back to me, and I shuddered. "We're out?"

"Of course. I carried you out the second you collapsed."

"I think I threw up." I wrapped an arm around my belly.

"It's okay. That place makes me wanna barf, too."

I wanted to smile, but reality was too much right now. "I want to leave." I asserted.

"Me, too. This place sucks."

I grabbed his wrist. He gazed at me with a question in his eyes. "What about Sadie?"

"I'll get her and then we can go." He paused. "You okay?"

I nodded firmly, and he left my side.

So she was coming with us, then. Of course she was. Leaving her here was not an option. I, of all people, knew what she'd been through. Even just the small portion I recalled was hell.

And she remembered it all.

She belonged in Lake Loch. She deserved to have her life back. Maggie was her mother's best friend. Joline and Jeremy knew her parents, and Eddie was her childhood love. Even Robbie had been her friend.

Those people, they were her people.

They were mine, too, right?

Everyone had been missing Sadie so much for the past eleven years. So much they'd all wanted to believe I'd been her. They opened their arms to me, their homes. Was it all because they thought I was her?

I know I wasn't supposed to feel I was living someone else's life because technically all the time I spent living in Lake Loch was mine.

But I couldn't help it.

I couldn't help but wonder just how drastically the answers I found today would change everything.

CHAPTER FOURTEEN

EDWARD

We needed to get the hell out of here. No one was here on Rumor Island, but that could change at any moment.

There wasn't one doubt in my mind that there was a man lurking somewhere, a man who'd hurt Amnesia and Sadie.

Holy shit, I found Sadie.

There was no way in hell the widow could have done all this on her own.

Leaving Am up top, I leapt back down into the hole, sort of surprised she hadn't followed us out when I rushed (rather awkwardly) up the ladder with Amnesia.

"Sadie?" I asked, not sure how to approach her. I wanted to snatch her up and run like hell, but I held myself back. She was fragile; that much was entirely obvious. My God, the way she cowered when she thought the man was coming back...

If I hadn't wanted him dead before, now the urge was tenfold.

"What happened?" she asked, her voice small in the dark.

"It's okay." I promised. "Being back here is, uh, hard for Amnesia." That sounded stupid to my ears. Stupid and insensitive. This was so much more than "hard" on her, and Sadie, too.

"You call her Amnesia?" she asked curiously, moving back into the soft glow of the lantern.

"That's the name she gave herself."

"What about her real name?"

"She doesn't know her real name." I paused. "Do you?"

"It's Lily."

Lily. Like the flower. It was beautiful. I could barely digest it, though, any of this. Swallowing past the massive lump in my throat, I asked, "How do you know her name?"

"We're sisters," Sadie replied. "Well, we *were*."

I had no idea what that meant. Sadie didn't have any sisters. She was an only child. She was probably confused, dehydrated. Who the fuck knew what else?

Shit. Lily might not even be Amnesia's actual name.

"Come on. We need to go," I said urgently. I could ask questions later. Our safety was more important.

"Go?"

"Yeah, we're leaving."

She seemed confused. Her hesitation was something I wasn't expecting. I shifted on my feet, gazing up at the opening. "I'll take you home, back to Lake Loch. People are going to be so happy to see you."

"My parents," she murmured.

My heart broke. Sadie wouldn't see her parents. Hadn't she endured enough? But now she had to be told they died in a horrible crash caused by her own father.

Now was not the time for that. I wasn't sure when the time would be, but it wasn't now.

I went forward and took her hand. She glanced down to where I held her. "Come on."

"I can't go," she said, digging her bare feet into the floor.

"What?" I spun around. "Why?"

I honestly thought she'd run out of this cave so fast it would make my head spin.

Her voice dropped low, the tone warning. "He'll come back."

"Which is exactly why we need to go now." I pressed, giving her hand a little tug.

She yanked it out of mine, wrapping her arms around her middle. "He said I couldn't leave. He said I had to stay."

"He's a psycho!" I roared, my patience snapping.

She wilted, and I cussed.

"I'm sorry," I said, contrite. "I didn't mean to yell. It just… it makes me crazy to see you here like this, knowing you've been tortured all these years."

"How long have I been here?" she asked. "I tried to keep track…"

I pressed my lips together, then replied. "A long time, sweetheart."

She nodded. "You look like a man now."

"I won't hurt you," I said, thinking maybe the fact I looked like a man scared her. After all, she'd suffered extensively at the hands of a man.

"I know," she said, but there was a hint of doubt in her tone. "But he said I was his. He said I belonged here, with him. I'm not allowed to leave."

She was brainwashed.

I moved forward just slightly. "You don't belong here, Sadie." I held out my hand between us. She glanced at it, but made no move to accept. "And the only person you belong to is yourself. I'm here now. I'll protect you. I'll make sure you do anything you want, including leave here."

I saw the glimmer in her eyes. She wanted to break free.

She was like a bird in a cage.

A small, fragile creature that craved freedom, but didn't understand what it was.

Even though the door to the cage was propped open and no one stood in the way of escape, she hesitated. Because if she spread her wings and flew away, it would be to places unknown.

All she knew now was life inside here. She was kept. Hidden away. A beautiful bird, broken and locked up. A beautiful bird that once knew freedom but now only knew inhibition.

I left the door propped open but took a step back.

"Remember that time we got up just after sunrise and rode our bikes all the way to town just so we could get a fresh-out-of-the-oven donut from Joline and Jeremy's bakery?" I asked, smiling a bit at the memory.

"It had rained the night before, and by the time we got there, we were covered in so much mud, Joline made us wash up in the bathroom before she would let us have our donut."

"I told you we shouldn't have taken the shortcut through the field."

Her words pierced me straight in the heart. She remembered.

I chuckled. It was slightly forced because it was hard to laugh in this kind of situation. "You were right."

"Joline and Jeremy," she murmured.

"They're still there. Same bakery, same donuts. We'll get one." I cajoled.

Still, she hesitated.

"It's okay, Sadie."

"He said he would—" Her voice caught. "Hurt me if I wasn't here when he got back."

My teeth ground together so forcefully a pain in my jaw spread down my neck.

"He lied," I said gently. "I won't let him hurt you."

She debated another minute, which felt like an eternity. But then she stepped forward, her hand reaching out for mine.

"Okay."

The weight of responsibility sank down on me. She was trusting me enough to take her out of here, to keep her safe and protected. Even after the part I played in her getting here. I couldn't fail her this time.

"C'mon." I led her to the ladder. "You first, okay. That way if you fall, I'll catch you."

"I won't fall. I've climbed this a lot."

"That's good." I encouraged. "Go on."

She went, her movements definitely experienced. She even managed to avoid getting caught up in the too-long gown.

I went up closely behind her, nearly running straight against her when she paused at the top.

Her face turned back down. "You're sure he's not up here?" She worried.

"I swear. I searched the island before I found you." *I searched and then wanted to leave. Leave you here again…*

If it weren't for Amnesia, she'd still be down in that hole.

The second Sadie cleared the top, I practically catapulted out of that den of evil. I searched immediately for Am, making sure she was still okay.

She was still sitting on the ground nearby, looking pale and quite frankly wrecked. I started to go to her, but Sadie called my name.

"Eddie?"

I swung around, caught in the center. Up here in the sunlight, I noticed how much they favored each other. It was easy to see why we all speculated Amnesia was Sadie.

But there were differences, ones that now made it obvious.

"I'm here," I told her.

She glanced around as though she expected a giant eagle to swoop down from the sky and take off her head. Wind blew and the sound of the waves seemed louder.

Sadie shivered. "It looks different up here during the day."

"You usually come up at night?"

She nodded. "That was the rule. He left the hatch unlocked while he was gone but made me promise I'd only come out at night. Someone might see me wandering here during the day. Someone might take me away from him."

How was a man—or any sane person really—supposed to listen to these things? These insane meanderings of a lunatic that this girl spoke as if they made perfect sense. How was someone able to brainwash another human being to, in a sense, make them think they were a dog and not in charge of their own life?

"It was you," Amnesia said from close behind me. "It was your lantern we saw here at night."

Sadie's eyes widened. "You saw me?"

I went forward, already knowing where her mind was going. "Just your light. But it's okay. You didn't do anything wrong. It probably was nice to get out of there and walk around."

"The stars are pretty at night." She agreed.

I wanted to scream. To yell. To punch a thousand things.

"I thought it was him," Amnesia said. "I came here to find him."

"Oh, he'll be back," Sadie said. She was so sure. She glanced past me at Am, her eyes changing slightly, but I wasn't sure how. "He's very angry with you. He says when you come home, he's going to have to teach you a lesson and that you won't get as many nice things as I do."

What. The. Ever-loving. Fuck?

Amnesia's face went white. So white I started toward her, worried she might fold to the ground again.

"And your hair…" Sadie went on. Amnesia's hand flew to her wavy, short strands. "He's going to get out the whip."

Amnesia whimpered. I caught her around the shoulders and pulled her in, covering her ear with my hand.

"He won't," I said fiercely, turning to look at Sadie. "He isn't going to touch her ever, ever again."

Amnesia trembled against me. Sadie just stood there stock still, almost emotionless. As though she had the inability to see what her words just did.

"Don't ever say anything like that to her again," I said, trying to be gentle. "Amnesia doesn't understand. She doesn't need that running through her head."

"It's what he told me," Sadie explained.

I was so close to yelling. So close to screaming. I held it in, feeling as if doing so might cost me an actual few years off my life.

I glanced down at Amnesia, pulled her away from my body, and looked into her face. "We're going home now."

She nodded and started walking in the direction of the boat.

"Boat's this way," I told Sadie, gesturing for her.

She rushed forward and took my hand, her fingers like ice. That gown was so thin I could see through it in the sunlight, and the wind was so cold her nipples were completely visible.

"Here," I said, unzipping my hoodie and putting it around her shoulders. "It's cold out."

She looked down at the shirt, then pushed her arms through. "Thank you."

It seemed to take less time to get to the dock. I thanked God for that. I was never coming back to this island of hell ever again.

Everyone was quiet as we made our way to the pristine white boat. Sadie was definitely weak and malnourished. She tired out halfway to the dock and began to stumble.

It didn't help she was barefoot and the sunlight seemed to blind her.

I picked her up and carried her the rest of the way. She sighed in relief and practically went limp in my arms.

"Be careful." I gently reminded Amnesia as she walked down the dock toward the boat. It made me nervous to watch her because so much of the wood was rotted out.

She didn't look back at me when we made it across, instead just jumping into the boat and moving toward the back where she'd sat on the way here.

I was worried about her. Unfortunately, my worry had to wait.

Once Sadie and I were in, I sat her down beside Amnesia and fired up the boat.

I didn't spare a single glance back at the island as I jetted over the water, but the creepy, unstable feelings it possessed definitely followed us home.

CHAPTER FIFTEEN

AMNESIA

The hospital was chaos.

The second Eddie pushed through the doors, carrying a newly found Sadie, me trailing along behind them, completely shell-shocked, everything seemed to snowball into an avalanche of activity.

There was some yelling. Some crying. Possibly even some fainting. I sort of felt I was walking through fog, in danger of being lost. I knew what was happening around me, yet it was like I wasn't participating.

Sadie was swept into a private room, and Eddie followed along. The next thing I knew, he was taking my hand, pulling me out of the chair I was in and leading me into the room with Sadie.

She looked like me. Or maybe I looked like her.

My hair was lighter than hers, and I had more freckles. Both of us had brown eyes. Both of us were too skinny, and we had the same shape face. I understood now why everyone was shocked when I first showed up.

I knew by the look on her face she was completely overwhelmed and scared. I didn't know quite how she felt, but I thought it might be similar to how I felt when I woke up from my coma. Except she knew these people. Or most of them.

Eddie stayed at her bedside, holding her hand. She kept her eyes on him most of the time, even when trying to answer any question directed at her. Eddie spoke more than she did. I saw his mouth moving, but I didn't hear his words.

I didn't need to. I knew what was going on.

A soft touch on my arm made me jump, startled. The world came back into focus. Mary Beth smiled down at me. "Why don't you come with me. Let us check you out?"

"I'm fine, thank you," I replied.

"You don't look fine," she said gently.

"I'm sure I don't."

"Go with her, Am. Just to be sure," Eddie said.

I glanced at him glancing at me. He was still holding Sadie's hand. I looked away, over at Sadie. She felt my eyes and turned her head. We connected for long moments; there was recognition there, but I didn't know how much or why.

There was also something else. Something I didn't understand.

Something I didn't particularly like.

"I'll come with you," I said to Mary Beth and stood from the chair.

"I'll be right there to check on you," Eddie called behind me.

We went to a small cubical not far away. They took my vitals, asked me a bunch of questions, and determined I might be in shock but my health was fine.

I didn't bother to say I told you so.

"You can go back in there now," Mary Beth informed me after what felt like a hundred-year exam.

I looked back toward the room where Sadie and Eddie were. Even Maggie was there, having just arrived several minutes before. Doctors and nurses would come and go constantly.

"Actually, would it be okay if I went home?" I asked.

She looked a little surprised, but her eyes softened. "Long day?"

"The longest." I tried to smile. I failed.

"Of course." She patted my hand. "How about I give you a ride?"

"Aren't you working?" I asked.

She shrugged. "Patient care is my job. Besides, everything's so crazy here right now. No one will notice if I'm gone for ten minutes."

"That would be great." I accepted the offer.

"Just let me get my keys. You go tell Eddie, and we'll meet at the elevators."

I nodded, and when she was gone, I walked to the elevators to wait. I didn't go tell Eddie where I was going. He was with Sadie, and right now, his focus should be on her.

My focus should be on me. I needed some time to myself. I needed to process… to cry.

I'd call him in a little while. He probably wouldn't even notice I was gone.

"All ready?" Mary Beth asked when she came, keys in hand.

I fake smiled and nodded, and we were on our way. Thankfully, she didn't want to make small talk or even go on and on about finding Sadie or how it happened. She was a comforting companion, actually, quiet but not cold. Silent but not awkward.

When she pulled up to Maggie's, I laid my hand on her arm. "You would make a really good friend," I told her.

She smiled. "I'm always here if you want to hang out."

"Thank you," I said and got out of the car.

When I walked into my room at Maggie's, tears of relief, pain—I don't know what else—filled my eyes and began to spill over. I ignored the wetness and the way it continued to rain from my eyes as I moved along selecting clean clothes and walking into the laundry room.

Elmo heard me and rushed downstairs. His little white body was like a ball of comfort. I sank onto the floor to greet him and ended up crying harder, holding him against my chest.

After a few minutes, the dog began to wiggle, wanting free. I set him down, and he licked my chin before running into my bedroom, probably looking for Eddie.

He wasn't there.

He was with Sadie.

After pushing up off the floor, I stripped off my clothes. If I had the luxury of tossing them all in the trash, I would. But I didn't have enough clothes to be so flippant with the ones I had. I would wash them up. The stench of the island would come out and the vomit would wash away.

Not that I would throw away the hoodie Eddie gave me. It could have the tears of Satan himself on it, and I still wouldn't give it up.

Sadie had one now, too.

He'd wrapped her in it on the island.

I was a terrible person because when I saw him do it, I felt pain. Jealousy. Insecurity. It was wrong to feel that way; I knew. Sadie was cold, scared, and a victim. She was also his long-lost love. Even if she wasn't all those things, Eddie would have given her the sweatshirt. Of course he would. That's just the kind of man he was.

Good.

Kind.

Strong.

The man I loved intensely.

After I added the detergent and turned on the machine, I went through the laundry room into the adjoining bathroom and closed the door.

I set the water in the shower to hot and stood outside, waiting for it to grow warm. I glanced in the mirror above the sink.

Who are you?

Quickly, I turned away and stepped into the shower. More tears ran down my cheeks, mixed with the spray from the shower. I cried as I scrubbed my skin. I was rough because I felt so dirty. I wanted that place off me.

Too bad the answers I'd been so desperate to find weren't that easy to wash away.

That was the thing about memories. About knowing vs not knowing.

You could never "unknow" it afterward.

Unless, of course, you jumped off something, tried to kill yourself, hit your head, and then were hit again with something else… Then you might unknow things…

Yeah.

I always feared I was living someone else's life. There was always that doubt I wasn't Sadie. Everyone voiced it. Over and over again. Even I doubted it at times. But time went on. It seemed more plausible every day.

Or maybe I just wanted it to be true more and more every day.

But with all the doubt, I never actually considered what would happen if I went to the island and found out I wasn't Sadie.

I never in my wildest dreams thought I would find her.

And now here I was.

Standing in the shower belonging to a woman who let me stay because she thought I was her best friend's daughter. Standing beneath borrowed water, using borrowed soap, and sobbing my heart out because I was back. Back in that terrible place.

The place I was in when I first awoke from the coma.

Alone and with no idea who I was.

I was shackled regardless, wasn't I? In the end, it seemed answers didn't matter, because no matter what I learned, I still ended up back here.

Despair threatened to swallow me whole. An image of open hatch in the ground swam into my mind. It looked like a black hole in the center of the sunshine. It was a hole that *did* swallow me once.

At least I thought so. I wasn't sure.

I knew I spent time down there. All the memories I had were of that place. How long was I there? What else happened? Was Sadie also there?

The distant sound of laughter echoed in my head, and the feel of someone tugging my hair gently, as if styling it into braids, was so strong a sensation, I reached up to finger the short, wet strands.

I sank onto the floor and covered my ears, squeezing my eyes shut.

"No," I begged. "No more. Please let my mind stay empty."

Sobs of sorrow broke out of me. I let them come. I encouraged them. The sound they made in the enclosed stall drowned out the laughter and the feelings echoing somewhere deep inside me.

Instantly, cold air whooshed around me. Strong arms and a familiar body hunched close. He was warm. The kind of warm I couldn't get from the water. It startled me at first. I jerked upright and peered over my shoulder.

"Eddie," I whispered.

He didn't say anything. Nothing at all.

But his eyes.

Dear God, his eyes. They said more than words ever would. The intensity he emanated vibrated the air around us. I loved that force, the near obsession I felt when he looked at me like that. If I were ever going to be the victim of an obsession, I would wholly surrender to him.

Leaning down, he gathered me close and stood, slowly turning so he was beneath the spray, blocking it from my eyes.

He was completely dressed—white T-shirt, jeans, and Adidas. His hair was now partially wet. I watched the dry stands drink up the moisture and melt around his head. Water dripped off his square jawline and onto his shirt.

He acted as if he didn't even notice being completely dressed in a shower and me being naked.

It was sort of symbolic, though, wasn't it?

It represented how I always felt with him. Exposed. See-through. An open book. Sure, a lot of my pages might be blank, but they were open to him.

And he was clothed, not quite so easy to figure out. Yet as he stood there, becoming more and more saturated, his clothes grew thinner… more sheer.

I loved him. I loved him so much it seemed the emotion had the ability to kill me. I didn't know it was possible to love someone that much.

To hurt for them.

To be jealous when I had no right to be.

To be equally obsessed.

I knew my eyes were swollen; my cheeks hurt and were puffy. My lips were likely red from me chewing them, and my nose was stuffy. He'd heard me sobbing. There was no way he didn't.

I couldn't even stand here and pretend I was fine, that everything was fine.

It wasn't.

He knew it just as well as I.

The second he lifted me off the shower floor, I stopped crying. All of him except for a few rogue curls was completely drenched now. His eyes remained trained on mine. I watched him stare at me, hoping my eyes conveyed even a fraction of what his did.

Water slipped in my mouth when our lips met and mine parted. He wiped it away with his tongue and kept going. I clung to his shoulders as he kissed me deep. Emotion rose inside me, and I forced it into my reply. I wanted to tell him how much I loved him, how scared I was, and how vulnerable I felt. I couldn't say the words, but my lips told him anyway.

Using my teeth, I bit down gently, tugging his lower lip and sucking it into my mouth.

Eddie backed me up until my back pressed against the shower wall, then lifted me. I wound my legs around his waist, wrapping my arms tighter around his shoulders. His mouth ripped away, a deep gasp filling the room as he sucked in air, then dove into my neck, sucking the flesh deep and then smoothing it out with his tongue.

My head fell to the side as he continued to suck and nibble across my collarbone and latch onto my shoulder. My hips spasmed against him, but neither of us acknowledged the movement.

I felt boneless, completely light, as if I were floating. My body was pinned between him and the wall, his fingers roaming everywhere. One of my hands found its way into his wet curls, fisted there, and tugged his face up.

His eyes flashed to mine.

There was anger there. Desire. Love. It all swirled together to create the kind of cocktail that got a girl drunk with just one sip.

Oh, I was drunk.

I might never be sober again.

I attacked his mouth. He groaned into me, and I swallowed the sound. We kissed fiercely, almost violently. It felt so good to channel all the emotion inside me, to get it out so passionately.

Eddie ripped his mouth away again and pulled back enough so he could latch onto my breast. I cried out and arched into him as he sucked deep. My body trembled, desire so great it made me quake.

He moved to the other breast, first licking off the water, teasing, caressing, and then sucking deep.

The ache between my legs tingled, growing painful. My hips began gyrating against him, begging for more.

Lifting his head, Eddie reached between our bodies, felt my slick heat, and without hesitation, slipped a finger deep inside me. I cried out and slumped into his chest.

He pumped a few times, then pulled out. I tried to clutch him back, but he moved away, easing me down. My legs wouldn't hold me. They absolutely refused to stand.

With a devilish smile, Eddie held me while I sank to the floor like a puddle. With the wall supporting me, he stepped back. I stared up his body in awe, unable to form a coherent sentence, my knees and core still trembling for more.

The white T-shirt made a sucking sound as he peeled it off his body and a slapping sound when it hit the floor behind him. I licked my lips, then bit down when he unbuttoned his jeans and worked them down his hips.

When they were gone, he reached for his boxers, which were molded perfectly around his insanely hard dick. They came off much easier than the wet jeans, and the instant he was free, my field of vision was reduced to just his hips.

His cock jutted proudly away from his body. It looked strong, just like he was, and I knew from experience it had plenty of stamina. I shivered just knowing what it felt like to be penetrated by something so hard.

I tried to stand up, slapping my hand against the wall for support, but it was a no-go. I was too far gone.

Eddie stared down at me, his eyes nearly on fire, hooded with desire. Water cascaded over his shoulders, down his chest, and slid over his cock and around his balls.

I was jealous again.

Jealous of that water.

I reached for him, but he pulled back. He picked me up again, kissing me so thoroughly I started to melt back down to the ground.

His low chuckle filled the space. I was lifted again. My legs wound around his waist at the same time he slid deeply into my body.

I collapsed against him, hugging him tight because without the support, I would fall. He held still, let himself claim the deepest part of me. At last, he started to move, pull in and out, pierce me again and again.

I moaned because there was no way I could hold it in. He pressed me against the cold tiles, but I didn't feel it. My body slid up and down the wet wall with every thrust, and I loved every single second.

I didn't feel empty just then. Or alone. I felt full to the point of bursting, exactly where I belonged.

With a final deep thrust, my eyes flew to his. He stared back, telling me everything I was feeling, he felt, too.

Telling me he loved me.

Our chests met again, and I held tight. Gripping my hips, he pumped rapidly, and black spots formed behind my eyelids. I whimpered, and he went harder.

My teeth sank into his shoulder as light exploded over me. Pleasure rocked my body so hard it was all I tasted. All I saw.

In the distance, I heard him shout. His cock pulsed inside me, brushing against my inner walls with every throb.

I drank him in, wanting it all. Needing it.

I clung to him even though I knew I probably wasn't the lightest weight in the world. I couldn't let go. Not yet.

Not too inclined to let me go either, Eddie held on, left his cock inside me, and spun so I was beneath the spray. It pelted my back and slid between our bodies. Using one hand, he smoothed it through my hair.

Lifting my head, I kissed him again, tasting him and rainfall, the scent of sex thick in the air.

"I didn't expect you," I said when I was finally able to find my voice. It sounded as though I'd been cheering at a football game for four hours straight.

He smiled. "I know."

I glanced away. "You heard me crying."

He grasped my chin, guiding my face back. "I did."

"I'm not Sadie," I whimpered. Why did it always come back to that? Even after the mind-blowing (and I mean *mind-blowing*) lovemaking, I still just had to say that.

"I don't care."

I blinked. Blinked again.

He smiled slowly.

I started to cry again.

Oh my God, I was a mess. The emotions were too real. Too raw. To overwhelming.

Eddie's eyes darkened, and he pulled me close. When my cries softened into sniffles, he sat me down.

He washed me, his hands like heaven. Far gentler than mine had been. When he was done and I was squeaky clean, I did the same for him.

By the time we were both washed, the water was cold and I was shivering. Eddie used the towel to dry me off, then quickly dried himself. After swiping the fog off the mirror, I stared at myself again.

"You're still the same as you were this morning," he said gently, appearing in the mirror behind me.

I tilted my head. "Are you?"

His eyes flickered. "Maybe not."

I turned my back on my reflection. His arms came around my waist.

Tipping my chin up, I studied him. "But you still love me?"

A definitive answer bloomed in his eyes. My heart sang.

"There is one thing you will always be able to count on. One thing that will *never* change," he told me.

I tilted my head to the side. "That the sun will always rise?"

He shook his head. "More surer than that."

"More surer?" I echoed.

"The surest."

My fingers played in the wet curls at the base of his neck. The blue of his eyes was so bright everything else looked black and white.

"How much I love you," he whispered, resting his forehead against mine. "That will never change. *Ever.*"

For the first time in quite a while, I remembered why it didn't really matter who I actually was… because he loved me.

CHAPTER SIXTEEN

EDWARD

I never wanted to hear her cry like that ever again.

Ever.

I knew today was hard on her, but I didn't think it resonated with me until the sound of her gut-wrenching sobs echoed through the laundry room, reaching into her bedroom, and effectively bottomed out my guts.

I was so horrified; I wanted to hold her instantly. The urge to rush to her was immediate. But the sound, it was so painful, so hollow I sank onto the end of her bed for long moments, just letting it beat me up until I was bleeding inside.

When I realized she'd left the hospital, my first thought was to find her and make sure she was okay. I knew she was tired. Her haggard appearance made that perfectly clear.

I didn't know, though.

I didn't understand until I heard that cry.

Regret was the sharpest sword because I hadn't left the hospital right away. I'd waited until Maggie was there. Until the doctor had seen Sadie and she seemed to be resting comfortably.

I should have come sooner. Am had been in this house alone, thinking I was going to abandon her. Probably thinking everyone was.

I wouldn't do that.

Ever.

I was lying here staring at the ceiling, my mind so wound up I genuinely thought it might never shut off. I could barely wrap my head around any of this. I didn't know what to do. What the right thing was. No one could tell me either because this was a rare situation. I was afraid I'd screw everything the fuck up. That mistakes I might make would damage two women who were already damaged beyond repair.

Beside me, Amnesia shifted slightly, whimpering softly in her sleep.

"I got you," I whispered, tugging her even closer.

Her arm, which was already draped over my waist, hugged tighter. Her cheek settled firmly against my chest.

Her hair was still damp from the shower, a shower I would never forget. That had been some hot, fucking epic sex.

If I did say so myself.

The chemistry between us was undeniable. The way I felt about her was seriously unmatched.

That was an answer all in itself. My love for her outweighed everything else. Therefore, my main priority was defined.

What about Sadie? a part of me whispered. My stare returned to the ceiling. God, this was fucking complicated.

A low, tentative knock disrupted the quiet. Lifting my head, I glanced over to the closed bedroom door. Another subtle knock.

"Yeah?" I whisper-yelled, cradling Am's head in my arm and covering her ear with my palm.

"It's Maggie," she replied.

Carefully, I slid out from beneath Amnesia and the blankets and quickly pulled on a pair of gray sweats I always kept here—you know, in case I decided to shower fully clothed.

I didn't bother with a shirt. It was late and Maggie knew I was in bed with Am. She wasn't dumb.

Before opening the door, I glanced back at my girl. She looked small in the bed, her body still turned to where I'd been lying. Sometimes I ached just looking at her.

The door was soundless when I pulled it open partway and stepped into the opening. "Is everything okay?" I murmured.

Maggie was standing there looking as tired as the rest of us. Her hair was disheveled, and she wore a pair of dark pants with a long sweater overtop.

"I wouldn't say everything was okay," she replied, "but it's as good as can be expected."

"You just came from the hospital?" I asked, keeping my voice low.

She nodded. "How's Amnesia? This has to have shaken her."

I looked back at her before answering. "Yeah." I sighed. "It's been a lot. She's finally sleeping."

Maggie wrung her hands, shifting from foot to foot. "What's wrong, Maggie?" I felt my gaze sharpen. "Did something happen at the hospital? Is Sadie okay?"

"Nothing like that." She assured me. "But..." Her eyes went to the crack in the door as if she were trying to see Amnesia.

"But?" I cajoled.

"She's asking for you. She's been agitated since you left."

Damn. "I thought they gave her something?"

"Yes, but some things not even sedatives can cover up. She's been asking for her parents. She doesn't understand why they aren't there."

My eyes closed. "No one told her?"

"To be honest..." Maggie began. "I thought it would be better coming from you."

I sighed.

"I know it's a lot to ask." Maggie fretted. "And if you can't, I completely understand. She's just calmer around you, something that became evident when you left. You were always the closest person to her beside her parents. Even more than me. I'll tell her, but maybe if you're just there..."

"I'll do it." I agreed. "I'll tell her."

"Are you sure?" Maggie said.

I nodded. "How was she when you left?"

"She made me promise to call you, ask you to come back."

The muscles in my neck were tight. I rubbed at them with my hand while I debated on what to do. "Am needs me," I whispered.

"I know," Maggie said. "Maybe just call the hospital and talk to Sadie. Tell her you'll be there in the morning. Maybe just hearing that from you will help."

God. It wasn't enough. Not really. When I brought Amnesia in, I sat in the waiting room the entire night and half the next day. I had to force myself to just go take a piss. If she'd been awake, if she'd been asking for me, I would have fought everyone there just to get back into her room.

And now Sadie—the actual Sadie—was here, and I wasn't there.

"I'll call right now." I promised. "Why don't you go get some rest? It's been a long day."

"I'll go back to the hospital tomorrow." I heard the worry in her voice. "Oh, I wish Ann was here."

My chest tightened. "So do I." On impulse, I left the doorway and hugged Maggie. She embraced me for a few seconds before sniffling and pulling back.

"I'll see you in the morning. Help yourself to coffee or anything in the kitchen, okay?"

"Thanks." I nodded, softly closing the door.

I took maybe two steps before Amnesia's voice stopped me.

"You should go."

My body froze, head rotating toward where she lay. She was still bundled beneath the covers, but her body was turned toward me and the door, her eyes wide open.

"What?" I asked dumbly.

"Go to the hospital, be with Sadie."

"I'll go in the morning. First thing."

"I know you want to be there, and knowing she's asking for you is probably killing you. You waited a long time to find her, Eddie. Just go."

I couldn't tell how she felt about it. Her voice was even and the room was dark. But she sounded sure.

"I want to be here with you," I admitted, feeling oddly ashamed. Sadie needed me.

Her pale arm appeared from beneath the blankets, stretching out toward me.

I took her hand. The mattress dipped when I sat on the edge. "I know."

A low rumble vibrated through the room. I glanced toward the windows. A flash of light cracked through the dark. "It's going to storm," I murmured.

Sadie hates the rain.

"Go."

I leaned down and kissed her, soft and not too quick. When I lifted my head, she cupped my jaw. "I'll see you tomorrow."

I went, but the entire drive, I wondered if I'd done the right thing. In the parking lot, fat raindrops began to fall—slow at first, but by the time I made it to the entrance, rain was hammering the pavement with an angry force and the sky had turned up the volume with sound effects.

On Sadie's floor, the night nurses saw me coming. I thought they might argue with me like they used to with Am, but this time was different.

"She's been asking for you," they told me.

I didn't stop or even comment; I just went on past and pushed into her room without knocking.

Sadie was curled up on her side, arms wrapped around her knees while she rocked back and forth.

Whenever I looked at her, it was like a shovel to the midsection. For a second, it was hard to breathe. She was the same, but she was also different.

A loud boom of thunder rumbled overhead, and she made a small sound.

The side of my lip curled up. "Still scared of the rain, huh?"

She jolted, surprised to see me there, but recognition was fast and her look turned to relief. "You drove here in this?"

"Heard you were asking for me," I said, pacing across the room and dropping on the end of her bed.

"I missed you," she said. "I've missed you for so long."

Another shovel to the stomach. This one left me feeling slightly dizzy. She reached her hand out to me, and I gave mine.

"I missed you, too," I told her.

"I think about that night a lot." She confided, leaning a little closer as she spoke. "The night I fell into the water."

"What happened to you that night, Sadie?" The words burst right out. I knew it was too soon to ask, but my God, I'd waited so long. Scenario after scenario had played through my head over the years.

Her brow furrowed as though she were thinking about it, trying to remember every last detail. "The current was so strong. I remember trying to swim against it, my arms burning with the effort. The water was so dark. It was so hard to tell which way was the right way."

"I searched for you. I screamed your name," I told her. "I swear to God, Sadie, I tried so hard to find you."

"I know you did," she whispered, holding my hand a little tighter. "I heard you screaming. I tried to call out."

"What happened?" I asked again, the pain from that night returning and making my chest hurt.

"I came up for air. My lungs burned so much. Just when I got a few breaths in, I was sucked back under. The next time I came up, your voice sounded so much farther away. I called out to you, but I was so weak I barely even heard myself."

"Ah, Sadie," I murmured, scooting a little closer across the mattress.

The room was lit with a bolt of lightning and thunder roared outside the window. Sadie jumped, her hand falling out of mine.

"It's just a little rain." I promised.

She didn't seem very convinced.

"Cross my heart," I said, making an X over my chest.

A smile I thought I'd never see again transformed her face. "Hope to die."

I grinned, and together we said, "Stick a needle in your eye."

She giggled, and I laughed.

The moment didn't last long, though.

Her voice went low once more, matching the gloomy tone of the pounding storm. "I started to run out of energy. I was so cold, sluggish. I thought I was going to drown. Drown while I listened to the sounds of your desperate yells."

I closed my eyes.

"Just as I started to slip beneath the surface, someone lifted me out of the water and dropped me into a boat."

My head shot up. "What?"

"I thought it was you at first. That you'd found me."

It wasn't me. We both knew it wasn't.

"It was *him*. I hadn't been scared at first. I thought he was going to help me. After all, he saved me from drowning."

I nodded, trying to encourage her.

"He said my life was his because he saved it. He told me right from the start I was his."

"I'm so incredibly sorry, Sadie. So sorry I couldn't find you that night."

"I don't blame you, Eddie," she said. "This wasn't your fault."

"I never should have gone out on the lake that night."

"You just wanted to complete the dare. The dare Robbie gave you."

I glanced up. "You remember?"

"I remember everything," she said, her voice kind of hollow.

The storm raged on, the rain pelting the windows. Sadie shivered, pulling in on herself.

"You okay?"

Slowly, she shook her head. "Will you hold me?"

Immediately, I went to her side and put both arms around her. She laid her head against my chest, clutching the front of my shirt.

We sat there a while, quiet, her in my arms. I stared at the wall, going over everything she went through that night.

If only…

"Eddie?" she asked, lifting her face.

"Hmm?" I replied, pulling back enough to look down. She had brown eyes like Amnesia, but hers were a deeper brown, wider, and something else… Older. Wiser.

Amnesia had a certain innocence in her stare. Noting the difference between the two women now, I wondered if it was because of the memory loss. I wondered if Am would look older if she recalled everything that befell her.

"Why aren't my parents here?"

I stiffened. How did you tell someone, after everything they already suffered, that they would never again see the two people they loved most?

"Did they move away? Are they having to travel back?"

"No, sweetheart, they didn't move away."

"I don't understand why they aren't here. Maggie wouldn't say."

"Maggie didn't want to hurt you," I said.

"I want to know!" She pulled back, a freaked-out look clouding her eyes.

"Your parents aren't coming," I said gently. "They would if they could. They would have been the first ones through that door."

"Why, Eddie?" Her voice broke. "Why?"

I swallowed, remembering how much her father hated me, how much he would hate I was here now.

"There, uh, was an accident," I explained, trying to ease into it.

"What kind of accident?"

"A car accident," I replied. "Your mom and dad, they, uh, they didn't make it."

Her eyes filled with tears. Her face screwed up as if she couldn't understand what I was telling her. "A car accident," she whispered. After a moment, her watery eyes connected with mine. "They died?"

I nodded, my own eyes stinging. "Yes, sweetheart. They did."

A low wail filled the room, and she collapsed in my arms, crying into my chest. I held her because there was nothing else I could do. Nothing that could make any of this even slightly better.

She cried for a long time, occasionally whispering, "Mommy," or, "Daddy."

Eventually, she stopped crying, but her pain still filled the room. She clutched at my shirt, leaving her face buried against me. A short while later, she turned her head, pillowing her cheek on my chest. "When I was... gone, I thought about them every day. I wondered if they missed me. If they looked for me."

"They missed you. And they never stopped looking," I answered, hoping it gave her even a small amount of peace. "The entire town searched for you. Even the island. More than once."

"I heard them." She confided. "But I wasn't able to call out. He wouldn't let me. Eventually, they stopped searching."

"Eventually," I echoed. "But no one ever stopped hoping."

She sat up. Her face was blotchy and her eyes were bloodshot. "Even you?"

"Especially me." I tucked some of her hair behind her ear. "Your hair isn't as blond as I remember. It's more gold now."

"He said it was my best feature."

He was a filthy, sick pig that I would gut like a fish if I got the chance.

"How long ago did they die?" she asked.

"It's been several years."

"Before they... before the accident, they were okay?"

I decided not to tell her about her father's drinking problem and the strain it put on her mother. I wanted her to remember them as the people they actually were, not the ones they became because of unfortunate circumstances.

"They missed you so much," I told her, taking her hand. "But yeah, they were fine."

"What about you?" she asked, staring up at me with wide brown eyes.

"I missed you, too."

"You never got married?"

I was too busy waiting for you.

I found Amnesia instead.

"I was too busy helping Dad with the store."

"But you're with Lily now," she said.

"She goes by Amnesia."

"You thought she was me, didn't you?"

I swallowed. "Um, yeah. At first."

She nodded slowly, trying to work it out in her mind. "Well, now you know she isn't."

"Do you know who she is?" I had to ask.

"I told you. She's Lily."

"How do you know her? Where did she come from?"

"I'm tired," she replied.

Of course she was. I was a damn insensitive moron for throwing out so many questions. Especially after I just told her about her parents.

"It's okay. You've been through a lot. Get some sleep, and I'll come back in the morning."

"No," she said, catching my wrist before I stood from the bed.

"What's wrong?"

"Stay with me, please."

I half smiled. "Still scared of the rain?"

"He's going to come for me," she intoned. "He's going to want me back. Just like he wants her back."

"Her?" I said, alarmed. Did she mean Amnesia? Or the widow? Did she even know the widow? "Her who?"

"Please stay," she whispered. "Just hold me."

She pressed against me, and I gave in instantly, lying back against the sheets. Sadie slid as close as she could, laying her head on my chest. I felt awkward and wrong for being here with her like this.

"You make me feel safe," she whispered, tucking her hand beneath her chin. "Safer than I've felt in a long, long time."

My hand hovered above her for long minutes. Eventually, her words and my guilt won out, and I smoothed my hand over her hair. "It's okay, Sadie. You're safe."

"Please don't go," she whispered.

"I won't." I promised.

She drifted off to sleep, but for me, rest was much harder to find. I lay there and wondered who *he* was and what kind of lengths this animal would go to in order to get back what he thought of as his.

CHAPTER SEVENTEEN

AMNESIA

I wasn't prepared. Not for the sight that greeted me when I stepped into Sadie's hospital room.

The box of muffins I held wobbled, as though suddenly they were fifty pounds too heavy. On top, the beverage holder began to slide, and visions of coffee and hot chocolate splashing all over the floor and walls flashed in my mind.

Moving fast, I caught the drinks, pushed them back on top of the box, and steadied both with two hands. With breakfast firmly in hand, all my focus went back to the bed where Sadie was sleeping.

With Eddie.

Her head was against his chest, her body curled up along his side. The blankets were over her, but not him. Eddie was lying on top of the covers, fully dressed in gray sweatpants and a long-sleeved black shirt.

One of his arms was around her, keeping her close. His hair fell over his forehead, and I thought about the way it looked just last night when it was dripping wet in the shower.

It shouldn't bother me. After last night, the moments we shared… I think parts of me were still trembling from it.

It did bother me.

Knowing he left my bed last night and came here was one thing. But seeing them together like this stung pretty severely.

Obviously, he loved me. I felt it whenever we were close. I tasted it when he kissed me, and I just knew it deep in my heart.

Could a man love two women at once?

Did he?

I wanted to be his only love. Sometimes we didn't always get want we wanted. I think I knew that better than most.

Standing there with my heart literally caught in my throat, chest tight, and mind overfull, I debated on what to do. I could wake them. Give them the breakfast I brought and maybe try and talk to Sadie.

Or I could go.

Slip out the door as if I were never even here. Let them wake up alone. Give them time. Give *him* time. He agonized over this girl for almost twelve years. It wasn't a shock to see her in his arms.

But it hurt just the same.

I was going. This was awkward. I felt self-conscious and wounded. Since my stomach felt hollow, I decided to just leave the food. I remembered all too well what it was like to be in the hospital, starving for something real to eat. Sadie would appreciate the muffins and coffee.

I would even leave my hot chocolate in case she preferred that.

Creeping over with barely a sound, I cautiously slid the food and drink onto the bedside table. A quick glance beside me caught a vision I didn't want, but would likely carry forever.

The two of them pressed close. Peaceful in sleep.

Quickly, I skidded away as though I were fleeing from a masked killer, in a hurry, but also not wanting him to hear.

The door made a loud creak when I opened it, which made me wince, but I didn't turn back. I slipped out, slowly letting it close behind me, staying with it until it latched with no sound.

Heaving a deep breath, I leaned against it for a long moment, trying to compose myself. My heart pounded beneath my ribs, and I felt oddly out of breath.

A nurse turned the corner at the end of the hall, and I spun away, walking toward the elevators so I wouldn't get caught in conversation. The tap-tap-tapping of my sneakers against the squeaky-clean tile floor was impatient. The ding of the elevator arriving seemed to take forever.

I stepped inside, thankful I was the only one in the car. Bracing my hands on the wall, I leaned my bowed head against it to look at the floor. Behind me, the doors began to close, so I pushed off, turned around, and watched the entrance to the hallway grow smaller.

Right before they shut completely, a flash of movement stunned me. An arm jammed through the narrow opening and damn near got crushed.

I gasped, covering both hands with my mouth, anticipating the doors snapping shut and the arm being lobbed off and landing at my feet.

My imagination needed a serious chill pill.

Instead of cutting off the arm, the doors bounced back open.

"Eddie!" I said, rushing forward. "Are you okay? Your arm!"

"You see that?" he asked. "Almost got it cut clean off."

I smacked him. "That was stupid!"

He was standing in the hallway; I was still in the elevator. The doors began to close between us again. I squeaked and backed up. All this talk of dismembering made me paranoid.

He cursed and jumped forward, landing inside the small box with me.

"What are you doing!" I exclaimed dubiously as the doors firmly closed and the car began to glide down.

Eddie swung around and promptly hit the emergency stop button.

Beneath our feet, the thing lurched to a stop, making us rock unsteadily.

"That was the stop button!" I yelled.

"What gave you the first clue?" he drawled quite sarcastically. "The bright-red color, the giant size, or the fact it says STOP in bold writing?"

"What's with the surly attitude?" I asked coolly, crossing my arms over my chest. If anyone had the right to be surly, it was me.

"You saw us," he intoned, stepping forward. It was a rather menacing step.

My body thought it was delicious.

I lifted my chin. "In bed together? Yep. Got an eyeful."

His lip curled. "You thought you could run out without a word?"

"You looked busy," I snapped.

He sighed heavily, rubbing a hand over his already wild curls. "This is why I hit the stop button," he murmured.

"What?"

His eyes flashed up to mine. He walked forward against me until my back was pressed to the wall, his hands flattened beside my head, caging me in. "We're not getting out of this elevator until I make something crystal clear."

"What's that?" I asked, holding his stare.

"What you saw back there wasn't what it looked like."

"I know that," I replied. "You were comforting her. She needs it."

His eyes narrowed slightly, but he nodded. "She had a rough night. It's, uh…"

I laid a hand on his chest. "You don't have to explain. I know. She was your best friend. Your first love. You spent a long time wondering what if."

His eyes bounced between mine. Searching. I didn't know what he was searching for, so I couldn't give it to him.

"I hurt you. Seeing me like that with her hurt you."

"Maybe a little," I admitted. Then quickly I added, "But I know it shouldn't. I know—"

"Stop right there, Am," he growled.

My eyes grew wide.

"Your pain isn't any less important than hers. If anything, yours is *more* important."

A little part of me sang a joyous song. Clearly, I had some real issues here. "Hers is much more recent." I allowed.

"No." He came forward, his body pressing all along mine so I was sandwiched between him and the wall. His nose caressed my cheekbone; his lips brushed against my jaw.

I sighed. His touch was always my undoing.

Drawing back, he said, "Look at me."

Obviously, I listened.

"I'm in love with you. *You.* No one else. I thought you understood that after last night."

"I do." I promised. "I was just caught off guard this morning."

"I get it." He nodded. "If I saw something like that, I probably would have given the guy a bloody nose."

I wrinkled up my face. "Probably?" I mean, we all saw what he did when I got shot with a paintball, during a game.

His head tipped back when he laughed. "Definitely." Taking my hand, linking our fingers together, his face turned serious. "I can't promise you won't ever see Sadie in my arms again. She was my best friend. She needs someone to be there for her…"

I put my fingers against his lips. "I know that. I completely understand."

He nipped at my fingertips, and I yanked them away.

"No, you don't. What I'm trying to say is Sadie is my friend, and I feel responsible for what happened to her. You know I do." I nodded, and he went on. "But I'm in love with you, Am. Not her. There are parts of me, so many, that will only ever belong to you. I might hold her when she cries, but you're the only one I will climb into a shower for, fully dressed. The only girl I would lose an arm over trying to get into your elevator. Yours are the only lips I want to kiss. The only one I reach for when I wake up in the morning. Your body is the only one mine craves." His head rested beside my ear, our fingers still entwined. "I love you," he whispered. "Only you."

That little piece of me singing a joyous song?

It turned into a full-on choral performance.

"I wish I could say I didn't need to hear that, but I did."

He grinned. "I saw you scurrying from the room like we were in some bad soap opera. I was afraid you were going to be like one of those overdramatic characters who jumps in her car, drives erratically, and hits a tree because her heart is eternally shattered."

I blinked. "What?"

Oh my Lord, his grin unraveled me. Both dimples appeared, white teeth flashing. "Honey, if you think reality TV is bad, you should try some soap operas."

Curious, I asked, "They're on TV, too?"

Chuckling, Eddie grabbed me and pulled me in. I forgot all about whatever he was talking about. My belly overturned, landing somewhere near my feet, when his body folded around mine.

It was the kind of hug that consumed me. His large, tall frame hunched in, closed around me, and I was entirely surrounded. The scent of his skin, the warmth of his clothes, the sound of his heart beating steadily. I hugged back, holding him tight. My eyes slid closed, and all the insecurity I felt completely melted away.

"You brought us breakfast?" He pulled away but kept our hands linked.

I nodded. "I remember how grateful I was when you brought me food when I was here."

He kissed my temple. "You're a good person, Amnesia."

"I was hoping I could talk to Sadie," I blurted out, as if him calling me good was too much for my conscience to handle. I had so many questions.

"Of course you do," he murmured. "So do I."

"How is she?" I asked. "Does she seem… capable of answering? Does she seem…?" I faltered.

"Sane enough to believe?" He finished.

I nodded, feeling guilty.

Eddie reached behind him, hitting the emergency stop button again. The elevator groaned and started moving instantly.

"For the most part," he answered.

I tilted my head, silently asking him to elaborate.

The elevator stopped and the doors opened.

Eddie leaned forward and hit the button for the floor we'd just left. Turning to me, he said, "I had to convince her to leave the island."

Shock rendered me immobile. "She didn't want to go?"

"She wanted to, but she's scared of him. I almost feel she's been brainwashed."

"Widow West sounded the same way when she was going on about him." Without thinking, I reached up and tugged the ends of my hair nervously.

Eddie's hand came over mine. "He's not going to hurt you."

He knew I was thinking about what Sadie said yesterday. It was very similar to what the widow had said. He was going to be angry I cut my hair. He was going to punish me.

The elevator opened, the familiar hallway back in sight. Eddie led me off, stopping by a few windows that overlooked a parking lot.

"Do you think she'll be up to talking?" I asked.

"I think there's only one way to find out."

As we went back toward Sadie's room, my tummy filled with nervous energy. I couldn't help but be a little scared of the things we might learn.

CHAPTER EIGHTEEN

EDWARD

Torn. I felt torn between two women. Stretched so thin I was in danger of ripping.

For so many years, I begged the lake to give back Sadie. I bargained. I threatened… I prayed. I sank deep into the depths of guilt, what-ifs, and unknowns.

The lake replied. And in true Lake Loch fashion, what I was given was a mystery within the mystery. An answer that unwrapped a million more questions.

Not one girl, but two. And me with only one heart.

The lake was probably laughing now, proud of the game it played so very well.

Be careful what you wish for?

No.

I would rather struggle than not be here today. It didn't matter that what I begged for came in a package I wasn't expecting.

I had Sadie back. And I had Amnesia.

Those were two regrets I would never have.

I did feel some remorse, though. This was hurting Amnesia. She tried to hide it, but her poker face was nonexistent. I was glad for that because it was easy to see when she needed something (except when it was dark). Or maybe I was just that in tune with her, that perceptive of her emotions.

She might not have much memory. Unfortunately, she made up for it tenfold with loss. For a while there, I really thought she was Sadie. After the allergy, I changed my mind, but I'd slowly been changing it back.

Now we knew who she wasn't. We just didn't know who she was.

Even though we were never sure she was Sadie, finding out she wasn't? It was like ripping away her identity all over again. Amnesia had lost herself twice.

That's twice more than most anyone ever experienced.

She thought it mattered to me. Her identity. Maybe at first it did. It was all I thought about. But the longer I sat beside her bed, the more and more I was around her, everything inside me shifted. Toward her. Like the cells in my body permanently rearranged themselves to match up to her indefinitely.

I was already gone, fallen deep. I fell in love with the person she was, not the name she might have had.

Amnesia halted just before I could open the door to the room. "I'm nervous." She confided.

"I think it would be weird if you weren't."

"Do you think she knows me?" Am asked, anxious. I knew she was afraid of what she would learn. She was also afraid she wouldn't learn anything at all.

Talk about a double-edged sword.

"She knows you."

Her eyes rounded, and suddenly, I had a craving for milk chocolate. "How do you know?"

"She told me she did. On the island."

Am gasped before I could even say more. "You didn't say anything to me!" I watched as she crossed her arms over her chest and glared.

"Don't look at me like that, woman. I don't like it." I reached out and tugged her arms, trying to rid her of that defiant pose.

"Well, I don't like you not telling me things."

"If you would let me finish," I drawled and took her hand. "She told me she knew you, but in the rush to get off the island, I didn't think it was a good time. And last night…" I cleared my throat. "You didn't need information last night, baby. You just needed me to be there."

Her eyes softened. "Just because you're right doesn't mean I forgive you."

"Aww, don't be like that, Am. I'm telling you now."

She rolled her eyes. I thought it was kinda cute.

"Tell me."

"She says your name is Lily."

"Lily," she echoed. I watched thoughts play over her features. I watched her try and recognize the name. She tried so hard my heart pinched when she looked up at me and frowned. "It means nothing to me."

"It's okay."

"It's not," she insisted.

"Hey." I cupped the back of her head and pulled her in. She resisted. I released her and bent so we were eye to eye. "Give. It. Time." I urged. "And who knows? Maybe Sadie is mistaken. That's all she told me about you. Maybe she was confused."

"That's all she said?" she asked, crestfallen.

"Well, she did tell me you two were sisters." Amnesia gasped, and I held up my hand. "But Sadie is an only child, so that's not true."

She slumped forward. I wrapped an arm around her. "If you aren't up for this, it can wait."

"No. I'm ready," she asserted, left my hold, and went through the door ahead of me.

Sadie glanced up the second we walked in. Her eyes went first to Am, then moved to me. She smiled. "Eddie, I wondered where you went."

"Just stepped out to talk to Amnesia. Didn't want to wake you."

She held out her hand to me, wiggling her fingers. Suppressing my inward cringe, I went to her. But instead of taking her hand as she wanted, I picked up the drink tray Am brought. "Look, Amnesia brought us some breakfast."

"It smells amazing!" she said and smiled at Am. "Thank you."

Amnesia came forward. "I wasn't sure if you preferred coffee or hot chocolate," she said. "But I brought both,"

Sadie glanced at me, and we both smiled. "Coffee," we said at the same time.

"There's cream and sugar in the empty cup holder, there," Amnesia said, pointing.

"Thanks, baby," I said, handing Sadie a cup of coffee.

I felt her eyes when she took the drink, but when I lifted mine, she just smiled. I grabbed the cream and sugar and plopped it in her lap. "You used to use this," I said.

"Thank you."

After I plucked the second black coffee out of the tray, I took the hot chocolate out and carried it over to Am. "How'd you know she'd pick coffee?" I whispered when I handed it over.

"I didn't," she said simply.

She would have handed over the drink I knew she got for herself if that's what Sadie had chosen.

"What's in the box?" Sadie asked, pulling me around.

"Monkey bread muffins," Amnesia said. "I've never tasted anything better."

"Joline is still the best baker in Lake Loch?" Sadie asked, stirring the add-ins into her coffee.

"Of course," I replied. "That woman can outbake anyone."

"Is everyone else still here in town?" Sadie asked timidly. "Has anyone else passed?"

My heart clenched. "We've had a few people move to town, a few people move away. Most everyone is still around, though."

"Except my parents," she murmured.

I cleared my throat.

"I'm so sorry to hear about them," Amnesia offered, moving closer to the bed. "I'm sure they loved you very much."

"I loved them," Sadie replied, her voice sad.

I pulled the chair close and gestured for Am to sit down.

"What about you, Eddie?" Sadie asked.

"I'm good," I said, sipping the coffee.

"Sit," Sadie patted the bed.

Instead of making everything more freaking awkward than it was, I sat on the end of the bed, leaving my feet on the floor.

"You must be starving," Amnesia said, setting aside her cup and picking up the box to offer Sadie a muffin.

Sadie glanced at the food, then away. "Actually, I really don't have much of an appetite."

Amnesia nodded, sympathetic. "I can understand that." She started to put the box back.

"What about me?" I complained.

She laughed, the sound like the sun peeking out on a cloudy day. "Here," she said handing me the box.

I snatched one up and took a huge bite off the top.

Amnesia laughed again.

I couldn't take my eyes off her face. She looked better this morning. Not as haggard. She was still obviously tired, and worry lined her eyes, but at least she didn't appear on the verge of falling.

"Bite?" I asked and shoved the muffin in her face.

Smiling, she plucked a piece off the top. It was extra gooey with icing—those were her favorite bites—and delicately put it between her lips.

"You take such girl bites," I told her and shoved more in my face.

"Because I don't eat like a pig?" Am retorted.

I snorted.

An odd feeling wrapped around me, and I glanced over. Sadie was staring between the two of us with an odd expression on her face.

Amnesia cleared her throat and put the box on the table. Both her hands wrapped around the hot chocolate, and she sat forward in her chair.

"Sadie? Would it be okay if we talked?"

Sadie looked at Amnesia. "About what?"

Am glanced at me, and I nodded. "Eddie said you told him you know me."

"You don't know me?" she asked.

Slowly, Amnesia shook her head. "I don't remember anything before waking up here in a coma."

"Nothing at all?" Sadie asked, pulling the coffee into her chest.

"Well, I do have a few memories that have come back, but nothing that tells me anything about who I am."

"What do you remember?"

Amnesia swallowed. "The cave we found you in, that place was familiar. And hair braiding."

Sadie's face lit up. "We used to braid each other's hair all the time."

Amnesia's body tensed. Admittedly, so did mine. I didn't say anything, though. This was their time.

"We did?" she asked, sitting back. "Every once in a while, I'll hear giggling, like maybe we liked it?"

"It was our favorite thing to do," Sadie said fondly. "It's how we passed the time."

"But he didn't like it," Amnesia said, her voice low and afraid.

Sadie nodded solemnly. "Oh no. He hated it. We weren't supposed to do anything he didn't allow. That's why it was our secret."

"But he found out." Amnesia pressed. "Didn't he? And I cut my hair?"

"You remember that?" Sadie's eyes widened.

"I think so. So it's true, then?"

I couldn't imagine what it was like to have to rely on other people to tell you about your own actions. Your own life.

"Oh yes," Sadie's voice dropped. "He was so angry that day. I don't know why you had to make him angrier. You should have just let him punish you. But you didn't. You fought back... I thought you learned not to fight back."

Chills ran down my spine. The way she talked. It was so normal to her, as if she didn't realize how twisted it was that she learned to allow herself to be "punished" and not fight back.

"I did fight back, though, right? I got a pair of scissors and chopped off chunks of my hair.

"We both got punished for that, you know," Sadie intoned, her eyes going blank. "He might have broken your arm, but he punished me, too."

"How?" Amnesia sat forward. "How did he punish you?"

Sadie turned her dark, emotionless eyes on Amnesia. "You know how. You know."

It took everything inside me to stay rooted on the bed. To not grab Amnesia by the waist and haul her the hell out of the room.

I didn't want to know any more. I didn't want to hear. The thought of any of this shit happening to either of them made me want to puke.

"I don't know." Amnesia's voice wobbled. "That's why I'm asking."

Sadie tilted her head and studied Am. "You don't remember anything?" she asked. "That's what everyone says."

"If I did, I wouldn't be asking to relive it all over again!" Amnesia exclaimed.

"Am," I said softly.

"I'm sorry," she said, directing the words at Sadie. "I know how hard this is, and I know you probably don't want to relive any of it either. It's just…"

Sadie watched her. "Just…?"

"I need to know."

Sadie leaned back against the pillows, set aside her coffee, and pulled her knees into her chest. I watched with trepidation as she wrapped her arms around them and stared ahead, as if she were seeing nothing but what was in her mind.

"I was the first." She began, low. "He scooped me out of the water one night and locked me in a bedroom in their house. I spent the first few days screaming and begging him to let me go. I would hear arguments somewhere in the house. Yelling… a lot of yelling.

Sometimes screaming. One day, he came inside and dragged me through the house. At first, I thought I was going home, that he was tired of my screaming and was going to let me go. Instead, he threw me down into the hole in the ground, shut the door, and locked it. I heard people searching the island, people calling my name. I screamed for them. I screamed so long I lost my voice."

"Sadie," I whispered.

"He came back when everyone was gone, told me I was his and this was my new home. He, uh… beat me… Raped me and then chained me up, naked."

"He never let us wear clothes," Amnesia murmured.

"Only when he let us out," Sadie answered. "I don't know how long I was down there. I couldn't count the days because it was always dark. The only times he brought me up out of the hole, it was dark outside. I fought back at first. Tried to escape. Each time, he beat me. Raped me. Sometimes he did, uh, other things…"

"You don't have to tell us," I said, my voice savage.

"She needs to know," Sadie echoed.

"It's okay," Amnesia said, her face pale and withdrawn.

"I don't know how long I'd been there, a long time, though… Maybe a year? Or more. I, um… stopped bleeding every month. I stared getting sick, throwing up a lot."

"Jesus fucking Christ," I said and jumped off the bed, pacing.

"What was wrong?" Amnesia asked naively. My sweet, innocent Am.

"She was pregnant." The answer ripped out of me like a roar. "He got her pregnant."

Amnesia covered her mouth with her hand.

Sadie nodded, that blank look on her face. "It took him a while to notice, but when he figured it out, he was mad. So mad. He said it was all my fault, that I knew better than to get like that."

I wasn't sure how much more I could hear. How much more I could take.

"It wasn't your fault," Am said, trying to comfort Sadie.

"Maybe it was."

I groaned.

"I can go get Dr. Kline. Maybe you should talk to her and not us. She can help you. She helps me." Amnesia pushed up from the chair and leaned over to set aside her drink so she could go get a doctor.

Sadie moved suddenly, lurching forward and grabbing Amnesia's wrist. She cried out in surprise and tried to jerk back.

"Don't you want to know?" she intoned. "Don't you want to know how you got to the island?"

Red dots swarmed before my eyes. I didn't think, only reacted to the fact that someone put their hands on Am and she was struggling to get away. Lunging forward, I brought my forearm down over Sadie's and dislodged her hold.

Amnesia stumbled back, and so did I. I fell into the chair, Amnesia on top of me. Breathing heavy, I sat forward, wrapped my arms around her, and held her against me.

"Don't touch her." I warned, trying to sound as unthreatening as I could. "Just don't, Sadie."

"You love her," she said, her eyes meeting mine.

It seemed cruel to say I did. It seemed somehow disloyal. I nodded instead, because not voicing it somehow seemed kinder.

Sadie's eyes flashed back to Amnesia, who was still sitting in my lap.

"He beat me. He beat me until I lost the baby. I bled so much, was so badly injured, he thought I was going to die. I almost did… That's where you come in," Sadie told her. The expressionless way she spoke creeped me the fuck out.

"Me?" Amnesia asked, her voice quivering.

My arms slid tighter around her as if I could somehow shield her from what Sadie said next.

"You were my replacement," she said. "He got you to take my place. Except I never died. Instead, we became sisters."

CHAPTER NINETEEN

AMNESIA

"This is all your fault. All your fault, Sadie."

"Saaaadie. Saadieeee."

The sounds of him coming were unmistakable. His intent even more so. He always came around this time. And every time, he said the same thing.

Over on the other side of the place he kept us chained was another girl. Someone who barely ever moved. Someone I had yet to even see.

I knew she was there because I could smell the blood. I could hear her whimper in pain. Sometimes an old woman would appear, carrying a bucket of water and some rags. She never came over here. I never saw her that clearly. She would go over to that side of the room, and the crying would start.

They never spoke. All I heard were the sounds of dripping water as though it were being squeezed out of a rag. And the crying. I could never tell who was crying, whether it was the girl who barely moved, the old woman… or both.

Then she would leave. Take her bucket and climb back up the ladder. The slivers of daylight I sometimes saw physically hurt because I knew above us, out there, life went on.

I was naked. The cold rocks beneath me were uncomfortable and dirty. He told me I could earn some blankets, maybe even a cot. He never said how I would earn it, but judging from the fact the girl across the cave had a cot, I always figured I didn't want to do what she did to earn a thing.

"Sadieee. Saaadiee."

I shivered every time he sang that name. I knew it was hers, but whenever he said it, I knew he was coming for me.

I scrunched up against the cold, hard wall, trying to make myself as small as possible. Hoping and praying he'd forget about me and maybe go to the other side of the room. Something I knew was wrong to hope for, but I did just the same.

He didn't, though.

The beam of his flashlight found me. I was dragged away from the wall, my legs cut relentlessly by the jagged floor. The sound of rattling chains turned my stomach; the weight of the metal cuff around my ankle was like an anvil.

The last time he came, I fought back. I tried to get his light and bash him in the head. I ended up with a swollen eye, a bloody lip, and a stinging bite. A bite in a place that made me shudder.

This time I just lay there, so taut I knew I would hurt tomorrow. But I would hurt tomorrow regardless. There was nothing about me that didn't hurt anymore.

"This is all your fault, Sadie," he yelled across the room as he spread my legs. "If you hadn't gotten pregnant, I wouldn't have needed another you."

I blacked out while he assaulted me. The entire time he grunted and groaned and sweated over me, he called out Sadie's name.

When he was done, he left my body but kept me pinned down. The splatter of his seed spurted all over me. On my chest and belly. He grunted and moaned. I gagged in the back of my throat.

When he finished, I tried to crawl away, but he grabbed my ankle.

"You know better, girl." He hit me across the backside, my skin stinging wildly. I lay back as he expected, my eyes watering from the hit. Or maybe from the assault.

His hand was rough when he swirled his finger around in the mess he made of my chest, and I recoiled as he lifted the saturated finger toward my lips…

"Ahh." I gasped, catapulting out of Eddie's lap and racing to the door. It was a heavy door, hard to yank open, but I did it, rushing out into the hallway, barely seeing anything, just desperately trying to get away.

Tears streamed down my face. My hair floated out behind me, and my knees threatened to give out.

Someone yelled my name, but I didn't stop. I couldn't. The images wouldn't leave me alone. The memory… the sick torture…

The sign for the bathroom came into view. I abruptly changed course and bashed my way inside. I didn't even look to see if anyone else was there. I rushed in and hit my knees in front of the first toilet I saw.

The stall door banged behind me; all the stall walls vibrated with the force of my entrance.

Vomit spewed out of me. My back hurt with the force of it, and my throat burned. I coughed and gagged as I threw up everything inside me, plus some.

I wished I could throw up that vile memory. I wished it would go back to where it came from…

Hell.

"Oh shit, baby," a familiar voice said from behind. Air whooshed around me as the stall door was yanked open. Eddie crouched behind me. I felt his palm on my back.

"Don't touch me," I said, then heaved some more. His hand left me, and I didn't turn back to see if he left.

I just cried and vomited until there was literally nothing left inside me but memories and pain. Collapsing against the wall beside the toilet, I leaned back and let it support my weight.

Movement out of the corner of my eye made me jump and put a hand to my chest.

"It's just me," Eddie said softly, holding his hands out in surrender. He was sitting in the door of the stall, just sitting there.

"Eddie," I moaned.

"I'm here," he said.

"I can't go back in there," I said, "I c-can't."

"You don't have to do anything you don't want to do."

"Is everything okay in here—" Mary Beth said, coming into the bathroom. She stopped short when she saw Eddie, then slowly crept closer to peek around at me.

"What happened?" she asked, her voice hushed.

"Sadie, uh… was telling us how she knew Amnesia," Eddie said, his voice flat.

Mary Beth paled.

"You might want to have Dr. Kline speak with Sadie." Eddie went on.

"Would you like me to have Dr. Kline come in here?" the nurse offered.

"No." The word ripped from me. I coughed then leaned against the wall. "I can't talk about it."

"Then you won't," Eddie said, soothing.

"Tell Dr. Kline if she would like to speak to me, she can call my cell," Eddie told Mary Beth. "Amnesia will be unavailable until further notice."

I felt rather than saw Mary Beth hesitate. A moment later, her voice reached out to me. "Remember what I said about a friend."

I looked up. She offered me a smile.

"Thank you," I croaked sincerely.

She left the bathroom soundlessly.

"Am," Eddie said. His voice sounded as broken as I felt. "I just…"

I knew what he wanted. I crawled over the floor toward him (If I were in my right mind, I would cringe, too. A public bathroom floor and toilet. Ew.). His body opened immediately, and I let him fold me into his embrace.

I started to cry. His comfort just trampled what was left of the walls I was using to keep me from totally falling apart.

"I got you," he murmured, clutching me close. "I got you."

"I don't want to know," I wailed. "I don't want to know anything else."

"Shh." He tried to soothe me.

You couldn't soothe a person after that kind of vivid memory.

"I'd rather have no answers than any more of that," I blubbered, grabbing his shirt by the fistfuls. "Please, no more," I pleaded. "No more memories."

I was still crying when he picked me up, cradling me against his body, and kicked open the bathroom door. He carried me out of the hospital and slid into the driver's seat of his truck, all the while keeping me in his lap. I was so closely plastered to the front of him, not even a pound of grease and a giant spatula could have gotten me loose.

He drove to the lake house, parked as close to the back porch as he could get, and carried me inside.

His muscles were vibrating against me as he kicked open every door in his way. In the bathroom, he sat me on the sink, moving between my legs.

I looked up at him, and he cupped my jaws in his hands. "He used to tell her it was her fault when he raped me." My voice cracked. "That's why I thought my name was Sadie."

A tear, glistening and actually quite perfect, slipped out of his eye and trailed down his cheek. I'd never seen him cry. He was so laidback, so strong, I never thought I'd see the day. In fact, it never even occurred to me there was anything on this planet that could illicit such a reaction.

"If I could take your pain, your memories… Hell, if I could've taken your place in that hellhole, I would do it. I would do it in a fraction of a heartbeat."

I grabbed his wrists, squeezing them tight even though I was so weak my grip was laughable. "I would never let you."

With a groan, he gathered me close. "I'm not letting go of you the rest of the day, Am. Not even once."

"Promise?" I whispered.

He vowed, "Cross my heart."

CHAPTER TWENTY

EDWARD

Her body trembled like the last leaf clinging to a bare tree on the cusp of winter.

Hours upon hours.

So long I actually internally debated if I should disregard her wishes and call a doctor.

Whatever memory crashed into her mind was worse than anything she remembered before. She wasn't ready to speak of it. Hell, I wasn't sure she ever would be. The small piece she told me, I knew, was only a tiny sliver of the whole.

I wasn't sure I wanted to know the details. Just seeing her this way, knowing the little I did, cut me deeper than I thought anything could.

Am had to live with it, though. The memory would always be there in the back of her mind, haunting, waiting to remind her. It made me feel like a wimp because if she had to live with it forever, then I should as well.

"Amnesia?" I murmured.

"Eddie," she replied instantly. I didn't think there would be much sleep for either of us tonight. Her voice was hoarse from all her crying.

"When you're ready, I'd like to know what you remembered."

"You don't." She protested.

"I do." I kept my voice passive and caressed her skin with the back of my knuckles. "We're in this together."

"If I was stronger, I'd let you go," she murmured as she dragged her finger over the fabric of my shirt. We were in bed, but after everything, I'd kept on my clothes. It seemed like the right thing to do. The honorable thing.

"What?" I said, my chest seizing. Lifting my head, I gaze down at her, shocked by that response.

"I would," she said again.

Slipping my hands under her arms, I lifted her torso so she was slightly above me. Her hair fell around her face and jaw, shading her slightly, but I was still able to stare into her eyes.

"Why would you say something like that?"

Her lower lip wobbled, and for several moments, I stopped breathing.

"I'm such a mess," she confessed. "And now you are, too. You're too good for a mess, Eddie. You deserve so much more."

"Look at me," I demanded. Her eyes lifted. "Don't say that ever again. If you're a mess, then I'm a pig who revels in mud. You belong here with me. In my arms. No matter what. Even if you let go, I'll still hold on. You hear me?"

"But—"

"No buts." I cut in.

"You don't understand." She reached out, trying to cuddle close.

I relented, letting her press near. Her hand clutched my shirt.

"Being with me puts you in danger. But I'm not strong, Eddie. I'm weak. I need you."

"I'm here," I murmured. "It's okay."

"It's not okay." Her voice cracked, and I was terrified she'd start crying again. "He's going to come for us," she added, a strange tone in her words.

I stilled. "What?"

"*Him.*" Amnesia warned. "Sadie was right. He's going to be so angry with me. For leaving. For my hair. For loving you."

"Don't you worry about him," I said, heat in my voice. "I won't let him hurt you."

"It's not me I'm worried about," she replied. "It's you. He's going to want you dead."

I shushed her gently and began pulling my fingers through her thick hair. I knew she was right. I also knew we were dealing with a man with no conscience. A monster.

Thing was I wasn't as concerned as maybe I should have been.

He's going to want you dead.

Yeah, well, the feeling was mutual.

CHAPTER TWENTY-ONE

AMNESIA

One foot in front of the other. One breath at a time.

One kiss at a time.

That's how I was going to take this.

My life felt altered. Irrevocably so.

The bits and pieces of memories I had were upsetting. But yesterday. That had been near devastating. Those bits and pieces came together, revealing a bigger picture. A horror picture no fully sane person could ever paint.

I knew my name now—well, my first name.

It wasn't my name, though. It was the name of the girl who lived before me. The girl who lived and ultimately died at the hand of a madman.

I was Amnesia now; though after yesterday, I wasn't sure that name fit either.

I knew things now. Felt things. Remnants of what I used to be. Remnants of who I never ever wanted to be again.

Thank God for Eddie. He was literally the glue for all my cracks. No, it wasn't his responsibility to fix me. Or heal me. But he helped hold me together until I could heal myself.

Really the only way to "heal" from the terrors I once lived was time.

And one hell of a prayer I didn't remember any more.

I didn't know how Sadie could even speak. Or smile. Or do anything other than cry or stare into space. I hated to say it, but the fugue state the widow was in? I understood it now.

It was beyond clear she lived the same kind of hell. That old woman who used to tend to Sadie when she was fighting for her life (from a beating and a miscarriage... *gulp*) was her. But she didn't live down in that hole with us.

So where had she been?

How could she sit idly by while two innocent girls were tortured, raped, and locked up?

I wondered if I had been as brainwashed as both of them? Probably. Maybe? I tried to kill myself. Did that mean maybe I wasn't as brainwashed, that I knew how wrong everything was, how inescapable, so I chose the only way out I could? Death would have been better than living that life.

This amnesia had been a blessing. I was the lucky one of the three of us.

Beside me Eddie stirred. The deep intake of breath and way he stretched up against me made me smile.

The amnesia was perhaps a stroke of luck, but the biggest blessing of all was him. I didn't know a lot, certainly not a lot of people. Only the few who had reached out to me in Lake Loch. It didn't matter if I knew one or a hundred people, though, because I understood there weren't many like him.

"Hi," he murmured, pulling me closer. I was on my back and turned my head toward his face. He kissed me on the tip of my nose.

"Hi," I whispered back.

His hands were large. He could easily palm the side of my face in one hand. He never used the fact that he was bigger to intimidate me. Or against me. Instead, he used it to make me feel safe.

Tucking the hair behind my ear, he asked, "You doing okay?"

I nodded slow. "Okay."

"You stopped shaking," he observed, hugging me close.

I kissed his cheek and smiled. "Thank you for being here."

"Nowhere else I'd rather be."

That made me think of the hospital and Sadie. A sick feeling churned in my stomach. I tried to hold it back. "I don't want to go back there today." After a brief pause, I added, "Maybe ever."

"Seeing her is hard." Eddie understood.

I nodded. "I know she said we were sort of friends." I shuddered inside, thinking of the way she called me her sister. "And I know we only had each other, but seeing her brings up things."

"Things that are better left forgotten?"

"I think so," I whispered.

"I understand."

"I feel selfish."

"Don't." He pushed up onto his elbow so he hovered above me. "Taking care of yourself is not selfish. It's human. And frankly, I need you to do it."

"You do?"

He nodded sagely. "I won't be okay unless—*until* you are."

I whispered. "I love you."

He dipped his head and kissed me. I could have melted into him, could have gotten lost with him.

Eddie ducked his head into my neck. "I really need to go check on the store."

"Of course." I'd forgotten about the store. I gasped. "I'm supposed to work today!"

He made a sound. "No. Management is giving you the day off."

"Management?" I asked.

His dimples showed. "That's me. I'm the boss."

I mock scowled. "Are you giving me preferential treatment because I'm sleeping with the boss?"

"Maybe," he drawled.

I giggled. It felt good. I didn't know moments of happiness and comfort could exist in a storm. But he taught me they did.

"Seriously though, baby. You're off today. And tomorrow. Take as much time as you need."

"I don't need time off," I told him. "I need to live. To have the life I've built here. It's the only way I can prove to myself that the past can't have my future. It's a lot to process and come to terms with, but I know I will. Especially with you by my side."

"You're sure?" He seemed concerned. "If you're worried about the money, I'll pay you. I don't want you to worry about that."

"I'm not worried about money." I laid a hand on his cheek. "I don't need money. I'm already a wealthy woman."

His eyes warmed, the corners of his lips tilting upward.

"That's how amazing you are, Eddie. After everything I lost, everything that was taken from me, I still feel I have so much. Because of you." My voice lowered. "All because of you."

He groaned. "You make it real hard to get out of this bed, woman."

"Can you take me home on your way to the store?" I asked. "I want to see Maggie."

"Of course."

"Are you going to the hospital?" My voice was timid. Just thinking about Sadie brought on a rush of difficult emotions.

His eyes turned sad. "Yeah. After I check in at Loch Gen. My parents are probably anxious to talk to me."

I nodded. "Maybe I'll take just today off."

Worry creased his forehead. The urge to play with his sleep-rumpled curls came over me, and I didn't resist. "Are you going to be okay today? Want me to stay?"

"I'm fine." I promised. "You need to see your parents, and I need to talk to Maggie."

"I'll come by after I get finished." He promised.

"Take your time." I fully understood that even though he was committed to me, there were many other commitments in his life.

"I'm only one call away, okay? If you need anything, anything at all, you call."

"What if I need a kiss?"

"Especially if you need a kiss."

I languished in bed while he showered and changed into his standard uniform of jeans, sneakers, and a Loch Gen shirt. When he was ready to go, Eddie scooped me up out of bed and carried me to his truck.

I held his hand the entire short drive to Maggie's. He walked me to the door and kissed me, then waited until I was inside to walk away.

I loved him.

"Amnesia?" Maggie called out, appearing at the top of the stairs. "Is that you?"

"Yeah, it's me."

Her shoulders slumped a fraction. "I've been worried about you."

"I know." I apologized. "I'm sorry, I guess I just needed a little bit of time."

Her eyes were wide when she nodded. "Of course."

"I was thinking maybe we could talk if you have time?"

She smiled. "You know I do! I was just about to make some breakfast. How about you come give me a hand?"

In the kitchen, we got out what we needed for scrambled eggs and toast. I wasn't sure, but when Maggie and I spent time cooking like this or watching bad reality TV, I felt maybe this was what it would be like to have a mother.

It was odd to think that out there somewhere I had a mother. Even odder that I couldn't remember even the smallest clue about her.

I didn't miss her. It was hard to miss someone you didn't know.

"Where is Eddie this morning?" she asked as she whisked together a few eggs. I felt slightly queasy still. The sight of food wasn't appealing.

"He went to work and to check in with his parents."

"I'm sure they are worried about him."

"A lot's happened." I allowed.

We didn't say anything else until the eggs and toast were on plates and we were seated at the table.

"They told me what happened at the hospital yesterday when I came to see Sadie."

I shuddered. "The things she told me, I remembered a little."

"It was bad," she observed.

I glanced away. "Very."

"Well, judging from the few things Sadie shared with me about her experiences, I can't even imagine."

"Sadie told you?"

She set aside her fork and looked up. "Not much, but she was upset, understandably, so I talked to her for a while."

"I didn't mean to upset her," I murmured.

Maggie's hand covered mine. "None of this is your fault. Hers either."

I cleared my throat. There was something I wanted to say. Or rather ask. It weighed on me, but it was an unnecessary burden. I needed to make things easier where I could, and while having this talk wasn't easy, it was within my power. I needed to use all the power I had right now; if I didn't, I might fold in on myself and never recover.

"Now that we know I'm not Sadie, I wanted to let you know that..." I paused and swallowed. This was hard. Hard to feel I didn't belong even though I so badly wanted to. "I..."

Maggie nodded encouragingly, looking at me as if I could tell her anything.

"I understand if you'd like me to move out. You've been very generous taking me in, someone you didn't even know." I murmured to add, "And still don't really."

Maggie gasped. "Amnesia!"

"I don't want you to feel bad, like you have to let me stay. I know you felt responsible for me because of Ann... and since I'm not Ann's daughter—"

"Stop right there," she said firmly. "While I appreciate your consideration of how I feel, I must say it's stupid."

My eyes shot up, I felt them widen into saucers. "Did you just call me stupid?"

Maggie sniffed. "Of course not. But the notion that I don't want you here because you aren't Ann's daughter, well, that's just cockamamie."

I assumed cockamamie was another word for stupid.

I started to giggle.

Maggie tried to keep a straight face, but then it dissolved as well, and we sat there snickering over our eggs.

When we were done, Maggie cleared her throat and looked at me with serious eyes. "It's true part of the reason I invited you here was because you might be Ann's daughter, but that wasn't the only reason. You needed someone. We all need someone sometimes. But now that we know, I don't want you to go."

"You don't?" I asked, hopeful.

"Of course not." She leaned across the table. "Can I tell you a secret?"

I nodded.

"The more time I spent with you, the more I secretly hoped you weren't Ann's daughter."

That surprised me. "But why?"

"It made me feel guilty for wishing you were mine instead."

I started to cry. Can you blame me?

"Oh, honey." Maggie came around the table and wrapped her arms around me. "I didn't mean to upset you."

"Y-you didn't," I wailed. "I'm crying because I'm happy."

"Well, thank heavens for that."

I laughed breathlessly. "You really mean that?"

"I really do. Having you here has filled up my life in ways I didn't know it was empty. I couldn't imagine watching bad TV with anyone else."

I smiled, watery.

"And teaching all my family recipes to you. I thought they would die with me."

"Don't say that," I swore fiercely.

Maggie patted my shoulder and sat back. "I know Eddie has been after you to move in with him and it's only a matter of time, but until then, you're welcome here. Even after. I want you to think of this place as your home, too. And I hope even after Eddie sweeps you away, you and I will continue with our relationship."

More tears streamed down my cheeks and I dashed them away. My heart was so full my chest felt it might burst. "I would very much love that."

Tears filled her eyes, and she hugged me again. "I'm so glad."

"I love you," I whispered as we hugged. "Thank you for being here for me."

"I love you, too, honey," Maggie replied.

It took us both a minute to compose ourselves, me longer than her. I'd been worrying about this even before we found Sadie. Worried I was living someone else's life and if we found out I wasn't Sadie, then all the people here would turn their backs. Well, part of it came true.

I'm not Sadie.

But I was starting to think maybe it didn't matter. I hadn't been living her life. I was living mine.

And the people around me liked me because I was... me.

"Your eggs are getting cold," Maggie admonished, slipping back into her chair.

I grimaced. "I'm really not hungry."

Coffee in hand, Maggie frowned. "How are you really?"

"I'm not sure," I admitted.

"Seeing Sadie triggered everything?" Her voice was concerned.

"Talking to her." I agreed.

Maggie withdrew then, sat back, and drank her coffee with a thoughtful look on her face.

"Is something wrong?"

She looked up, setting aside her coffee. "I had wanted to talk to you as well, but after our talk, I'm worried it might not be a good idea."

"What?" I could tell she was debating to even tell me, so I gave her a hard look.

She sighed. "Sadie doesn't have the extensive injuries you did when Eddie found you. She's dehydrated, malnourished, has some bruises, cuts and scrapes... nothing a few days in the hospital won't get on the healing path."

"What are you saying?" I asked.

"She's going to be getting out soon."

"And you want her to stay here," I surmised.

"Well, yes. She is Ann's daughter. She doesn't have anywhere else to go."

A brief vision of her staying at Eddie's intruded on my mind. I hated it.

"Of course." I agreed. "She should stay here."

"I don't want to cause more stress on you if seeing her brings back memories."

I sat forward. "I'll be fine. I think the initial shock of finding her and learning who she is and where I'd been before Eddie found me is over. I can't say I will ever be completely comfortable around her, but she and I have a lot in common. And if there is anyone in this town who can help her heal, it's you."

"Are you sure?" Maggie pressed. "This is your home, too. You have a vote."

"I vote yes," I said, even though I felt apprehensive and squeamish about seeing her again. About living under the same roof.

"I'll give her a guest room upstairs so you'll still have privacy downstairs," Maggie added.

"It's going to be fine." I assured her, wishing I felt as confident as my voice sounded.

CHAPTER TWENTY-TWO

EDWARD

It was afternoon by the time I made it to the hospital. I had shit to catch up on at Loch Gen, and when I walked in, both my parents were there. Waiting.

Finding Sadie sent a shockwave through our sleepy lake town. More than when Amnesia showed up. The surprise of not one, but two missing girls, both of whom could have been the same girl, was something no one ever expected.

Of course rumors and speculation abounded; not everyone knew the truth. No one else heard the grisly details right out of Sadie's mouth.

I told them a watered-down version. Basically, Sadie and Am were victims of the same man. Both kidnapped, held hostage, and abused.

It took a while to assure them I was handling it, a fact that sort of pissed me off. I mean, I was a grown man, for fuck's sake. Yet at the same time, I understood. I was a complete mess for years after Sadie disappeared.

It took a long time to get me back on track, and they'd watched the entire thing.

I was older now. Stronger. And my heart knew love. My entire body knew it. People often said love made you weak.

Maybe it did because it allowed you to get hurt. I sure as hell hurt when I saw the pain in Amnesia's eyes.

Love wasn't a weakness, though.

It was a strength.

Probably the strongest bond I'd ever felt. I wouldn't crumble under any of this because I had everything to protect.

Thank God for my parents, though. Without them, Loch Gen would likely sit unopened, and the residents here would be pissed. Especially Ms. Scarlet; she needed her nightly apple.

They were keeping the place going, and I was able to focus on the shit in my life that was a lot less stable. At least today. Amnesia was right this morning when she said we had to live. We had to go on. Stability within chaos. As an adult, I was learning that was key.

The hospital was so familiar to me now. I probably knew it as well as the staff. It wasn't a place I wanted to be so well acquainted with, but wants and needs were entirely different.

I felt guilty for not being there more. For not coming back yesterday after Amnesia ran out, and I hoped Sadie wasn't angry with me. Or hurt. The last thing I wanted was for her to endure more hurt.

The nurses waved as I went past. I nodded and kept going.

Just as I was about to knock, the door swung open and Dr. Kline stepped out. Her eyes widened when she saw me on the other side. I stepped back to make room for her exit instead of brushing past.

"Doctor," I said, letting the door close behind her.

"Mr. Donovan." She inclined her chin.

"Eddie." I corrected. "How's she doing?"

"You know I can't discuss my patients with you."

I sighed. "Look, I don't need anything private. But a general update isn't something that's out of the realm of reason. Especially in this situation. I think you know that."

Dr. Kline hesitated then sighed. "She has a long way to go. The things that happened to her… some of them are very difficult to heal from."

"Impossible?" I asked.

Again, she hesitated. "I can't really say."

"Because you don't know or because you're obligated not to?"

"I don't know." Her voice was low. "I haven't dealt with this degree of PTSD."

I didn't know why, but the diagnosis caught my off guard. "PTSD?"

She shifted. "It's not just for military veterans. Any kind of traumatic situation can result in a victim suffering from post-traumatic stress."

"She said some things to Am yesterday. She had a memory and was very upset, but didn't want to call you."

"Amnesia is much stronger mentally than Sadie," Dr. Kline remarked.

That made me feel better, more hopeful.

"Because of the amnesia?"

"Likely."

Fear stabbed me in the gut. "So if she keeps remembering?"

"I can't really speculate." Dr. Kline put me off.

I levelled her with a flat stare, cooling my eyes to a shade of ice. "Level with me," I demanded.

The doctor swallowed thickly. I saw the intimidation in her eyes. I didn't even feel bad for it. I wanted her to be intimidated. I wanted answers. "It could have a negative impact."

"How negative?" I barked.

She drew up. I thought she might argue, but I narrowed my eyes. "Trying to guess what the mind will do in these situations, Mr. Donovan, is like playing the lottery. I don't know."

I cussed, running a hand through my hair roughly.

She watched me. Whatever she saw made her soften. "Eddie." She relented. "I know you're very worried about Amnesia."

"Of course I am. I love her."

"I see that," she observed. "While I still think you two are very dependent on each other, I do see the love between you. The love itself is healthy."

I suppressed the urge to roll my eyes. She was trying to head shrink me.

"I'll level with you about Amnesia because I don't feel it's a breach of confidentiality. You're practically family."

I made a rude sound. "She *is* my family."

Dr. Kline nodded. "Amnesia has had six months of stability. Six months of care, love, and therapy from those around her. The memory loss aided a great deal in helping her heal, helping her learn about people in a way she probably wasn't able to before. She's in a much better place than Sadie. While I can't say for sure, I believe Amnesia will be able to live a normal life."

"And Sadie?" I pressed.

"It's too soon to say."

I was silent, digesting the words, and she used it as an escape. "Excuse me. I have other patients."

I let her go, knowing I got more information out of her than she wanted to give. It wasn't much, but it was hopeful. At least for Am.

Inside the room, Sadie was sitting in the center of the bed, dressed in a hospital gown and the black Loch Gen hoodie I gave her the day I found her on the island. A strong sense of déjà vu came over me as I recalled what it was like when I first started coming to see Am after she woke. The two really were very similar in looks.

Clearly, the psycho had a type.

And, uh, maybe I did, too.

"Eddie!" Her face brightened, and I smiled.

"How ya doing today, Sadie?"

"Better now that you're here."

I pulled a chair up beside her bed and dropped into in. "How are you feeling?"

"Okay. I'm ready to get out of here."

"Not liking the hospital food?" I joked.

"Oh, no, it's fine." She promised, not realizing I was teasing. "It's just not home."

My stomach clenched. Her home wasn't hers anymore. After her parents died, the house sat empty until it was auctioned off by the bank. "Are you talking about your parents' house?" I asked carefully.

"No," she said.

Holy shit, she doesn't mean that hole in the ground, does she?

"I'm ready to spend more time with you." She finished.

She thought her home was with me. Oh, that stung. Like saltwater in a deep cut. She looked small and wounded in the center of the bed, buried beneath my hoodie and gazing at me with wide brown eyes. I was her home.

I wouldn't tell her otherwise, even though I knew she couldn't move in with me. It would break Amnesia.

"What do you want to do first?" I asked, shifting the subject. "See Loch Gen? Go to the bakery? Go shopping?"

Her eyes clouded over, and I worried I said something wrong. "Is everyone in town talking about me?"

I couldn't lie. I leaned close, as though I were telling a secret, and made sure my dimples were on display. "You know the people in Lake Loch. They love a good rumor."

She smiled. "They always did."

"Ms. Scarlet is still obsessed with apples."

She giggled. It was a pure sound that made me feel everything was going to be okay.

"Do you need anything?" I asked. "What can I bring you?"

"I don't need anything but you," she said. After an awkward silence, she went on. "I thought about you all the time. I wondered if you thought of me. He always told me I was his… but I remember Eddie. I remember I was yours first."

I thought I'd waited to hear those words for twelve years. Hearing that, seeing her… it's what I'd wanted more than anything. I'd thought it would fix everything.

I was so wrong.

So utterly mistaken.

I felt almost gross hearing her say them. Not because I loved Amnesia. Not because I didn't love Sadie (I did in my own way). Because I was naïve.

That didn't fix anything. It almost made everything worse.

I didn't know what to say or how to react. It seemed everything I could say was wrong. She waited and watched me, openly wanting an answer I didn't have. Carefully, I chose what to say. "You were—no, *are* my best friend. Of course I thought about you. Every day."

She nodded. "I was yours," she whispered again.

"You aren't anyone's Sadie. You belong to yourself. You have control over your own life."

Her brow furrowed as if she didn't quite understand. As if she didn't know how to be in charge of herself.

"But I…" Her eyes lifted, confusion swimming at the surface, and I saw tears about to fall.

I went to her, hugging her close. She put her arms around me and held tight. I stroked my hand down her long, soft hair until I felt her body relax.

We sat like that for a while. The entire time, I marveled about how I'd imagined this moment a million times, and each of those million, I never once imagined it to feel the way it did now.

Sadie wasn't my future. Maybe she never was. Maybe she was just a catalyst, an unfortunate victim of life bringing me to where I really belonged. With whom I really belonged.

It wasn't fair. Life rarely was.

After a while, Sadie pulled back but took my hand and held on. "You thought she was me, didn't you?"

"Everyone thought so," I said, knowing she meant Amnesia. "At least at first."

"That's why you love her," she murmured. "Because it was supposed to be me."

Everything inside me revolted, sickened. It was a stronger reaction than even I expected because, yes, it was true. I was first drawn to Am because of Sadie. Because I thought she was her.

But now, knowing both of them, the differences were astounding.

There was no mistaking one for the other.

I only loved one.

And it wasn't the girl whose hand I was holding.

"I do love you, Sadie," I said gently. "As a friend. A best friend. Just like all those years ago."

"We were more," she insisted.

"We could have been," I echoed. It still hurt to think about that, even knowing where my future lay.

I eased off the bed, worried where this conversation was going. She was already mixed up enough. I wanted to be here for her, but I wanted to be clear about our friendship.

There was a knock on the door, and the interruption was welcome.

I glanced around at Sadie with a huge grin. "Another visitor? You're one popular lady."

Her eyes grew wide and fearful. "Do you think it's him?"

Schooling my reaction so I didn't look angry, I said, "No way. Maybe it's Maggie. I'll see."

"Maggie is supposed to bring me clothes," she said.

"You girls and your clothes," I teased, even though I felt tense inside.

Before opening the door, I looked out the small, square window and sighed in relief. "It's a friend," I told her, then pulled open the door.

Robbie stood on the other side, looking anxious and a little uneasy. "Hey, man. What are you doing here?" I asked, stepping into the opening.

"It's her?" he whispered.

"Yeah. No question this time."

"Can I see her?"

In reply, I stepped back and pushed open the door. He walked inside, dressed casually in a pair of jeans and a black pullover. His creamy-coffee-colored skin was paler than usual, and beneath the rich color was a sheet of white. His dark eyes instantly went to Sadie and rounded.

"Hey, Sadie," he said, clearly nervous. "I heard you were back and wanted to come see you."

Sadie said nothing, just sat there and stared at him.

Robbie and I glanced at each other, then back at her. I cleared my throat. "Sadie, do you remember Robbie? We went to school with him."

"I remember," she said suddenly. "You're the one who got me kidnapped."

Robbie jolted as if she'd slapped him. Hell, even I was shocked as hell.

"Sadie, it wasn't Robbie's fault." I tried to reason.

"You're the one who dared Eddie, weren't you?" she asked, her stare on him.

He swallowed. "Yeah and I came to apologize. I wanted you to know it was stupid and something I'll always regret."

She stared at him. Just stared. The tension in the room grew and grew until it was nearly suffocating.

Her eyes suddenly shifted to me. "You forgave him?"

Damn. Nothing like being in the hot seat.

I nodded. "Yes, Robbie's a good guy. He and I both went through a really hard time when you were kidnapped. He helped search for you. We both felt so fucking bad."

Next to me, Robbie nodded sagely.

"This wasn't your fault, Eddie," Sadie told me. Then she glanced at Robbie. "Thank you for helping look for me. And for coming here to visit."

Robbie's shoulders relaxed. "I really am sorry," he poured out. "When I saw Amnesia, all the old guilt and shame came back. When she told me she didn't blame me, I felt a weight lift I didn't even know I carried. So when I heard you were found, I knew I had to come. I knew I had to tell you just how much I regret making that dare."

"You apologized to Amnesia?" Sadie asked.

He nodded. "We thought you might be her." Robbie grimaced and glanced at me. Out of the corner of his mouth, he said, "Was I not supposed to say that?"

I slapped him on the shoulder. "Nah, she knows."

"Well, if she can forgive you, then so can I." Sadie reasoned. It didn't make much sense to me, but if it did to her, that was all that mattered.

"It's okay, Robbie. I forgive you."

I was the largest ass in the state because I wondered if she even meant it.

Robbie moved toward her, and she shrank back. I went forward instantly, sliding between the pair. "She's a little shy still," I said, trying to make him feel better about it.

"Of course," he said, stepping back. "I'll, uh, just go."

I nodded. Talk about awkward.

He leaned around me to look at Sadie. "Thanks for seeing me. I'm really glad you're back."

"Thank you," she answered.

"Be right back," I told her as I walked Robbie to the door.

Out in the hall, he turned to me. "Dude. She hates me."

"No. She's just been through a lot."

Robbie shook his head. "I know hate when I see it. You looked at me the same way once."

"Yeah, and that changed. Give her time. She will, too."

"I don't know, man," he murmured. "There was something about the way she looked at me. Something in her eyes yours never held. I don't think she's going to change her mind, and really, I can't blame her."

"Robbie." I tried to think of something encouraging to say. I was coming up blank because I, too, saw the look on her face.

"I shouldn't have come." He went on. "It's just… Amnesia made me feel better, less guilty. Maybe that should have been a clue she wasn't Sadie. I should have known…"

"Don't do this to yourself, Rob. This entire situation is fucked the hell up."

"Yeah, maybe," he murmured. He started to say something, then stopped.

"What is it?" I cajoled.

He shook his head, rubbing his palm over the buzzed top. "It's just that, man, Sadie and Amnesia, they're completely different."

Yeah.

Obviously, they were two different people. Obviously, they wouldn't be the same. It was still a shock. For all of us. It was hard to separate the two women at first because, in our minds, they were one in the same for so long.

But *oh*…

It wasn't as hard now. The similarities between Amnesia and Sadie were dwindling down to nothing but appearance.

Now I was seeing just how very unalike the two women were.

CHAPTER TWENTY-THREE

AMNESIA

An entire week passed. I only stayed with Eddie twice, though I really wanted to stay more. My relationship with Maggie was also important, and I wanted to make sure she knew. Plus, it gave me time to think and really digest the memory I'd had. Not completely, of course, but enough I could put it into perspective some and not feel sick over it.

It would probably always be a struggle to remember that the past was just that—the past—and it couldn't intrude upon the future unless I allowed it. I think coming to terms with the realization I could be haunted forever by things that happened to me—and there *would* be times it did intrude upon me—was the hardest to grasp.

And then there was the fear. The fear I would remember more. That the more those feelings of being violated and abused came back, the more I might be crippled. I was scared of that, scared my past had the ability to rob me of my future.

Don't allow it.

It was sort of a mantra now, when I felt the stirring of panic deep inside my stomach. When it seemed hard to keep a grasp on reality and I felt myself slipping into some sort of foggy anxiety, I would breathe deep and tell myself I was in control.

Sometimes it worked. Sometimes it didn't. It was a process. I was coming to learn that's what life was. A process. A series of highs and lows.

The light knock on the doors across the room made me smile. Like a giddy child, I threw the covers off and pranced across the room, my bare feet and legs blasted with the cool morning air.

Hopping from foot to foot, I opened the door so Eddie could slip inside.

He grinned at me, all dimples and white teeth, as he shut the door. "You look like a little rabbit."

"It's freezing this morning!"

He caught me around the waist with one arm and lifted. My legs went around his waist, and I cuddled into his neck. "How come you're warm? You were just outside."

"I'm always warm for you, baby," he murmured.

Lifting my head, he stuck the tall cup beneath my nose. "Extra whip, just for my girl."

The warmth seeped into my palm when I wrapped it around the cup, and he carried me back over to the bed. The blankets were still warm from my body, and my toes curled into the soft head and I sighed.

Eddie slid in beside me and pulled the covers up over our lower halves.

I sipped at the cocoa, enjoying the way the liquid heat slipped all the way down my throat and into my stomach.

Not staying with Eddie every night was something I didn't like. But I did like when he snuck into my room early in the morning with a hot chocolate.

"How's my girl?" he asked, stroking the side of my head.

I leaned over and kissed him.

"You taste like chocolate," he murmured. I kissed him again, this time licking into his mouth, stroking our tongues together.

"I have something else for you," he said when I pulled back.

"You do?"

Leaning sideways a little, he reached under him into the back pocket of his jeans and pulled out a white envelope that was folded in half.

"May I present to you," he said with flourish, "your first paycheck."

Excitement and pride sparked inside me. Pushing up, I folded my legs under me and balanced my drink in my lap. Carefully, I pulled the check out as though it were something precious and rare.

It kinda was. I'd never earned a paycheck before. Or had a job. Or money of my own.

The paper was long and rectangular, a light-blue shade. It looked professional and serious, and right there on the side was the amount with my name on it.

"This is all mine!" I exclaimed, bringing my hands down and nearly dumping hot chocolate all over us both.

"Whoa." He chuckled. "How about I hold on to this?" He picked up the cup and set it aside. When he turned back, I was still marveling at the check, waiting for him to tell me it was just a dream. "It's all yours."

His confirmation lit my face with a smile. I felt so much pride in that moment, knowing I'd earned this money. That I could buy myself something that was all mine.

"Thank you," I said.

His eyes softened. "Don't thank me, sweetheart. You earned it. You stocked a lot of shelves and made polite conversation with curious townies."

"I've never had any money before," I said in awe.

A sad look passed behind his eyes, but then it was gone, and I was glad. This was a happy moment.

"I wish it was more. At least it's better than minimum wage."

"What's that?" I asked.

He groaned and hooked his arm around me, pulling me close. "So innocent," he murmured.

I was too happy to worry about whatever I didn't understand. Instead, I squealed lightly and hugged him hard.

Jerking back, I looked at the check again. A thought occurred to me, and I frowned. "Oh," I said, glancing up. "I don't have a bank account. How will I cash this?"

"I got you," Eddie said and again dove into his back pocket to produce another white, folded envelope.

I peeked inside and saw a stack of green bills. I gasped and looked up.

"Your pay's under the table, at least until you have a full name and a bank account. The check isn't cashable. I just printed it out so you could keep it. Remember your first pay."

"What's under the table mean?" I asked, slightly confused.

Eddie laughed. "It just means you don't have to cash the check. That money is yours. Just take it."

"I'm going to keep this," I said, clutching the paper to my chest. "Thank you for giving it to me."

"So what are you going to do with your first check?" he asked.

I wanted to go shopping. To get something for myself, to pick out a new outfit or two. "I'll probably give some to Maggie, you know, to pay her back for all her generosity." I thought a moment, realizing Eddie had done just as much for me. "And you, too."

"You're pretty amazing," he said, leaning close to kiss me softly. "But forget it," he added, his voice much firmer. "There's no way in hell I'm taking any money from you, and I know Maggie will say the same."

"But—"

"No buts," he concluded.

I glanced down at the envelope in my hand. "Well, I have hospital bills."

He groaned, forcing my chin up with his finger. "What do you *want* to do with it, Am?"

"Go shopping," I whispered.

He laughed. Then laughed again.

I scowled. "What?"

"Spoken like a true girl."

"Is there something wrong with shopping?" I demanded.

"Of course not."

"It might be nice to pick out a few things for myself."

His gaze was warm as it swept over my face. His thumb and forefinger tugged on the ends of my hair. "Get dressed. You can ride with me to the store and spend some time shopping on Main Street."

"I have to work!" I declared.

He made a sound. "I'll cover the store this morning. It's just a couple hours. You can work this afternoon."

"I don't think most jobs are like that," I pointed out. I was pretty sure I couldn't just come and go as I pleased because I felt like buying new jeans.

"Guess you're just lucky," Eddie quipped.

I definitely couldn't disagree.

After a kiss, I bounded off the bed to get dressed. I had shopping to do.

As excited as I was to shop, my nose had other ideas.

And apparently, I was ruled by my nose and stomach.

On my way to the shops, I was distracted, very decisively, by the sweet and buttery scent of monkey bread muffins and the other mouthwatering concoctions at Joline and Jeremy's bakery.

Of their own accord, my feet stopped and turned. The bell on the door jingled as I entered. I drew in a deep breath of cinnamon-scented air.

Joline popped her head around the corner and saw me, her face lighting up. "Well, look who it is!" she exclaimed and stepped around. "Good morning, Amnesia!"

"Good morning," I chimed, gazing into the glass case.

"Where's your other half?" she asked.

"Working. I'm supposed to be shopping, but my nose led me here."

She beamed. "Have you had breakfast?"

"Actually, no," I said. "Just a hot chocolate."

"Ah, yes." She nodded. "Eddie has become quite a regular in here in the mornings, picking up your favorite drink."

I smiled. I loved him. So much.

"Well…" Joline gestured toward the case. "Pick something! A girl's gotta eat!"

She had a point. "Everything looks so delicious, but you know my favorite is the monkey bread muffin," I said, glancing at the lone muffin.

"We had a big order for those this morning. Nearly cleaned out the case. I was just in the back, making another batch."

"Oh?" I perked up. "Maggie's been teaching me how to cook. Is baking much different?" I loved cooking. It was quickly becoming a favorite hobby of mine. It made me curious if I would enjoy baking just as much.

She smiled. "It's a whole other ballgame." Lifting a section of the counter, creating a path, she gestured to me. "Come on back and I'll show you how it's done."

"Really?"

"Definitely. You can have a fresh from the oven muffin when we're done."

"I would love that," I said, hurrying back. "I love to cook."

"Well, you're going to love baking, too," she said, guiding me into the kitchen of the bakery.

It was like a whole new world back there. Large sacks of flour, mixers, ovens, and more filled the small space. There was a tall, long table with the most beautiful-colored counter Joline called marble. It was white with veins of dark grey running through it.

Jeremy appeared out of what looked like a stockroom, carrying a huge sack of flour over his shoulder, a white apron covering his chest.

"You got a coveted invite into the back?" he asked, raising his eyebrows when he saw us there. "Oh, ho-ho, that's a high honor. Jo never lets anyone back here!"

"I let you back here, and you're nothing but trouble!" she retorted.

He laughed. "That's 'cause you can't carry these bags of flour." As if to prove his point, he swung it down onto the end of the table, and a large white cloud puffed out around him.

I giggled.

"Men," Joline muttered. "Jeremy, man the front. I'm about to put Amnesia here to work."

"Well, kid, it was nice knowing ya," he said, stopping beside me on his way out front. "Once she gets a hold of ya, you'll never want to come back." Then he laughed as if it were the funniest thing he heard and disappeared around the corner.

"Forgive him, hun. He's clearly not as charming as your Eddie."

My Eddie. I liked the sound of that.

"I think he's great," I told her.

"I heard that!" he yelled.

Joline rolled her eyes. "Now he's going to have a big head for days."

I smiled and took the apron she offered. "Better put this on. It's about to get messy."

Joline wasted no time getting back to work but at the same time bringing me right into it. Before I knew it, my hands were covered in dough, my face dusted with flour, and the intoxicating scent of sweets clung to my skin.

She played a radio while we worked. I had no idea what kind of music it was or who sang, but I loved it. The overall energy of the bakery was infectious. It was almost like getting lost in a good TV show; between the music, the company and the constant activity, there was no room for thought.

She taught me how to grease the muffin tins (hers were a little larger than most muffin pans sold at stores) so the monkey bread didn't stick. She shared secrets, like putting the bread dough in a warm spot to help it rise better and keeping a damp towel draped over the top of the bowl to keep the top from drying out.

I learned measuring was much more important in baking than cooking. With Maggie, we were guided by taste—a pinch here, a spoonful there—but in baking, you had to be more precise.

We made two dozen monkey bread muffins. Half of them had apples and raisins; the other were just cinnamon. Both were buttery and sugary, making my mouth water before they even went into the oven.

As they were baking, she got out everything we needed for the glaze that would be drizzled overtop. After piling everything on the counter, Joline stepped back and just told me what to do, and I made it all myself.

"You're really enjoying this," she remarked as I was adding the simple ingredients into the bowl to whisk it together.

"Oh yes," I practically gushed. My cheeks felt flushed from the warmth of the ovens and the happiness I felt. "This really has been so fun. Thank you so much for sharing this with me today."

"You're a fast learner. You should come back again. I can teach you even more. I'm usually stuck here with Jeremey, and sometimes he can just be an insufferable bore."

I laughed.

"I heard that!" he yelled from the front.

"I wasn't whispering!" Joline yelled back.

We both snickered as I began whisking the powdered sugar with the cream, turning it into a shiny, sweet concoction.

All of a sudden, I saw a cloud of white out of the corner of my eye, and Joline made a strangled sound.

I spun around as she was gasping and slapping at her apron. The action was only creating a larger cloud. "You didn't!" she swore, staring straight past me. I spun again to see Jeremy standing just at the corner, his hand covered in flour.

"Who's the insufferable bore now?"

"You threw flour at me!" Joline exclaimed.

"No one said she was the brightest of the bunch," Jeremy told me, sly.

Joline gasped. I pressed my lips together as she darted past me and another cloud of white erupted. Fine white dust flew everywhere, floating through the air and grabbing at everything it touched.

When it cleared a little, we were left with the view of Jeremy standing at the center, his hair completely coated. His eyebrows, too.

I burst out laughing.

"Oh, you think that's funny, do you?" he intoned, stepping forward. His hand went to the pocket of his apron.

I backed up, putting my hands out in surrender. "Oh no," I said. "Not funny at all."

He pulled his hand out, revealing a palm full of flour.

"You keep flour in your apron?" I asked, amused.

"You betcha," he roared and flung it at me.

I shrieked and lunged back to avoid it, but of course I was too late. The powdery substance smacked me right below the chin. I felt it coat my neck and ends of my hair.

I gasped. Joline and I looked at each other, smiling wickedly.

"Oh shit," Jeremy exclaimed.

We all lunged for the closest available flour and started flinging it at each other, everyone shrieking and exclaiming. The shrieks turned into laughter, and soon, the entire back room was filled with a white cloud.

The bell on the front door jangled, and the circus the three of us made halted almost instantly. Silence pressed in, and flour settled around us. The three of us looked from one to the other and then at the massive mess we'd made.

Pressing my lips together, I worried about how much extra work this would create.

But Joline and Jeremy started chuckling, which then turned into full-blown laughter. "You look like a snowman," she told her husband, smacking him in the middle, creating more dust.

We dissolved into hysterics again.

"Hello?" a familiar voice called out.

"We have customers!" Joline hissed at Jeremy.

I rushed around the corner, knowing who was there. "Maggie?" I called out.

The second I appeared, Maggie's mouth dropped open. "Amnesia!" she exclaimed. "What in the world happened to you?"

I glanced down at myself, then back up. "Joline was teaching me how to bake."

"Well, honey, I hate to tell you, but it looks like you're not very good."

I burst out laughing, then noticed Maggie wasn't alone. Slapping a hand over my mouth, all the joy I felt began dissolving into panic.

"Sadie," I said, unable to keep the shock from my voice. "You're here."

Sadie stepped out from behind Maggie. She was dressed in a pair of jeans, yellow sneakers, and the hoodie Eddie gave her.

My stomach twisted uncomfortably.

This was the first time I'd seen her since the day she told me I was meant to be her replacement after our captor beat her so badly she almost died.

My throat suddenly felt very dry. As if I'd swallowed a pound of the flour.

"They released me from the hospital this morning," Sadie said, glancing at my flour-covered attire. "We were on the way to see Eddie."

I tried so hard not to be bothered by that.

I was. On all accounts.

"We thought we would stop in, get some coffee. See Joline and Jeremy."

"Oh my goodness, is that Sadie?" Joline cried, coming out from the back. "Jeremy! Sadie is here!"

She rushed around me and swept Sadie into a hug. Jeremy was close behind her. They fawned all over her, talking and smiling. I was glad for it. I needed a few moments to compose myself. I hadn't been expecting to see her here this morning. It threw me for a loop.

It was a jolt of reality in what started out as a pretty dreamy day.

Soon, the chatter calmed down and the pair retreated behind the counter to get some coffees and a few pastries for Maggie and Sadie.

The timer in the back went off. Joline perked up. "There's our monkey bread, Amnesia. I'll go pull it out. Then you can glaze it."

Maggie came to my side, brushing the flour from my shoulders and hair.

I smiled. "We got a little carried away."

"It's nice to see you having such fun."

"I got my first paycheck today," I confided. "I'm supposed to be shopping."

"The day is still young!"

My eyes drifted back to Sadie. She was taking a coffee from Jeremy and going to the nearby table to sit down.

"She's coming home with me," Maggie said, her voice hushed. "I would have told you, but I didn't know she was being discharged until this morning."

"It's okay," I said.

Maggie stared at me a heartbeat longer before nodding. "You have a good time today. I'll get her all settled in."

I nodded. Feeling her eyes, I turned my head, our stares colliding. She stared at me without blinking, her brown eyes holding something that made my toes squirm around inside my Adidas.

I wanted to run. To squeeze my eyes closed and forget she was there. I was afraid to remember. So afraid.

Instead, I stepped around Maggie and went to the table, dropping down in the seat across from her. "How are you, Sadie?"

"I'm good, Lily. It's nice to be out of the hospital."

My stomach dropped when she called me that. My hands grew clammy. I pushed it all back and focused on the current moment. I nodded enthusiastically. "Yes, I felt the same."

"You live with Maggie, too?" she asked, taking a drink of her coffee.

I glanced at Maggie, who was at the register, handing Jeremy a few dollar bills. "Yes, since I got out of the hospital."

"What about Eddie?" she questioned.

"The doctors all thought it was a better idea if I stayed with Maggie," I explained.

She nodded, slow. "They told me the same thing."

"You asked to live with Eddie?" The words came out before I could snatch them back.

"Of course," she said, as if it should have been obvious. "We're going to visit him right now at Loch General."

I smiled, hoping it looked genuine. It frustrated me the way I felt when I was around her. I was uncomfortable. Awkward. Slightly intimidated... and a little bit jealous.

Okay. Fine. Maybe more than a little bit.

"I'm sure he'll really like that," I said, reaching out and putting my hand over hers. "He's really happy you're back. The whole town is."

Her hair was long and shiny around her shoulders. It looked freshly washed and brushed. It made me think of how chopped up and uneven mine had been when I got out of the hospital.

Joline poked her head around the corner and called my name. I perked up, grateful for the interruption. "The glaze waits for no one!" she told me.

I chuckled beneath my breath and stood. "I'm helping Joline. I should go finish up."

Sadie stared at me, focused. After a second, she blinked then nodded. "You didn't come back to see me," she said, mild accusation in her tone.

"I know," I replied. "I'm sorry. I had a memory and it overwhelmed me. Scared me. I was afraid it would happen again."

"You can't pretend," she said.

"What?"

"You can't pretend it didn't happen. It did. All of it."

I felt my insides tremble. A fine tremor shook my fingers. I got up from the table. "I know it did," I told her quietly. "I'm not pretending."

Joline called my name again.

"Coming!" I answered. Then I looked back at Sadie. "I really have to go."

"I'll see you later," Sadie said. "At home."

Chills raced up and down my arms and legs, the back of my neck prickled with discomfort, and I practically ran into the back.

Sadie and I were roommates now.

Or should I say *again?*

CHAPTER TWENTY-FOUR

EDWARD

Every time the bell on the door jingled, I looked up. It was pretty fucking stupid because I knew it wasn't Am. I knew she was down the street, shopping, but still, every time the bells made their distinct announcement, my eyes shot up, hoping to see her.

It made for a slow work morning. Getting things done was hard when I was constantly looking at the door.

Eventually, I gave up on the shit that required the most attention, putting it aside until she came in this afternoon. At least I hoped her presence would allow me to stay focused enough to get it done then.

For now, I settled on restocking a few shelves and doing a few tedious things on the computer (AKA register) at the front counter.

There was the typical morning rush, mostly regulars but with a few non-regular morning shoppers who dashed in needing something last minute.

After the latest customer walked out with paper sacks in hand, I went into the back to grab a cup of coffee. The one I drank earlier was starting to wear off. I thought about Am, hoping she was enjoying herself, hoping she found something for herself she truly loved.

Truth was I padded her paycheck a little. She didn't know it and I would never admit it, but I could do shit like that because I was the boss. No one told me what I could and couldn't pay my employees.

Favorable treatment? You bet your ass. But she deserved it. No one deserved it more.

That thought made my mind turn to Sadie. I felt a twinge of guilt for my last thought. Perhaps Sadie deserved some favoring as well. It was hard to wrap my head around the fact that Rumor Island had two victims (three if you counted Widow West, but I didn't feel like counting her). Even harder to accept that Sadie wasn't the one I was most focused on.

For so long, she was it. The be all, end all. Odd how she had more of my attention in absence than now in her presence. The shame of that made my face burn. Even though I went to see her every day, even though I cared about her—hell, part of me even loved her—I still felt as though I were somehow betraying her.

Truth was it didn't matter how much time I spent with her, sat at her bedside, or reminisced, I didn't connect with her the way I used to. There was something between us. A barrier I was starting to believe only I felt.

I knew it was probably the twelve years we were apart. The heinous, crippling things that happened to her. How whenever I looked at her, I saw a girl who was beaten so badly she lost a child and almost died. It made me sick… sick I didn't stop it. I felt responsible, even though I wasn't the one who inflicted all her wounds.

I felt her reaching for me. I felt her eyes, heard her voice when she told me she was mine before she was anyone else's.

I could be a friend to her, but I couldn't be anything more.

That made me feel guilty, too. Now, after all this time, I had a chance to make it up to her, make amends for all the shit I hadn't done.

I couldn't. Not in the way I was beginning to see she wanted.

How could a mere man make right the sins of a devil? How could I reverse the horrible things that changed her irrevocably? It was impossible. There were some hurts in this life that were so severe, so unflinching they laughed in the face of apology.

I learned something as I continued to visit her. As I saw how different she was from not only Amnesia, but from the Sadie I remembered from childhood.

She wasn't the only one who was changed by the events that happened.

I didn't realize it until she came back. For years and years, I gripped so tight to that night all those years ago; I didn't allow myself to see something that was so completely essential.

I changed, too.

I was no longer my fourteen-year-old self. I was nearly twenty-six. A man. A man who was jaded, almost wearily so.

A man who was in love with someone who wasn't Sadie. Funny how you looked in one direction and life pulled you in another.

Out in the store, the bells announced someone else's arrival.

The pot clattered a little as I shoved it back on the burner. In my haste, coffee sloshed over the rim of my mug and slapped against the floor.

"Shit," I muttered, glancing around for a few napkins, which I promptly tossed onto the floor. The white material began greedily soaking up the liquid. To hurry it along, I stomped on it with my shoe, rubbing it up a little.

When that was done, I left the saturated napkin where it lay and headed out front.

I felt a little flutter low in my stomach, a feeling I would never admit to having. Anticipating Amnesia all morning was turning me into some whipped little puppy.

Maybe if I tell her that, she'll scratch my belly... then allow her hand to travel lower.

Coffee nearly sloshed out of the mug again with that seductive thought. Smiling, I walked out front toward the door to see if it was who I awaited.

"Eddie!" a familiar voice called out. But it wasn't the one I was expecting.

My eyes widened as I rounded the display aisle and saw Sadie standing there with Maggie at her side.

"Sadie?" I announced. "You're here."

She giggled. "That's what Lily said when I saw her."

She saw Amnesia? Without realizing it, I again started looking around for my girl.

Maggie noted and spoke up. "We just left her at the bakery. Joline was giving her an impromptu baking lesson."

My eyes met and held Maggie's. "Is she having a good time?" *Is she okay? How did she do with seeing Sadie?*

Maggie heard my unspoken questions and nodded. "She was having a wonderful time."

I let out a silent breath, relief flooding through my middle

"The doctors let me out." Sadie began. "So of course I wanted to come by and tell you, see the store." She looked small standing there, my hoodie still swallowing her whole. Her hair was down around her shoulders (I'd never seen it any other way), and she had on a pair of jeans and yellow sneakers.

"Oh!" She went on. "We got you a coffee from the bakery." She jolted forward to extend the large white cup in one of her hands. Noting the cup already in my hand, she frowned. "Oh, you have one already."

"Meh." I scoffed. "I made this in the back. It's terrible. I suck at making coffee." I accepted the one she offered and took a sip, ignoring the fact it scalded my tongue. "Much better." I lied.

She beamed. That made the small lie okay, didn't it? The fact it made her happy.

"You ladies are straight from the hospital?" I asked, leading them over toward the front counter where I set my first cup of joe underneath.

"Yes, on the way home," Maggie said.

I glanced at her quickly, then away. This wasn't something Am and I had talked about. The fact they were going to be under the same roof. She still hadn't gone back to the hospital since that memory. She remained adamant about not wanting to see Sadie, and now she was going to be living with her.

Maggie's eyes flashed with apology, but I understood her position. There was no need for regret.

She was caught between the two women just as I. Stuck trying not to favor one over the other, being tugged in both directions, and knowing eventually, something would snap.

I thought vaguely of offering to take Sadie home with me because it would give Am the space I knew she needed. But if I did that, what message would it send?

"I'm going to be making a special dinner tonight," Maggie told me, picking up a basket near the counter. "I hope you'll join us."

"Wouldn't miss it," I said.

Sadie beamed, came to my side, and slipped her hand in mine.

"I'm going to get a few things for the meal tonight. Sadie, would you like to help?"

Sadie shook her head, sidling closer to me. "I was hoping Eddie would give me a tour. I want to see what's changed."

"Of course." I agreed.

"I won't be long," Maggie said and went off in search of her ingredients.

"What do you want to see first?" I looked down at Sadie.

She shrugged. "It doesn't matter."

"How about all the merchandise we sell now? You can pick a T-shirt." With her hand in mine, I led her across the store toward the merch section near the bathroom. "I designed all this stuff myself."

"You did?" she asked, glancing over it all. Her fingers caressed one of the dark-blue shirts with the words "Lake Loch" on the front.

I nodded. "I had fun with it."

The words, though innocent, were like a knife in me. "I'm sorry." My voice was rough and low.

She perked up, focusing on me. "For what?"

Rubbing a hand over my face, I moaned. "Because that seemed insensitive. To say I had fun doing something while you were out there being…"

Sadie grabbed my other hand, turning so we were facing each other. "Don't be sorry about that," she whispered.

"I am," I rebutted

"I wanted to call you this morning. The doctor wouldn't let me."

Alarm pushed back my sorrow. "Are you okay? What's wrong?"

She smiled softly. "You always worry about me."

"Always." I agreed.

"Everything's fine. They let me out, didn't they?" She glanced away. I saw the ghosts in her eyes. They were hidden when she looked back up. "I want to stay with you, not Maggie."

I swallowed thickly. "The doctor said that's not a good idea."

"I don't care what the doctor said."

"They think it's best you be with a woman after everything that's happened to you—"

"I want you!" she burst out, her voice echoing around the store.

All the muscles in my body stiffened, my senses on high alert. "Sadie."

She shoved me away but then just as suddenly came back, wrapping her arms around my middle and pressing her face into my chest. "I want you, Eddie. You'll protect me. I know you will."

I hugged her back. I felt the tremble of her body. "Protect you from what?" I whispered.

She lifted her head. "From *him*."

I felt my eyes narrow, white-hot anger whooshing through me. "Who is he, Sadie? What's his name?"

"We weren't allowed to call him by name," she whispered, her voice hollow.

I hugged her tighter. I didn't want to ask, but damn, didn't I have to? How would I protect anyone if I had no idea what I was up against?

"Do you know his name even though you never used it? Did you ever hear anyone call him by it?"

She nodded. "*Her*."

"Amnesia?"

"Daniel," she whispered. "She called him Daniel."

"Did you tell the police, Sadie?" I asked. "Do they know who to look for?"

She looked back up at me, pleading with her brown eyes. "I can't tell anyone but you. I can't. He'll know."

"Shh." I soothed, pushing her head back into my chest. "It's okay. Telling me is enough."

"You have to let me stay with you," she pleaded, her voice muffled. "He's coming. He wants us back."

"Us," I echoed, everything inside me icing over.

She nodded. "Lily and me. We belong to him."

Chills raced up my spine. She sounded haunted by him, as if a piece of him lived inside her.

"Where is he?" I demanded, pulling her away from my body, giving her a slight shake. "Where is he, Sadie? Tell me."

"He's watching," she murmured, her eyes glazed over. "Waiting." She blinked, brown eyes again focused on me with perfect clarity. "He's coming, but I want to stay with you."

A tear spilled onto her cheek, and her lower lip wobbled.

I cursed, knowing I pushed too far. But damn, someone had to. We needed answers, and we wouldn't get them by tiptoeing around.

"Eddie?" Sadie clutched at my back.

"I'll stay at Maggie's tonight, okay? I won't let him hurt you." I assured her.

That seemed to pacify her, which was good.

But it did *very* little to pacify me.

CHAPTER TWENTY-FIVE

AMNESIA

She called us sisters. Called me by name. A name I didn't identify with. I remembered, albeit briefly, us braiding each other's hair and feeling glad she was down in that hole with me.

Did that make us friends?

Could two tortured women forge a friendship under such dire circumstances, or was it purely survival instinct?

Maybe it wasn't friendship, but instead a sort of bond. Bonded together by something only the pair of us could experience. I would think a bond like that would be stronger than friendship.

Why, then?

Why did it feel I was looking at a stranger when I looked at Sadie?

Was it the amnesia, the reminder, or was it something more?

I said it before, and I would say it again. Sadie made me uncomfortable. The kind of uncomfortable that felt as though there was something lodged in your throat. Something thick and unforgiving, something bone dry that would never go down no matter how many times I swallowed, no matter how much water I drank.

My body remained in a constant state of hypervigilance when she was in the same room—hell, under the same roof. I hated it. I felt guilty for it. I tried to reason it away.

That was the thing with feelings, though, wasn't it? You felt them whether you wanted to or not.

I felt her eyes all evening long—when she wasn't looking at Eddie, that is. The area between my shoulder blades tingled when I excused myself for bed later that night. Eddie was staying here tonight, something I didn't find unusual, except there was something about him tonight. Something unspoken.

I asked of course. He'd been this way since I went into work this afternoon. He denied it, and at first, I believed him, but as the night wore on, my nerves began to crackle with intuition.

I was dressed in one of his T-shirts I'd stolen from his drawer when he quietly slipped into the room. We didn't say anything, but I went to him, stepping right into his arms with a deep sigh.

After a moment, I pulled back, gathered the hem of his shirt, and pulled it slowly over his head. He helped by lifting his arms, allowing me to remove it totally.

Once it was gone, I stared at his skin, which seemed to glow in the dark of the room. Smoothing my hands over the expanse of his chest, I pressed a single kiss above his heart, then climbed into bed.

Stripped down to nothing but his boxers, Eddie slid in beside me, making sure to tuck the covers around us. Shifting close, I fit myself along him, pressing my ear against his chest.

There was a lot to say it seemed, a lot of currents traveling through the room.

We didn't say anything, though, not a single word.

All that mattered was he was here. That I was here.

That we were together.

Darkness closed around us like a thick blanket. The steady rise and fall of his chest beneath my head was soothing. My eyes grew heavy to the steady sound of his heartbeat.

Deep sleep wrapped around me, finally relieving me of the hypervigilance stringing me tight. I don't know how much true rest I got. I just knew, eventually, something stirred around me. Disrupting those currents I'd mentioned before.

A new one vibrated throughout my room, sort of like a rock song layered on top of a Top 100 hit. They didn't mesh well, didn't play nice.

The sound of Eddie's heartbeat came back to me. The very sound that just lulled me to sleep was now the very thing keeping me awake.

My stomach turned uncomfortably. I lay there with my eyes closed, wondering if I'd had some kind of nightmare that left me feeling sick and shaken. Nausea sat deep in my stomach like a coiled snake waiting to strike.

I shifted, trying to move away from the feeling, but I couldn't get away from something that was already inside me. I squeezed my eyes shut and told myself it was only a dream, trying to find solace in the steady pounding of Eddie's heart.

There was no solace there. Not right now. Now, twistedly, the sound unsettled me more. Caused cramps to squeeze my insides, making my toes curl into my feet.

The sound of his heartbeat was like a ticking clock. A ticking time bomb. Every beat took him closer to death; every rhythmic thump could be his last.

The sound was pure frailty, reminding me just how fickle life could be. How I could lose him in just an instant.

I lay there silently, squirming against him beneath the covers that felt like electric blankets turned up extra high.

It's just a bad dream. Eddie's fine. Everything is fine. I promised myself, beginning to take deep, soothing breaths.

Just as I began to calm, the sound of his heartbeat grew faint until I was gripping his arm, straining for the sound.

And then it stopped completely.

The very last beat echoed through his now-silent and empty chest, bouncing around the hollow cave of his ribcage.

With a gasp, I jolted up, pressing a hand to my chest as tears dampened my cheeks. Instantly, I looked down at him, shoving the hair away from my eyes. He looked peaceful in sleep, curls falling over his forehead, his arm still thrown out beneath where I'd just been.

The steady, reassuring rise and fall of his chest proved he was okay. Proved he wasn't lost. Just to be sure, I reached out, pressing my palm against his skin. The second his heart thumped against my touch, I sagged forward in relief.

But just as soon as the relief came, something stole it away. Violently. Coldly. Unexpectedly.

My head snapped up; my eyes widened.

Even though my mouth fell open, not a single sound came out.

She was there. At the foot of the bed. Staring at us through the dark with an ominous presence. Her eyes unblinking. My hand flew to my chest, and we locked eyes.

I couldn't see her expression, but I didn't have to. I felt it.

How long had she been standing there stalking us while we slept, vulnerable?

Anger radiated off her, jealousy a close second.

My hand slapped down in the center of Eddie's chest. "Eddie!" I whisper-yelled. "Eddie!"

He jolted up so fast it scared me. In one swift move, he bolted up and shot his arm straight out in front of my body, creating a barrier. Then his entire body rotated, blocking me, shielding me.

He did all that without even knowing what it was I wanted.

"What?" he said, sleep evaporating at an impressive speed. "What's wrong?"

I clutched his arm, which was sort of like a personal seatbelt, and glanced back to the foot of the bed. "She's in here."

"What?" He twisted around, following my gaze.

I blinked. Blinked again. "I don't understand…"

Eddie looked between me and the spot where Sadie had been lurking. "Who's here?"

"Sadie," I whispered, still searching the dark. "She was here, watching us."

Eddie didn't ask anything else. Instead, he clicked on the bedside light. I recoiled almost instantly, unprepared for the harsh light.

"Sadie was in here?" he asked. "Where?"

Blinking, I pointed toward the foot of the bed. "Right there!" I insisted.

"Baby," he said, his voice soft. "There's no one there."

"I know," I wailed. "But she was. I swear."

He pulled me close. "It was just a nightmare."

"No," I insisted, clutching his arm. "I know what nightmares are. This was real. She was *real.*"

"Why would she come in here in the middle of the night?" he asked, smoothing the hair back from my face.

"I don't know," I whispered. I felt stupid, and doubt started to cloud my own judgment.

Had I been dreaming?

Pulling back, I looked down at the end of the bed. A creepy feeling came over me. "She was here." I decided firmly. "She was."

"Okay." Eddie relented. "I believe you."

"You do?" I lifted my eyes.

He cupped my face in his hands. "Always."

The worst of the anxiety inside me calmed.

"Come here," he murmured, lying back down, tugging me with him.

I lay against him again, curling my arm tightly around his middle.

"I'll leave the light on until you fall asleep," his voice rumbled.

I nodded. The sound of his beating heart catching my attention. I lifted my head and scooted up his body so my ear rested against his shoulder, not directly over the sound.

"She was in here," I told him again. "Watching."

"But why?" he wondered around a yawn.

I had no idea. But I did know one thing. Whatever I'd known about her in the past, friends or bonded by situation, that didn't seem to matter anymore.

Those things were gone just like my memory.

Whatever she'd been doing in here tonight wasn't anything a friend would do.

CHAPTER TWENTY-SIX

EDWARD

The low tone of repeated vibrations broke into my rest. Amnesia was practically lying atop me, draped across my chest like skin. The first thought I had was of Sadie, of how, just hours ago, Am woke up insisting she was in here.

Right after that thought, the reason I even awoke took over. Flinging out an arm, I snatched my phone off the bedside table and hit the screen without looking at it.

"Yeah," I nearly barked into the line. It was early, and we hadn't slept the best last night.

"Eddie?" Mary Beth said, her voice hushed. I knew that tone.

Fully alert, I sat up, holding on to Am so she didn't go rolling off me. "Mary B, what's wrong?"

"I thought you'd want to know," she quickly said. I could hear the stress in her voice. Mary B stressed wasn't something I often heard; she was usually pretty cool. "Robbie was just brought in."

"What!" I exclaimed, totally awake now. "Why?"

Against me, Amnesia stirred.

"He's, um, badly injured. In and out of consciousness. We haven't gotten ahold of his parents yet. It's very early, and—"

She was rattled.

"Mary," I snapped, gripping the phone tight. "What happened to Robbie?"

The words tumbled right out, nearly tripping over each other. "Someone tried to kill him."

My entire body jolted. Am pushed off me, sitting up in the center of the bed to blink widely at me. I catapulted out of the bed and began to pace.

"I'll be right there," I insisted, then cut the call.

"What's wrong?" Am asked, fear in her expression.

"Robbie's been brought into the hospital," I said gently, not wanting to upset her. "I need to get down there."

"I'm coming, too." She scrambled out of bed, nearly falling over on her ass.

I caught her, pulling her up. "You don't have to."

She made a rude sound, pushing at my chest. "He's my friend, too!"

Pride swelled within me. "Get dressed."

We rushed out the door, ran through the yard and around the house, and jumped into the truck.

On the way there, Amnesia turned to me. "Did she say what was wrong with him? Is he sick?"

I grabbed her hand, wishing I had something not quite as heinous to impart. "No, baby," I said and swerved around a corner. "Robbie isn't sick."

"Then what!" she demanded.

"Mary Beth said someone tried to kill him."

Am gasped, flattening against the back of the seat.

We went the rest of the way in silence, then ran hand in hand into the ER entrance.

"Robbie," I said, slapping my hand down on the desk.

"Are you family?" asked the nurse who'd known me since I was a kid.

I felt my lips curl up. "You know damn well who I am to him!"

"Eddie," Mary Beth called out, appearing around the corner.

We left the idiot nurse in our dust as we rushed down the hall. She tried to call out we couldn't go down there, but I gave her the finger.

She was totally going to tell my mother.

Oh well.

"Mary, what's going on?" I demanded.

"Is Robbie okay?" Amnesia worried.

Mary gestured for us to go back around the corner. We stepped into the hall from where she materialized.

"He was stabbed. Twice. They're prepping him for surgery now."

"Surgery!" Am gasped.

I cursed low. "What the fuck happened?"

"We aren't sure yet. He managed to call 9-1-1, but when they arrived at his place, he was unconscious. He's been in and out since. They haven't been able to get any information from him."

"Can we see him?" I asked.

"Surgery." She reminded me and shook her head.

"Is he going to be okay?" Amnesia asked.

Mary Beth hesitated, and that's when I knew it was really bad.

Running a hand over my head and down the back of my neck, I paced the hallway, trying to figure out how something like this happened.

We had a lot of weird things happen in this town, a lot of secrets and rumors. But murder? I was thinking that was a first.

"Go sit in the waiting room," Mary Beth instructed. "I'll let you know as soon as I hear anything."

I felt helpless in the moment. I wished there were something I could do. "I'll keep trying his parents," I offered. It wasn't much, but it was something.

Mary nodded, grateful, and went swiftly down the hall.

I took Am's hand to lead her toward the waiting room. As we went, the sound of squeaking came from behind.

Amnesia glanced over her shoulder, jerking to a halt. "Robbie!"

I spun. It was him lying prone in a hospital bed, an oxygen mask strapped to his face, a surgical cap that looked like a hair net over his head, looking like death was definitely knocking on his door.

"Rob." I let go of Amnesia and rushed to the beside.

"You need to wait outside," an orderly insisted.

Keeping pace with the bed as it rolled toward the elevators, I stared at my friend. His eyes were closed, his entire face drawn. I wasn't used to seeing him so lifeless. "Everything's going to be okay, Robbie. Amnesia and I, we're here. We're not going anywhere."

Amnesia rushed to the other side of the bed and touched his arm. "We're here," she told him. "We love you."

My heart pinched a little. I wasn't sure I realized before just how unconditional Amnesia's feelings were. She was innocent despite so much "experience." It was proof good existed.

The bed stopped in front of the elevators, and the orderly pushed the button on the wall.

I watched Am reach out to adjust the cap on my best friend's head. As she slowly pulled away, Robbie's hand shot out, grabbing her by the wrist.

Amnesia gasped. Her body fell forward as he yanked. Her chest came right up against the bedrails at his side.

His eyes were wide, kind of wild and filled with pain.

"It's okay." Amnesia assured him. "Everything's fine."

"You need to go!" the orderly demanded.

The elevator dinged, and I knew it would open in seconds.

Robbie turned his head back and forth, making noises.

"He wants to say something." I reached for the mask covering his nose and mouth.

Despite the orderly's protest, I lifted the mask, hovering it over his face. Robbie turned his head toward Am, still gripping her arm.

He said one word.

One word before his eyes closed again and they rushed him off to the OR.

"What is it, Robbie?" Amnesia asked, leaning close.

He drew in a ragged breath. The sides of his eyes crinkled in pain.

"Sadie," he rasped, clear enough there was no mistake.

"We're going," the orderly demanded, pushing the bed onto the waiting elevator. As if the guy hadn't just heard his patient drop a name… drop an accusation.

We both stepped back without a word.

The second the doors closed, we glanced up at one another.

I knew the same look Amnesia wore was mirrored on my face.

Sadie.

CHAPTER TWENTY-SEVEN

AMNESIA

"Maybe he was confused." His voice was filled with disbelief.

When I didn't say anything right away, he glanced up at me. I knew he wanted me to agree. It was just too horrible to consider anything else.

Cautiously, I nodded. "He definitely could be. He looked terrible." Not at all like the guy we'd just gone paintballing with. He always had a ready smile, a wisecrack for everything.

Not today. This morning, his warm skin was sallow, almost ashy. His lips were dry and cracked, making the word they'd formed seem extra shocking.

Eddie was rubbing his palm repeatedly over the back of his neck, eyes downcast toward the floor. "Maybe when he saw you, he thought of Sadie... you know, because you look similar. Because for months, we thought you were her."

"Maybe," I echoed.

Eddie glanced up. My heart squeezed because I knew he was in pain and also denial about what was going on.

"It's going to be okay." I assured him, closing the distance between us to hug him close. "Robbie is strong,"

"I should call his parents again," Eddie murmured, pulling back.

We needed more details. What happened to him?

Mary Beth turned the corner, carrying a chart. I rushed forward, nearly colliding with her. "What happened to Robbie?" I asked. "What kind of injuries does he have?"

The nurse glanced around as though she were making sure she wasn't divulging any information in front of people who would slap her wrists for it. "He has multiple stab wounds, as I said. The deepest wound is in his side. He—ah, lost a lot of blood."

I gasped, staggering back. How horrible!

Eddie stepped up, his front connecting with my back. He was a wall of strength for me, even when he himself was upset. "Do they know what kind of weapon?"

Mary Beth didn't seem to think that was an odd question, which made my stomach twist. I didn't want to think about all the different objects someone could stab another human being with.

"It was a large kitchen knife," she confirmed. "I'm not exactly sure which kind. I think the blade was serrated, though. The blade did some damage when it went in and then was pulled out."

I sucked in a breath. Eddie put his arm around my middle.

"Did he say anything when he was brought in? Did he say who did this to him?" he demanded, his voice harsh.

"Not that I've heard. He was unconscious for a while. The police won't be talking to him until after his surgery and the anesthetics wear off." I watched Mary Beth tuck the chart under her arm, then dab at her eyes.

She noted me watching her and spoke. "We grew up together. All of us, you know? Who would do something like this? Why?"

I went forward and hugged her. I was new to hugging people. I usually only hugged Eddie and sometimes Maggie.

Mary Beth hugged me back, though. She must not have thought it was awkward.

"Keep us updated, okay?" I whispered when I pulled away. "We'll be waiting."

"Of course." She nodded, sniffling a little.

She went off to do her work. Eddie and I went silently into the empty waiting room.

"I hate hospitals," he muttered, slumping into a chair. Almost immediately, he got back up and started to pace.

"I should call Maggie," I said. "Tell her what's going on. Ask her…"

He spun around, his jaw like granite. I knew he was upset, but it had to be said. Didn't it have to be said?

After that "dream" that I was sure wasn't a dream, after seeing Sadie standing ominously at the foot of my bed, staring at us with accusations I didn't quite understand and now Robbie being here, fighting for his life.

He whispered her name. We both heard him.

"It's not her," Eddie intoned.

I wasn't so sure. There was something about her… something broken. He didn't want to see it. I understood. It would be hard to wait for someone for twelve long years, get her back, get that chance to make amends for everything you thought you were responsible for, then have that chance taken away, too. To feel responsible for what she'd potentially become.

"Probably not." I assured him. "But we need to at least know if she's home. For Robbie. For her own protection."

A low curse dropped from his lips. "I know."

Instead of dialing the phone, though, Eddie shot forward to wrap me against him. "I'm sorry," he murmured. "I didn't mean to snap at you."

"You didn't." I clutched at his back. "It's okay. This is terrible."

He lifted his head, and I smiled up at him. Even in this dire circumstance, smiling at him wasn't hard. Ruffling the hair falling over his forehead, I tilted my head. "Can I use your phone?"

He nodded, producing the cell. Maggie's number was programmed in. I hit the button and listened to it ring.

Just when I started to think she wasn't going to answer, her sleepy voice came on the line. "Hello?"

"Maggie," I answered.

"Amnesia?" Her voice became more alert. "What in the world?" I heard her moving around. "What time is it? Are you calling from downstairs?"

"It's early, and no. I'm at the hospital."

"The hospital!" She gasped. "What's happened?"

"I'm fine." I quickly assured her. "Eddie, too. It's Robbie, Eddie's best friend," I explained. "He was stabbed. He's in surgery."

"Good heavens!" she exclaimed. "How did this happen?"

"That's sort of why I'm calling," I told her timidly. As I spoke, I looked at Eddie. his face was drawn, his lips a hard line. "I need you to do something."

"Of course, honey. Anything!"

Swallowing thickly, I plowed ahead. "Can you look and see if Sadie is in her room?"

"Sadie?" she wondered, then suddenly gasped. "You can't possibly be suggesting…"

I felt like a villain. Like the only person who could possibly believe what Robbie said.

"Robbie said her name," I tried to explain. "He grabbed my arm and said her name."

"I see."

I didn't know what that meant.

"If you hold on, I'll go check."

I let out a sigh. "Thank you," I murmured.

I heard her place the phone down. I closed my eyes tight. *Please let her be asleep in bed. Please let it not be her.*

Maggie was gone for what felt like forever. So long, in fact, I pulled the phone away from my ear to make sure it was actually still connected.

Eddie glanced at me, questions in his eyes. I shrugged.

"Amnesia?" Maggie said suddenly.

My reply was instant. "Is she there?"

"I checked her bedroom." Maggie's voice was shaky. "I checked the whole house."

My heart sank. "Maggie," I pleaded. *Tell me she's home.*

"She isn't here, Amnesia." My eyes snapped up to Eddie's. "Sadie isn't in this house."

CHAPTER TWENTY-EIGHT

EDWARD

I didn't want to believe it.

Everything inside me revolted, wanting to vomit out the very idea.

How?

How did you totally disregard the truth when it stared you boldly in the face?

"It wasn't her." My ass hit the chair as I said the words. My own voice sounded hollow and disbelieving.

It was a feeble attempt at lying to myself.

"Eddie." Am perched in the chair beside me, angling her legs toward me. She was so close her knees brushed against my legs. Her pale, small hand reached out and covered mine. Her skin was cold, which was a jolt to my senses.

My eyes snapped toward her, taking in her appearance for the first time since we'd first run out of the house. She was only wearing a pair of jeans beneath the T-shirt she'd slept in. My T-shirt.

Her eyes seemed haunted, and beneath them were dark circles that looked like bruises. Her lower lip was slightly puffy from her chewing on it. It was a habit she had when she was upset.

It was my job to protect her. Even in the middle of a shit storm. Even when I wanted to rage about the unfairness of it all, when I wanted to deny what I knew deep down.

Nothing else mattered quite as much. Not my parents or the store. Not Robbie. Not even Sadie and the fact she might actually be… Well, I wasn't sure.

"You're freezing," I murmured. "Where's your coat?"

"I didn't think about it," she replied. "It's fine."

"No." My voice was hard and loud. I pulled my long-sleeved T-shirt over my head, immediately transferring it to hers. I heard her protest while her face was stuffed inside my shirt, and I told her to hush.

The second her head appeared, I demanded. "Arms."

With a thick sigh, she pushed her arms through. The fabric was so long it covered her hands. "What about you?" She worried.

I glanced down at the fitted shirt I'd worn beneath the thicker one. "I'm fine."

Amnesia leaned forward, pressing her palm against my cheek. "No. You aren't."

No. I wasn't.

"I noticed." I admitted, my voice low, almost ashamed.

"Noticed what?"

"She's not like you," I murmured.

"Of course she isn't. We're different people." Her voice was gentle and patient. My heart squeezed a little.

This hurt. I hated to admit it, even to myself. To acknowledge this situation was fucked up and there was nothing I could do about it. It hurt to even think Sadie could do something like this.

I shook my head, trying to clear it some. "I mean, she's broken. There's something inside her that didn't survive all these years. Something essential. She's not whole, not like you are."

"My mind protected me," she whispered.

I grabbed her face, putting my forehead against hers. "Thank God," I rasped. "Thank fucking God."

The thought of Am being so damaged was more than I could take.

"I tried to ignore it." I went on. "I made excuses. She was healing. She was traumatized. It would take time for her to adjust."

"Those aren't excuses. It's the truth," Am insisted.

"She needed more help than any of us realized. We all got lost in the fact that she came back, that she was 'saved.'" I made a humorless sound. "She wasn't saved. Not really. We failed her. *I* failed her."

Am made a sound of protest, but I wasn't about to allow her to try and talk me out of what I knew was the truth.

With a growl, I jolted up, pacing the length of the room.

"She's said things, things that didn't quite sit right with me. I ignored it, though. I wanted to believe she was okay." I wanted this shit to be over. Twelve years was a long time.

"What kind of things?"

I spun. "She told me she belonged to me first. Told me the reason I loved you was because I thought you were her."

"I think we've all thought that," Am said, her voice quiet.

I knew those words hurt her. It was just another reason I tried to keep it all under wraps.

"No," I insisted. "It was more. She was angry." I thought about it, really allowing myself to see. "There is an underlying anger in her that she tried to hide. That no one wanted to see."

"She has a right to feel angry. She lost so much."

"Fuck," I swore.

Amnesia stood from the seat. The hem of my shirt fell to her knees. "What?"

"Robbie came to the hospital. She blamed him, actually accused him of being the reason she was kidnapped."

"Because of the dare," Am surmised.

My stomach twisted, my heart beating rapidly. Oh my God. It was true.

Sadie was angry with Robbie. She blamed him for everything that happened to her. Everything she lost.

I glanced at Amnesia, thought about how she insisted Sadie was staring at us in the middle of the night... right before someone tried to kill Robbie.

I couldn't bury my head in the sand, not anymore. Lives were at stake.

Lives of the people I loved.

"She doesn't know what she's doing." I groaned. "She just doesn't understand."

Amnesia came forward, placing her hands on my chest. "We're going to help her." She assured me. "No one is going to blame her after everything she's been through."

Gazing over Am's features—her freckles, brown eyes, and golden hair—my chest squeezed. If Sadie blamed Robbie so much she tried to kill him, would she come after my girl, too? Would she blame her for capturing my heart?

I couldn't let that happen.

"We need to call the police."

CHAPTER TWENTY-NINE

AMNESIA

So many unanswered questions. The more answers we found, the more we needed.

It was beyond frustrating that I probably had everything we needed to know locked away inside my mind. Kept hidden even from me.

I knew pleading with myself wouldn't work. Bargaining, even trying to force the answers out— nothing worked. I'd tried it all.

The only memories I did have came at heavy cost, when least expected. In short, they came when they wanted to, not when I asked.

I felt helpless as I sat in the center of the waiting room, waiting to see if Robbie would live or die. Waiting to hear from Maggie, from the police... from Sadie herself.

The cops were out searching now—an APB was put out on Sadie—and Eddie was just outside in the hallway, speaking to a few uniformed officers himself.

I knew they would want to question me as well, but I had nothing to offer.

No insight. No answers.

Just blank pages. Pages filled with words written in invisible ink.

Eddie was beyond himself. The blame he placed on himself and the responsibility he shouldered was palpable. I knew it cost him something great to admit to himself Sadie was further gone than any of us realized.

I knew the only reason he admitted it at all was because of me. *For me.*

I wanted to give something back to him. To give instead of take.

The only thing I could think of that would equal what he'd done for me was answers. I didn't have them… but I knew where to get some.

Slipping out of the waiting room, I moved stealthily down the hallway and around the corner. The elevator was just beginning to close, so I rushed forward and slipped inside before the doors closed completely.

Alone in the small car, I leaned against the wall and tried to tame the wild beating of my heart. I didn't know if this was going to work, but I had to try.

True, some memories were better off forgotten… but we couldn't truly be free until some things were remembered.

Actually, I didn't even have to *remember.* I just had to know.

The elevator opened to reveal the floor I selected. I stepped out into the quiet hall. I walked carefully along the wall, trying to remain as inconspicuous as I could, hoping no one would see me and if they did, they wouldn't bother telling me to stop.

I made it all the way to the large room door, but then someone called out my name.

Wincing, I rotated, knowing the look in my eyes was sheepish. "Dr. Beck," I said. "Nice to see you."

"Amnesia." He came to a stop in front of me. "You know you aren't supposed to be here."

I sighed, dropping the innocent act. "I assume you heard about Robbie in the ER? About Sadie being missing and suspected of his stabbing."

"You still can't be here," he said, firm.

"C'mon, Dr. Beck!" I burst out. "I have to be here! If I can't rely on my own memory to help everyone I care about, then I have to at least try this!"

He studied me for a long moment, then sighed. "She's still catatonic."

"I don't care," I answered, firm. "I just want to talk to her. Maybe she'll hear me. Maybe she'll answer."

"It's been over a month." He cautioned. "I'm not even sure she can hear us."

"Then it won't matter if I go in there," I told him. "*Please*, Dr. Beck. Widow West is my only chance at learning anything. The townspeople's safety could rely on this."

He glanced down the hall, then back at me. "Just a few minutes."

"Thank you," I said, sagging with relief.

"Amnesia." He cautioned, putting a hand lightly on my shoulder. "Do not touch her. And if she does anything at all, leave this room immediately."

Even though I wasn't facing him, I smiled. My hand covered his. "I care about you, too, Dr. Beck."

He withdrew his hand. His voice was gruff. "Five minutes."

I didn't waste any time, but let myself right in. The room was quiet, sterile, and dim. Memories of how my own room looked when I first woke from my coma came flooding back to me. I remembered how confused I'd been. How weak, mentally and physically.

I was stronger now, on both accounts, but I knew I still had a long way to go. This was a step in the right direction, though, facing my demons head on.

Widow West was lying on her back in the generic hospital bed. Her thin frame was covered with a hospital gown, and standard-issue blankets were pulled up to her waist. There was an IV in the back of her hand, but otherwise, there were no other machines. Her eyes were still open, just like the last time I saw her. They were glazed over, kind of milky. Utterly creepy.

I expected them to follow me as I passed by the end of her bed and moved around to the other side.

They didn't. They remained fixed, staring ahead and slightly up at the ceiling.

Her long gray hair was down around her shoulders. It was thick and coarse-looking, her skin pale, but all the bruises from before were healed.

She might seem almost peaceful if not for the way her eyes appeared. If not for the way her lips seemed permanently twisted in a painful grimace.

There were no flowers in this room. No cards or get-well balloons. The walls were all bare, the room cold and plain. Not even the noise from the TV was there to fill the void.

What was it like?

To be lost in your own head. Lonely day in and day out. Was it preferable to what she lived before, or was it merely a defense mechanism just like my amnesia?

I didn't want to admit it. I hated to acknowledge it, but Widow West and I had some things in common. I wondered if maybe we once shared the same kind of bond I had with Sadie.

"It's me," I said, quietly dragging a chair up to the side of the bed. "Amnesia."

It was disconcerting to speak and not know if you were heard. To not be acknowledged at all. But I pushed it back and spoke anyway. Pretending I was indeed being heard.

"It's been a while since I was here," I told her. "I know we don't really like each other much."

No point in lying, right?

"Truth is I'm not mad at you anymore. I had been, you know. So angry. You tried to kidnap me, knocked out Eddie. Stalked me. You, ah, told me once you wished I'd died."

Nothing. Silence.

I swallowed.

"I understand." I leaned back and decided just to pour it all out. Not for her, but for me. "You were probably in a hard position. Confused and trapped just like me. Just like Sadie. I know he hurt you, too. The doctors told me. I saw the bruises. I remember that night when you said if you didn't do what he wanted, he would punish you." I paused a second, sweeping my eyes over her gaunt face. "I'm sorry. I know I'm not the one who hurt you that way, but I'm still so, so sorry. I only remember a little, and that alone is enough. I wouldn't wish what happened to us on anyone, not even you. What you did, what I did... even what Sadie did. It was survival, wasn't it? And we did survive. All three of us."

A nurse went by the window, down the hall. I folded my hands in my lap.

"I guess that makes us sort of bonded. Not really friends, because I think we're past that kind of relationship. In the way we're the only ones who can ever really understand what he did to us.

"He's missing, by the way. *Him*. The man who hurt us. I still can't remember anything about him. His face. His name. I know he hurt me." I choked back the memory. My voice was slightly shaky when I went on. "I know he, um, raped me. Sadie said I was her replacement when he thought she was going to die. There was this woman. She would come down into the ground sometimes. She would go to where Sadie lay and tend to her. Sometimes I heard her crying. That was you, wasn't it?" I stared down at my hands, which were now tightly clasped together. "You cared about us, even though you helped him."

I sat forward, emotion making it impossible to sit still. "I just don't understand! I don't understand why you helped him. Where did you stay on the island? Where did he keep you? Did you stay in the house? Did he know your husband? I just need to know. I need to know something. Anything. Who is he? What did he want with us?”

A tear escaped my eye, and I furiously brushed it away. “Sadie told me my name was Lily. I don't know if I believe her, but really, why would she lie about that? I don't know where I came from, who I was, or who I left behind. I don't even need to know. But I need to know who he is. *Where* is he?”

The widow remained unchanged. Her milky eyes still staring up, her body unchanged. Not even the air around us shifted with any kind of indication she was listening.

“Maybe you really don't care,” I murmured. “Maybe you're just completely loyal to him and you'll lie there like that until you die. But please,” I begged. “If you can hear me, if you can understand me at all, please wake up. Please just tell me where he is and what he wants.”

Silence.

Absolute nothing.

I fell back in the chair, slouched into it, and crossed my arms over my chest. My thoughts wandered to Robbie. I wondered how he was, if surgery was nearly complete, and if he was still alive.

“We found Sadie. We went to your island, and there she was, down inside the hole. It wasn't even locked like usual. She said he wasn't there, but he was coming back and she had to stay. Eddie convinced her to leave the island. She's been here for a while now. She just got released from the hospital.”

Something in the room changed.

The air shifted; a knowing feeling moved down my spine.

I sat up, staring at her still form. "I don't think Sadie can handle everything that happened. She seems angry. She keeps saying he's coming back. She, um, stabbed my friend today, tried to kill him, and now no one can find her. He's in surgery right now. I don't know if he'll live. The police are out looking for her, but I can't help but feel like this has to do with him. If only I knew who he was. Where he might be. Do you think she's with him now? Do you think he's still controlling her?"

I waited for an answer. I waited so long for her to blink, for a random beep from the IV machine. I watched her fingers for even a flinch.

I poured out everything. I begged for help.

I got nothing in return.

Eventually, I grew weary, my patience and hope dimmed. I wanted to go find Eddie, who was surely wondering where I'd gone by now. I should have told him, but I knew he'd only try and stop me. I wanted to know about Robbie and to call Maggie.

"It was worth a try," I told myself, using the side of the bed for balance as I pushed myself to my feet. After dragging the chair back to its rightful place, I moved back to the side of the bed and stared down at the widow.

I reached out and grazed my fingers over her hand. "I hope at least wherever you are, you have some peace."

As I was drawing away, her finger moved. A sudden jerk, perhaps an involuntary reaction.

"Widow West?" I whispered, leaning over her, looking into her foggy eyes.

She didn't move again. Her hands stayed still.

With a sigh, I pulled back. Her hand shot out and gripped my wrist. I squeaked, taken completely off guard.

"Did you hear anything I said?" I asked, letting her continue to hold my arm. "Please, if you know anything, *please* tell me."

Her mouth worked slowly, as though it were trying to remember how to form words. My patience nearly crumbled, waiting, trying not to grab and shake her. All at once, her eyes closed. I saw them shifting beneath her lids.

Please, I prayed silently.

When her eyes reopened, they weren't quite as glazed over, though they still had a film over them, making me wonder how coherent she was.

"He's my son," she rasped, her voice a near whisper. "My... son."

There was no way to contain my reaction. I gasped and my wrist dislodged from her slight grip. Her hand fell back onto the mattress beside her body.

Her son? How could that be?

"I thought your child died," I said, recalling the *Beloved Child* headstone next to the one belonging to her late husband.

"Where... is... he?" she croaked, her fingers trying to find mine once more.

I grabbed her hand, squeezing it lightly in mine. "I don't know. No one knows. Where would he have gone?"

"Not... well," she said, her eyes slipping closed. "Find him. He will..." Her voice stopped mid-sentence.

"He will what?" I demanded, almost desperate. I lifted her hand, giving it a shake. "He will what, Widow West?"

"My son," she moaned. Then her grip went slack.

"Widow West!" I exclaimed, lifting her hand again. "Ms. West!"

She didn't respond. Her eyes remained closed, her body limp against the bed. I launched over her and put my ear to her chest. The sound of her heartbeat was there and strong. With a great heave, I pushed off her.

I wasn't going to get any more answers out of her. Hell, I was incredibly lucky to have gotten what she said at all.

I raced from the room. Dr. Beck was standing at the nearby nurses' station.

"She woke up!" I told him, rushing over. "She moved and blinked her eyes. I think she fell asleep, though."

"Are you okay?" he asked, studying my frantic movements.

"Yes!" I insisted and started to hurry away. "I'm fine. Just help her!"

Running down the hall to the elevators, all I could think of was getting to Eddie, telling him what new information I had. I knew it wasn't a lot, but it was something.

The middle set of doors dinged open, and I charged ahead. A body rushed out, and we both nearly collided.

"Amnesia!" Eddie exclaimed, catching me by the shoulders. "Thank fuck! Where have you been?"

"I talked to her!" I burst out. "She told me!"

"Told you what?" he asked, giving me a gentle shake.

I looked up into his worried face, but the image began to fade, began to change… until it wasn't him I saw at all anymore. Until I wasn't standing in the hospital hallway.

My fingers dug into his biceps as I fought what I knew was coming.

"No," I said, but it was futile.

I was taken from the present and dragged brutally back into the past.

CHAPTER THIRTY

AMNESIA

The musty, overpowering smell of damp earth burned my nose. You'd think by now I'd be used to the scent, but I wasn't. I might never be.

It was worse when it rained, and tonight (or today), there had been one hell of a rainstorm. Even we could hear it down here. Sadie cried and screamed from her cot on the other side of the room as rain pelted the ground above us and thunder boomed so loud the stone around us shook.

I told her a few times it would be okay, that the storm wouldn't hurt us down here. I didn't know if she heard me over the rain and her own cries, but I kept telling her anyway.

I was chained. I think she was, too. The rocks were cold against my flesh, but when I sat huddled in on myself, it wasn't as bad. My corner of rock stayed sort of warm from my body heat, but I wasn't sitting back there now.

I'd stretched out, crawled across the floor as far as I could, moving as close as I could get to Sadie.

I hated hearing her cry. It seemed that was all she did. When he came down in the middle of the night as we slept. And now during the storm. There was no peace here. Not for anyone.

Eventually, the storm subsided and the smell of damp earth pressed in. I drew my knees up to my chest, wrapped my arms around them, and buried my face against myself to try and keep out the worst of the stench. Sadie was quieter now that the rain had stopped. I thought she might be sleeping.

I had trouble sleeping down here. I was afraid he would do worse things to me when I was unconscious. I'd rather just stay awake and know the pain for sure.

The familiar, distinct creaking of the overhead trapdoor made me stiffen. I sat up, plastered my body back against the wall, and stared up. When no sunlight shone down, I felt a pang of deep sorrow. I missed the sun. He didn't know it and I would never say, but whenever he came down here, there was one thing I liked.

For brief moments, sometimes even a full minute, sunlight would stream down into this damp, dark prison. Reminding me there was life above us, that the sun still shone even though I couldn't see it.

I wondered if it would still feel warm against my cheeks, if the air would still linger with the scent of sunshine.

All too fast, he would shut that door, though, closing us off from any kind of pleasure, climbing down into this hole to bring us more pain.

I still ached from the last time he'd been down. My body felt torn and swollen. My flesh still bore the sting from his bites. I'd made the mistake of crying out the first time he'd bitten me.

He liked that.

He did it over and over again.

I felt like a chew toy.

I didn't cry out again, even though inside I screamed. Eventually, he grew bored of the biting and moved on to new horrors.

My body shook violently as I waited for him to climb down. I knew Sadie was still pretty bad off, though I knew he went to her the day before.

I didn't know who he was coming for this time, maybe me. Could be her. If he went toward her tonight, I would call out, draw him away, toward me.

I could take another night. I wasn't sure if she could. The storm seemed to wring out everything she had left tonight.

A flashlight clicked on and swung down. I saw the feet of a woman and sighed audibly. It wasn't him.

It was her.

I didn't know anything about her, only that she came to see to Sadie. She'd never come near me, never even glanced my way.

I couldn't help but wonder about her, who she was, why she was here. Why she didn't live down here with us.

She walked quietly over to Sadie, dropped down beside her, and spoke softly. After tending to Sadie's healing wounds and assuring her the storm was indeed done, she packed up her little sack of supplies and started to leave.

"Wait," I called out, my voice meek but heard.

The woman's footsteps stopped shuffling over the rock. The beam of the flashlight swung toward me.

I cringed away from it, not wanting to be seen, not wanting to see myself. "Do you have an extra Band-Aid?" I asked, timid. I knew I could get in trouble for this, but really… wasn't I already being punished?

"For what?" she said, her voice low.

"I… I have a bite on my shoulder. It won't stop bleeding." I felt my lower lip wobble. I bit it to make it stop. "It hurts."

She stood there for a long time, so long I thought maybe she didn't believe me. Why would I lie? It wasn't as if I had anything to gain.

When I thought she was turning to leave, she didn't. Instead, she walked over, crouching in front of where I sat. "Where?" she asked.

With shaking hands, I leaned forward, showing her the side of my aching shoulder. "Here."

The light spotlighted the injury, and I squeezed my eyes shut at the vision it made. I knew it was bad. I felt the warm trickle of blood around it, felt the way the skin throbbed and burned.

But oh…

It was worse than even I imagined.

It was as if he chewed on my flesh. Not just a clean bite, but as if he tried to make my shoulder a meal. He enjoyed it, though, gnawing on me as if I were rawhide, licking at my blood while I whimpered against the floor.

The woman made a sound, then dropped her sack on the floor and used the light to fish through its contents.

She ripped open a small wipe of some kind and, without warning, wiped it over the area. I cried out a little, then stiffened, worried my show of pain would get me beaten.

"It's okay," she said. "It looks painful."

I merely nodded, afraid to say anything else.

She cleaned it up, made a few tsking sounds, then rubbed on some kind of cream before covering it completely with a large bandage.

The second she was done, I sighed in relief.

The woman began packing up her supplies, then tied the sack closed.

Before she stood, I grabbed her wrist. "Thank you," I said.

She seemed surprised I would thank her. Maybe I shouldn't. But this was the first show of kindness (no matter how terrible it was) that I'd known in a long time.

If I forgot how to appreciate kindness of any kind, wouldn't that make me a lost cause? Wouldn't that make me less human?

"Why?" she whispered.

"Because now it hurts less."

Something passed around us in the air, but I couldn't name the feeling. She started to move away again. I let go but stopped her with my voice.

"Who are you?" I asked. I had to know.

"I'm his mother," she replied after a heartbeat.

Shock rippled through me. "He's your son?"

"Yes," she said, emotion clogging her voice. "I'm sorry."

Her apology caused emotion to well up inside me. Anger. "You know." I sat forward, making the chain around my wrist clatter. "You know what he's doing to us is wrong," I accused.

"Yes."

"But you help him."

"He... he's not well. He doesn't understand what he does is wrong."

"That doesn't make it okay!" I demanded. "You should get him real help."

"I can't," she whispered.

Nearby, I saw Sadie sit up, listening intently. No doubt she had all these questions, too.

"Why can't you?" I demanded. I was in no position to demand anything.

Actually. Yes. Yes, I was in every position to demand answers.

"They'll take him away from me. He's all I have left."

I fell back against the wall, shocked and shattered. She knew what he was doing was wrong. She knew, and she didn't care.

"I'm sorry," she rushed out, then hurried away, toward the ladder that led to freedom.

"How could you?" I yelled after her, anger burning my throat. "How could you let him do this to us?"

I didn't expect an answer, yet one came out of the darkness.

"Because if not you, then others. The two of you are a small price to pay for his freedom, for the safety of everyone else."

I said nothing to that. I was too shocked and horrified to even comprehend.

We were nothing but a sacrifice. Playthings to a madman.

The sound of her climbing out of the hole made me look up.

The sound of the deadbolts locking us in made me cry.

Here I'd hoped I'd found an ally. Instead, all I'd found was another foe.

CHAPTER THIRTY-ONE

EDWARD

"You shouldn't have done that," I scolded, even though it really wasn't a scold. How could I reprimand the woman I loved when she was tucked into my lap, curled against my body, and shivering from whatever the fuck just took over her body and mind?

I was mad, though. Flaming, red hot, wanting to leave a fist-sized dent in anything nearby.

"I g-got some in-information," she said, her teeth chattering slightly.

"It wasn't worth the price you paid."

"I think maybe it was," she refuted.

The way she shivered proved her wrong. The way she collapsed into my arms when I stepped off the elevator proved me right.

My heart damn near stopped in my chest when she was immobile in my arms, unresponsive to any of my attempts to wake her.

I'd never seen anything like it before. Not until Am. The way the past took over, sweeping in without even a second's notice to push out all the present and quite literally drag her back into the bygone.

Even though she appeared somewhat peaceful as I supported her body in my arms, it was anything but. I knew a war waged inside her mind. I knew she wasn't really present with me when a memory took over.

The minutes I had to wait it out, to keep myself from literally losing my shit, were long and arduous. I took her down the elevator, back onto the floor where we'd been waiting. Mary B saw me step off the car with her and opened her mouth to yell for help. One firm shake of my head and the words died against her tongue.

She led us into an empty room, the closest one she could find. It was way better than the waiting room, as I wasn't sure what kind of condition Am would be when she came back to me.

This time she didn't run from the room or vomit all the contents of her belly. But it hadn't been a cakewalk either.

The second the past let her go, her body went rigid in my lap. I stayed still for long moments, my arms and hands hovering around her in case she jerked so fast she tumbled off me toward the floor. I didn't touch her, though. I was afraid to. I had to see what kind of condition she was in before I wrapped her close.

The last thing I wanted was for her to feel trapped or confined.

She glanced up, breathing heavy, wetness covering her cheeks. I clenched my jaw, my back teeth slamming together as I tried not to react the way I wanted, instead trying to be what she needed.

Am reached for me, fisting her fingers in the front of my shirt and curling into my center. That was my cue, the signal it was okay to hold her tight.

We sat there a while. I didn't say anything, though I sorely wanted to give her hell.

What the fuck was she thinking just disappearing like that? Slipping out of the waiting room while I talked to the cops. When I saw she was gone, my fucking chest nearly collapsed.

Wild fear shot through me, adrenaline surged, and I searched everywhere I could think of. Just when I was about out of my ever-loving mind, I remembered the widow.

"Don't do that again," I intoned. I guess I wasn't done scolding her.

"I'm sorry," she whimpered. "Please don't be mad."

I groaned. I swear, women (this one in particular) would be the death of me. "I'm not mad at you, baby." My fingers dragged up and down along her side. "You scared me."

"I just wanted to help."

"I know." I kissed the top of her head.

"Are the police still here?"

"Not a clue," I remarked as though it didn't even matter. Though, inside, everything was on high alert. Why would she want to know about the cops? Did she have something to tell them? I wanted to demand the answers, but I knew better. Pushing her would cause her pain, and frankly, that outweighed my need for info.

"Where are we?" She glanced around, still not lifting her cheek from my chest. It was telling, you know. The clinginess.

That memory hadn't been pleasant.

I was starting to wonder if she had anything good at all from her past to remember. All she ever remembered was hell.

"Just a private room. Same floor as the waiting room."

"Any word on Robbie?"

"Not yet."

"I had another memory," she informed me. Her voice was low, scared to even bring it up.

"Because you saw Widow West," I whispered.

"She's the only one with answers." Am defended herself. "I had to try."

"Seeing her triggered a memory." My voice was flat and unhappy.

Amnesia pushed up in my lap, sitting so we were face to face. "No," she refuted. "It was what she said."

My eyebrows shot up. "She woke up?"

She nodded. "I told her about Sadie, Robbie… everything. I begged her to tell me where he might be. At first, I thought she couldn't hear me, but then… she replied."

"What did she say?" I demanded.

"It's her son," Amnesia intoned, dropping back against my chest. Her fingers returned to the front of my shirt, twisting the fabric. "The man who kidnapped us, it's Widow West's son."

"Her son," I echoed. My mind was spinning. "But…"

"I know. The headstone we saw. She must have had a baby who died… before she had *him*." Then almost to herself, Am added, "It's why she didn't want to lose him. Too much loss."

"Daniel," I whispered.

"Who?"

"That's his name." I glanced down. "Sadie told me."

"I didn't remember."

"She said you weren't allowed to call him that," I explained, trying to make her feel better about not knowing.

Amnesia shivered into me. "He's not well. There's something wrong with him."

I grunted. That much was blatantly obvious. No one in their right mind would do to them what that sick fuck had done. "What else did she say, Am?"

"Not much, really. She wanted to know where he was. Seemed almost desperate we find him. I got the feeling she was scared he was out there… unsupervised."

I made a rude sound, my chest jerking with the force of it. "Yeah, 'cause he was so much more in control when she was *supervising* him."

Amnesia tilted her head up. "I think… I think maybe he was."

My jaw clenched. "What did you remember?"

Her voice slipped into monotone, her limbs rigid even though I tried to comfort her.

"She helped me one night, gave me first aid on an…" She glanced up, timid. "An injury on my shoulder—"

I was the one who was rigid now. "What kind of injury?"

"You don't want to know."

"Yes." I shook her lightly, trying to make her understand. "Yes, I do."

I had to know. I had to at least try and understand, to be burdened with the same memories as her. She wasn't alone anymore. I would shoulder this with her.

"It was a bite." Her voice was strained. Tired. "He liked to bite me… chew on my skin."

I bit the inside of my mouth, bit down so hard the metallic tang of blood hit my tongue. "Go on," I rasped.

"It was the first time I'd ever spoken to her or really had contact with her at all. She usually only ever bothered with Sadie. I asked her. She told me she was his mother. She seemed sorry…"

"Not sorry enough." The remark ripped right out of me.

"No. Not sorry enough. She said she knew he wasn't well. She seemed to believe he didn't understand what he was doing to us was wrong."

I laughed. This was disgusting.

"Why would she help him? Why would she let us be tortured that way? Locked in a hole, no sunlight… no hope."

"Am." I stroked her hair. For a moment, she paused, rubbing her cheek against my chest.

"Your shirt," she whispered, still rubbing her cheek over the fabric.

"What about it?"

"I don't like it," she whispered. "There's too much between us."

I ripped the shirt over my head, throwing it onto the floor in front of us, where it slid a few feet before stopping in the center of the room.

Amnesia wound her arms around me, scooting so close it was almost as if she were trying to climb beneath my skin. The second her cheek hit my bare chest, she sighed and her body gave a great shudder of relief.

I swallowed thickly. Emotion so dense made me feel I might choke.

"You make me feel safe," she whispered.

"You are safe," I swore.

"She said she couldn't lose him. She didn't want him to be taken away. She hid him there, on the island. I doubt anyone even knew she had a son."

"No one in Lake Loch knew," I said, sifting through a lifetime's worth of gossip and town knowledge. "She was always alone when she came for supplies."

"She thought people would take him away if they knew what he was."

"She was right," I growled.

"She made it sound as though we were responsible for keeping him contained. She told me… She said we were a small price to pay for the safety of everyone else."

The widow lost her husband, and her son grew up to be insane. I could feel sorry for her, the fact she lost a child, a husband, and all she had left was her son. I could sympathize with her pain and understand she was afraid to lose everything.

I didn't.

In my eyes, this woman was no better than the son she unleashed on two innocent girls. Look what she'd done! She'd broken Sadie and drove Am to suicide. All to try and keep her son in control.

You can't control darkness, though, not when you have no light.

"Did she say where he could be?" I asked. The need to find this guy and rip him apart was so strong my fingers shook.

"No. But I have a feeling he wouldn't go far, not with all three of his possessions here."

"You are not his," I demanded.

"He doesn't see it that way." Her voice was small. "Sadie and the widow seem to think so as well."

"No," I ground out. "I don't give a fuck what anyone thinks, says, or does. You are not his."

Her hand flattened on my chest. "I know."

I clutched her close, thinking about how all this time, evil lived right in our backyard. Did that make us all responsible? Was the entire town of Lake Loch at fault for not realizing what was happening right beneath our noses?

"I still don't know where I came from," Am said, drawing my attention back. "I have a feeling not even the widow knows. It's like he just left one day, probably in a fit of rage about Sadie… and came back with me."

And that psycho mother of his acted as if he'd brought home a dog and chained her up. Let him "keep" her.

Sick fucks. Both of them.

"It doesn't matter where you came from," I told her passionately. "Because you're now where you belong."

The door opened, and Mary Beth came in. My head snapped up so fast, my protective instincts on overdrive. Mary must have seen the wild look in my eyes; hers widened and her lips formed a small O.

"I, uh… Robbie is out of surgery," she said, taking a step back toward the door.

Forcing myself to relax, I waved her closer. "How is he?"

"He's stable but still in serious condition. The doctors are optimistic, but of course not promising anything. They want to give him a couple days."

"Can we see him?" Am asked, perking up.

Mary Beth shook her head. "He's still in recovery, heavily sedated."

"How long?" I asked. It felt we'd been waiting here for days already.

"I'm not sure. They probably won't let you see him until tomorrow."

"Are the police still here?" Am wanted to know.

Mary B nodded. "They're putting one outside his room once he's moved. His parents are here, too."

"Thank you," I told her, sincere. "I really appreciate you calling me."

She nodded and whispered, "You really think it was Sadie?"

Word got around fast. Big surprise there. Not.

"We can't be sure," Amnesia said, but at the very same time, I said, "Yes."

She glanced up at me, surprised and worried. "Eddie…"

I touched her face, smiling sadly. "It's okay, Am. I don't want to believe it, but who else could it be?"

After hearing about Sadie being not only abused and tortured, but exposed to two freaking whack jobs for eleven years, it seemed nearly impossible for it not to rub off.

Brainwashed + Battered + Imprisoned = enough to turn anyone crazed enough to kill.

Glancing down at Amnesia, I couldn't help but marvel at how fucking lucky she was. How fucking lucky *I* was.

She could have been just like Sadie. Just like the widow. But she wasn't. Her mind figured out the greatest defense of them all.

Amnesia.

Protecting her seemed more important than ever.

"I hope they find her," Mary Beth said morosely. "I hope she gets the help she needs."

"Me, too." I agreed.

"Okay, well, if you want to go home, I can call with updates on Robbie. I really don't think you'll be able to see him until tomorrow at the earliest. He's going to be in recovery the rest of the day. The police probably won't even be able to question him."

"Thanks." I nodded.

She turned to go, looking back. "Can I just say you two look like shit? I really hope you take my advice and go home. Get some rest."

I laughed. "Way to keep it real, Mary B."

Amnesia giggled.

"That's what friends are for," she quipped, then went back to work.

"I need to tell the police what I know. It's not much, but maybe his name will help. It's something."

"Yeah," I murmured. "It's something."

"Eddie?" Amnesia lifted her cheek.

I grunted.

"If you want to be out there looking for Sadie, I understand. You should go."

"Are you kidding?" I scoffed. "I turn my back on you for one second and you're off interrogating patients and having memories."

Okay, I tried. It was a joke, but that shit just wasn't funny.

"I promise I'll behave," she vowed, a little sparkle in her eyes.

Maybe it was a little funny.

"I'm staying with you." I committed. "You're the most important thing to me." It wasn't as if I wasn't freaked out of my mind for Sadie. Part of me wanted to go search for her. I felt I might be the only one who could reason with her. Even though she probably tried to carve up my best friend, I still cared about her. I still wanted to get her help.

"This isn't her fault," I murmured. "She's just…"

"I know." Amnesia put her hand over mine. "I know."

I pressed my lips to her forehead, and we fell into silence.

The whole time we sat there, I couldn't help but wonder…

Where the hell could Sadie be?

CHAPTER THIRTY-TWO

AMNESIA

Exhaustion clung to me like sweat in the summer. By the time we spoke to the police and waited around for more updates on Robbie, it was dinnertime when we left the hospital.

My eyes felt gritty, like there was a pound of sand beneath each lid. My mouth was dry, uncomfortably so. All of my body felt as though I'd taken some wild exercise class that made me exert every last bit of energy.

We went to Maggie's first, where we found food warmed in the oven and a note on the counter. She was out looking for Sadie and would be back later.

I knew Eddie was torn about wanting to be out there looking, too, but his great sense of loyalty to me kept him back. It was touching but also made me feel guilty. I didn't want to be the reason he did something he would regret.

"C'mon, baby," he said, lightly touching my elbow. "You gotta eat."

I glanced down at the plates he was holding. They were filled with baked chicken, mac and cheese, and vegetables. My stomach grumbled, but the rest of me revolted.

"I'm not hungry."

"I hear your stomach," he deadpanned.

My stomach was stupid.

I followed him out into the breakfast room and sat down. He dug in immediately, while I was more content to pick and push food around.

"I'm sorry," I finally said.

His fork froze partway to his mouth. His gaze slid over. "For what?"

"For putting you in the middle. For making you feel you have to choose between me and Sadie. You don't, you know. I would never ask you to not see her. To not care."

A loud clattering sound filled the silence when he dropped the fork. His entire body rotated toward me, his knees bumping the side of my leg. "You didn't put me in the middle," he said, firm.

"But you feel like you have to choose."

He pressed his lips together. "Yeah, maybe."

My heart sank a little.

"But really, there is no choice. I think that's what makes me feel the worst."

I glanced up. He met and held my stare with his own. Love shone in the depths of his blue eyes. "Remember what I told you, Am. I choose you. Always. No matter what."

Moisture prickled the backs of my eyes. He was everything to me. Eddie had given me so much. "I love you," I whispered.

"Ditto." He twisted his lips in a smile.

I laughed.

"I'll come with you!" I said, realization dawning.

"What?"

"I'll come help look for Sadie. Then you can be with me *and* look for her."

His face darkened. "No."

"But why?"

"I am not exposing you to any more shit that could traumatize you. Jesus, Am. You've been through enough."

"I'm stronger than you think."

"Oh, I'm well aware. It's your strength that scares me, baby. But even the strong can become weak."

I frowned, not quite sure what he meant. Was my strength a good thing or a bad thing?

"You've been strong a long time. All by yourself. You don't have to do it alone anymore. Let me protect you."

Maybe I should have fought him, but I was too weary to try. Truth was I wanted his protection. I craved it.

"How about we stay at my place tonight?" he suggested, pushing back from the table.

"How about we stay there from now on?"

He stilled. "What?"

I stood, taking his hand. "Is that invite to move in with you still good?"

Eddie's eyes flared. "Of course."

I smiled. "Good, then I'd like to come home."

He swept me up and spun me around. I giggled. When his feet stilled, he let my body slide down his. Our faces became parallel, my feet still hovering over the floor.

Eddie came forward and linked our mouths. I held my breath the entire time we kissed, not even missing the air.

When at last we parted, he smiled the biggest smile I'd seen light his face all day. "Get a bag," he told me, swatting my ass. "Let's go home."

CHAPTER THIRTY-THREE

EDWARD

I felt it again.

The pull of the lake. It was like a magnet, a song that only I could hear. The urge to go to the shore, to allow the icy lances of the waves grab at my flesh and chill me to the bone, was massive.

I don't know why, but I had a connection with Lake Loch. Almost as if the body of water and I were friends. Or maybe enemies.

Either way, we were close. The lake played a large role in my life, as if it were a person, a character I knew. It spoke to me, took from me, gave back to me.

All I knew was when it wanted something, no matter what it was, I was powerless to fight it.

I was hard pressed to carefully slip out from beneath Amnesia. Her bare, silky skin directly upon mine was almost more powerful than the summoning of the shore. I could roll over, press her body into the mattress, and bury myself in her liquid heat just as I had the minute we stepped into this room just a few hours before.

But I was intrigued. Intensely so. There was always a connection with the water, but nothing like it had been the night I found Amnesia.

The night the lake gave me back my heart.

A hollow pit formed in my belly, a feeling I remembered well. Back when my heart still belonged to the sea and the hollowness owned my chest, how it echoed with the sound of emptiness, reminding me day in and day out of what was missing.

The feeling scared me. Scared me more than almost anything, because it was the feeling of loneliness. The feeling that perhaps the lake changed its mind and wanted to take back what it had gifted me.

Friend or enemy?

After tugging on a pair of sweats, I stood at the side of the mattress and stared down at my heart. My gift from Lake Loch.

Please don't take her away from me.

Moonlight shone through a small gap in the curtains, a slice of silver streaking over her, illuminating her short hair, making it glow. Her skin was creamy and pale in the dark, her body still curled toward where I'd been, her cheek resting against the pillow.

Cross my heart.

Hope to die.

You will be forever mine.

I turned away, left the bedroom silently, and moved through the familiar darkness. I would abide the pull of the lake tonight if for no other reason than to deny whatever it thought to take back.

Even though the temperature outside was cold, I went bare-chested. My feet were also bare. I felt the first slap of wintry air as I stepped off the porch into the grass, more like tiny ice daggers than the green, friendly carpet.

After the initial shock of my skin meeting the air, I forgot about it. Tightened nipples, contracted muscles, and blowing hair—I ignored it all and stalked across my yard down toward the black, ominous water.

The whistling of the wind flew past my ears. My hair tugged fiercely away from my face and forehead as if it were trying to pull me back into the comfort of my house.

Go back, it warned.

I kept moving forward.

The moon hung low tonight, partially blocked by dark clouds but visible enough to shine a spotlight that stretched out over the water, highlighting the way it churned rather portentously. The trees all rustled, leaves scattering the ground pushed and pulled in various directions.

A few stars shone overhead, but not enough to make an impact. Not enough to draw the eye.

The sound of the shore grew louder, seemed more violent as I approached. Stuffing my hands in the pockets of my sweats, I carried on. My shoulder blades drew together with tension. I didn't bother to try and fight.

I had a feeling the lake wanted a fight tonight.

So a fight was what it would have.

The toes of my right foot hit the water first. The skin began tingling immediately. The inclination to recoil from the frigid temp was natural, but I held firm. Both feet sloshed into the dark waves. I walked forward just enough that the water was able to swallow both up to my ankles.

I spread my arms wide, staring out at the unforgiving body of water. Marveling at the secrets it held and the way it so casually homed an island of a madman.

"I'm here!" I yelled. "I know you want me. Here I am!"

I sounded like a lunatic, appearing to yell at no one. But I knew to whom I spoke. My words might have fallen on deaf ears, but the lake heard regardless.

"I don't understand why you took Sadie. Or why you gave me Amnesia." I went on, hurling the words into the wind. "You can't have her back!"

A wave crashed close, splashing up my legs and saturating the lower portion of my pants. Maybe I was dreaming. Perhaps I was going insane, but my words seemed to evoke a reaction. A great gale blew off the water, and the waves became defiant.

"What do you want?" I flung the words. I was angry and confused. I was also slightly embarrassed.

I was standing in a freezing cold lake in the middle of the night, with barely any clothes on, challenging it as if it were suggesting war.

The violent reply from the wind and water was all I got. I stood there until my feet were numb and the numbness began moving up my legs and teasing the tips of my fingers.

I didn't know what I expected, but it was more than I got.

Suddenly, a sick feeling plunged into me, coming up so quick my stomach revolted and the urge to vomit tickled the back of my throat. My body flung around. Turning my back on the water, I stared at my house. Scanning its outline, the yard, and everything around it, I searched for something. Anything. My eyes ultimately landed on the bedroom window, where Amnesia lay sleeping in my bed.

Knowing I left her in there alone gave me a creepy feeling. Maybe that's what the lake wanted. Maybe it wanted to tear me away so I *couldn't* fight.

A large wave crashed into me, hitting me just behind the knees. My legs buckled, but I didn't go down. The drenched material of my sweats clung to my legs, the weight shackles around my ankles.

A sound ripped from my throat, and I lifted one foot to trudge back home. Something bumped against the other leg. The one still anchored in water. I paused. It collided into me again, briefly tugged away, then clashed against me once more.

Whirling around, I stomped down, and the water splashed around me.

It took a moment for the sight to register. For the actuality of what I was seeing to seep into my mind.

The boat appeared out of nowhere. A small wooden craft not much larger than a canoe. The front end was pointed. The point was what bumped me, the surface rough even though it was wet. The edge caught my pants, snagging the material as if to yank me out to sea.

I kicked it back, sending the boat sideways. It was long, enough for a few people to fit inside. On the edge was a long wooden oar anchored by a clamp.

On the back of the boat, I could make out what appeared to be a tall metal rod sticking straight up into the night. There was a hook on the end, and I knew it was for a lantern that wasn't there.

I didn't know the boat; it wasn't one I'd seen before. The idea of using a lantern seemed archaic but also served as a precursor to other thoughts.

Visions of blinking, bobbing light out on Rumor Island replayed in my head. The glow of what we always thought was Sadie's lantern. Sadie roaming the island at night, waiting for her… master to return.

To bring back her sister, her replacement. What was his.

I gasped, the sound more like a yell of enlightenment.

Holy shit.

The boat rammed into my shins, forced close again by the ferocious water. I might have thought the lake was working against me, trying to stop me from rushing back to Amnesia's side.

I have to get back to Am.

But it wasn't.

The lake was warning me.

Friend or enemy, I still didn't know. Maybe it was ever changing like the tide. But tonight? Tonight, Lake Loch appeared to be a friend.

As I shoved away the wooden vessel, just beyond it, something rose from the water. A paper-white arm shot up from the inky depths. From finger to elbow, the arm reached up as if it were trying to grab hold of some invisible rope to tow itself up.

I watched as the figure emerged from the water, inch by inch at first, then surged up the rest of the way, water droplets spraying out around the body like Jaws coming up for a bite.

The man was tall and stocky, not built, but not thin. His hair was dark, of undeterminable length, and plastered to his head. Dark brows slashed thickly over his eyes, harsh and garish against his deathly pale face.

The white button-up shirt he wore was see-through from the water. It too was plastered against his body, showing off soft areas, for example, around the middle.

The shirt was buttoned up all the way, appearing like a noose around his neck and wrists. He moved stiff and slow, and I wondered why the fuck he was in the water and not inside his boat.

Dark dress pants covered his lower half, at least at the hips where he wasn't under the water. He was wearing a belt, his shirt tucked in, as if he were on his way to a business meeting and not literally birthing out of a dark, cruel lake in the middle of the night.

All the muscles in my body coiled, preparing for a fight it instantly knew was coming. Water swelled around me, giving me a buoyant feeling as though it were trying to build me up.

Yes, the lake was definitely friend tonight, for it summoned me down here not to take something away, but to help me keep it.

"So you're the one." The man's voice overpowered the wind.

"The one what?" I spat. I wasn't sure what the fuck was going on, but I knew whatever it was didn't call for pleasantries and happy greetings.

"The one who thinks he can claim what's mine."

Realization hit me so hard I would have fallen backward, but as I mentioned before, the lake tonight was like heavy shackles keeping me in place.

"You," I growled, my eyes going over his shoulder to the looming presence of Rumor Island.

He glared, measured me in a single sweep, then disregarded what he saw. "You might have been strong enough to thwart past attempts to gain back what is and always will be mine," he intoned, cutting through the water toward me. "But you aren't any match for me."

I laughed. The sound actually caused my own hair to stand up on my neck. "You're *him*," I spat. "The man who chains up women and keeps them in a hole. The man who robbed two girls of their lives and made one so desperate to get away she tried to die."

There were no words, not even thoughts that could come close to how much I hated this man.

"I've come for her." He didn't deny what I said. He didn't have to. I might never have seen his face before, but I knew him. Daniel. He reeked of havoc and mental illness.

The final step he took brought us face to face. Wind whipped around us; water churned beneath us. Inside me, so much anger burned I felt like a flint ready to ignite into a flame that could never burn out, even in a body of water.

I leaned in so close I knew he could feel my hot breath on his face. His eyes were dark, empty, and cold. There was no man here. No feeling. He was a shell, the mere house for the devil.

"The only thing you're getting here is a one-way trip back to hell."

The second the words left my lips, I reared back and launched my fist at him. All the force I had went into that blow. The momentum spurred me forward. The sound of cracking bone crunched around us the second my fist collided with his face.

His head snapped back, his body jerking as though it took a bullet. Then, just like rubber, he snapped back. I reared back to hit him again, but he caught my fist midair and squeezed. The bones in my fingers screamed in pain, but I didn't show it. Instead, I felt the water let go of me, and I kicked upward, driving my toes into his kidney. The grip on my hand slackened, and I lunged forward like a linebacker, catching him around the waist, and shoved. We both fell, him going backward and me on top. The water sliced into my arms and waist as I scrambled up, straddling him. He pushed up, but I buried my fist in his face again, knocking him back.

I stomped down, right in his midsection, making him curl in on himself a little. I watched his body disappear beneath the water, only to jackknife back up.

Teeth bared, water dripped from his features, making him look rabid. He lunged at me. This time I fell backward and he was the one on top. He punched me, then wrapped his hands around my neck and squeezed.

I brought my leg up between his, going straight for his balls. His thighs slammed shut, trapping my ankle and protecting his junk. Frustrated, I tried to pull back, but he lifted me with one hand, by the neck, out of the water. Beneath me, I heard the waves scramble about, but my eyes never left his face.

"She's mine," he intoned. "I'm not leaving without her. Without both of them."

He body-slammed me back into the water, shoving me down until my bare back scraped against the rocky floor. Dark water washed over my face, clouding my vision, as his hands tightened around my neck until it felt as though my windpipe might collapse.

I squirmed and kicked, prying at his hand with mine.

I could have sworn, as I struggled beneath the surface and my lungs started to plead for oxygen, that above me, I heard him laugh.

CHAPTER THIRTY-FOUR

AMNESIA

Discerning dream from reality was becoming a problem for me.

And maybe so was trusting myself to know the difference.

My arm stretched out, seeking the comfort I had come to rely on. When my palm met sheets, which had gone cold, alertness saturated the rest I'd been getting.

Opening my eyes, I glanced at the space Eddie always occupied. He was gone. I was beneath the covers alone.

The room was still very dark. Day had yet to break. It was too early for him to be up making coffee, and I didn't hear him in the bathroom. Anxiety pierced me; my chest squeezed uncomfortably as I rolled onto my back.

Something was wrong.

Without hesitation, I pushed up, nearly falling back when I realized I wasn't alone. The gasp was so unexpected, my surprise so great, I started to cough.

With watering eyes, I forced the reflex back and stared at the foot of the bed.

At Sadie.

I blinked. Blinked again. Was she really there? Or was this just a dream?

"I'm real," Sadie spoke. The sound of her voice sent goose bumps over my naked body.

I gasped again, folding my arms over my exposed chest.

"It's nothing I haven't seen before," Sadie remarked. "Both of us. We're very familiar with the sight of each other naked."

A sudden, terrible flash of memory cut through me.

Both of us on our backs. Both of us shoulder to shoulder. Him switching off between us… The sound of his heavy breathing.

"No," I exclaimed, slapping my hands over my ears as if it would somehow stop the images.

Remarkably, it did.

Thank God.

Chest heaving, my stare cut over to the empty spot beside me. Where was Eddie?

"He's busy," Sadie informed me.

Forgetting I was naked, I burst up, angry. "What did you do to him?"

"Nothing. I would never do anything to Eddie. I love him." She said it so calmly, without passion, as though she were speaking about shutting off the water or taking out the trash.

"If you loved him, you wouldn't have tried to murder his best friend!" I yelled. Adrenaline pumped through me, and I clutched onto it.

I moved around the side of the bed, grabbing the pair of panties I'd abandoned to the floor when we got home. Sliding them up over my legs, I had a brief memory of how they felt being dragged by Eddie's fingertips, down over my hips, over my knees, until they were gone.

Last night had been the first night we'd made love since the memory I had at the hospital. After I remembered being raped and used as a replacement to Sadie.

I thought it might be hard to be intimate like that after the memory rooted into my brain. After just recalling I was basically a human chew toy and reliving the soreness of my body after that man did unconscionable things to it.

It wasn't difficult at all.

That man didn't even factor into the moments I shared with Eddie. When I was naked beneath him (or over him) with his hands all over my skin, all I felt was love.

He'd been nervous. I knew he thought about what I'd been through. Eddie was cautious with me, but then pure passion came over us both, and nothing else mattered.

"I don't know why you're even bothering with clothes." Sadie interrupted my thoughts. "You know he won't let you keep them."

"It doesn't matter what he wants," I said, tugging on a pair of sweats, reaching for a T-shirt.

"Are you sure about that?"

Whatever I heard in her voice scared me. I stopped cold, looking up. "Where is Eddie?"

"Outside."

Rushing to the window, I shoved at the curtain to peer into the backyard. He was easy to spot among the darkness.

He wasn't alone.

I gasped.

Not even considering Sadie, I ran forward to help him. Sadie shoved me back. I stumbled, gaping at her. "Eddie is going to get hurt!" I raged. "We have to help him!"

"He's fine."

"You said you loved him." I flung the words at her. "If you truly did, you wouldn't just stand here like this."

She stared at me. Something flickered in her eyes, as if what I said struck a chord. Whatever. I wasn't waiting, and I wasn't about to reason with someone who was clearly unbalanced.

Instead of going past her, I went over the bed, taking my shirt with me. Pulling it over my head, I ran out the bedroom door, yelling Eddie's name.

The sound of pounding feet behind me wasn't a surprise, but I ignored them.

Down the hallway, I pivoted into the kitchen, racing to the back door. I grabbed the handle and yanked. Sadie slammed into me from behind, forcing the door closed. Sandwiched between her and the wood, I jerked back, trying to throw her off and pull it open again.

Reaching around me, she banged it shut.

"Sadie!" I gasped. "You have no idea what you're doing!"

The distinctive sound of a sharp blade scraping over a nearby surface made me pause. "Wha—"

Pain, sharp and shocking, burst along my body.

A gurgling sound sputtered out of my throat. I fell into the door, making it bang again. Instinctively, my hand moved to the source of my pain, knocking into the handle of a knife.

Wheezing, I glanced down. There was definitely a knife sticking out of my side.

I turned, leaned back against the door, and stared at Sadie. Her eyes were glittering, her chest heaving.

"Oh, I know," she said. "I know exactly what I'm doing."

True fear cracked through me like the brightest bolt of lightning in a thunderstorm. She was acting as though we were enemies. As though she hated me.

Maybe she does.

"You stabbed me," I said, even though it was perfectly clear. My legs were beginning to wobble, and blood gushed out around the blade, saturating my shirt. I glanced down, wrapping my palm around the handle. Should I pull it out? Leave it in?

Both seemed equally painful.

The knife didn't seem overly large. It was only halfway driven into my side.

"Did you really think I would let you get away with this?"

I began sliding down the door. I thought of Eddie and prayed to God he was okay. I knew who was out there with him.

I knew it was *him*.

He'd come for me just like everyone said he would. He wanted me back.

I'd die before I went back to that island.

But first, I had to make sure Eddie was safe.

I fought my folding legs, my drooping body. I drew in breaths and blew them out quickly, anything to delay the pain.

"Get away with what?" I asked, losing the battle as my ass hit the floor. The movement caused the knife in my side to jar, and pain made me cry out.

"She told me, *Amnesia*," Sadie yelled, emotion I hadn't seen from her before erupting from her pores. "She told me all about your *plan*."

"My plan?" I panted, my hand hovering over the knife.

"It wasn't enough to get away, was it?" She stood over me and raged. I glanced around for anything I could use to defend myself. "You had to take my identity. My life!"

"What?" I forgot about the weapon and looked up. My side was throbbing. I wanted to pull out the knife. Having it sticking out of me was torture.

She made an angry sound and stomped forward, bent, and ripped the knife from me in one savage move. I screamed and fell over, sprawling out on the floor.

"She watched you all those months, Lily! She stalked you, and you didn't even know. Or maybe you just didn't care. Everyone thought you were me, and you saw a chance to have the life I know you always wanted."

I pressed my hand against my bleeding side, trying to apply pressure, as slick, warm blood coated my hand.

"You told everyone you were Sadie. You cuddled up to Eddie and used the fact that he loves *me* to get close to him. You fooled everyone, the townspeople, the hospital. Even *my* Eddie."

"No," I insisted, sitting up. "I didn't know who I was. I had no idea who you were!"

"Lies!" She raged. "The widow told me. She would come back from watching you and tell me everything. How you planned to take my life and leave me on that island to die. You never planned to come back for me. You didn't even care!"

Oh my God. We always suspected she was brainwashed... but this? I never in a million years expected them to poison Sadie against me.

"That's not true," I implored, struggling to stand. I felt slightly dizzy, but I shoved it away. "We weren't sure who I was. I couldn't remember anything. Nothing at all. When we realized I probably wasn't Sadie, I was the one who pushed it. I'm the one who wanted to find out for sure."

She stared at me as I cried. I couldn't tell if she believed me or not.

"Eddie does love you. He—"

"Don't you talk about Eddie! It makes me sick to see you sleeping in his bed, in his arms! He's mine! He always was. You took him away from me!"

"No." I made it to my feet, straightening, still keeping my hand on the wound.

The knife was still in her hand, gripped so tight her fingers were white. I was scared she would try and stab me again, but this time I would be alert, prepared.

"They lied to you, Sadie. Widow West and him. They lied."

"It's all his fault, you know."

"Daniel's?" I asked, trying to follow the conversation as I inched toward the door handle.

"Robbie's! If he hadn't made that stupid dare, I never would have gotten kidnapped. You never would have been brought to that island, and I would be with Eddie."

"You tried to kill Robbie," I said.

"I wanted to live here with Eddie. Did you know that? I didn't want to go with Maggie. Eddie was afraid to let me. He was afraid to hurt *you*. I know he wants to be with me. I see it in his eyes. He missed me. He said so himself."

"Of course he missed you."

"I came into your room that night. I saw him in your bed. It's disgusting. It's everything she said. You're nothing but a liar. You hate that he found me, don't you? You wanted me to stay gone."

I could barely keep up with her crazy ranting. My God, she was completely twisted and confused. They'd been feeding her lies since I escaped that island, slowly turning her against me...

Had this been the plan all along?

All Widow West's attempts to get me back to the island failed, so instead, they decided to try something else.

"You're helping him." I gasped, reaching toward the door handle, wrapping my slick hand around it. "You're helping him drag me back."

She smiled. "I'm taking my life back, Lily. Your time as Sadie is over."

"I'm not Sadie!" I yelled. "I'm Amnesia."

"No," she intoned, taking a step forward. "You're *his*."

If I flung open the door and ran outside, what would be waiting for me? Was I running right into a trap?

What about Eddie? I couldn't just leave him out there.

Tears flooded my face; blood ran down my hip, saturating my pants. "You can't really think he'll only take just me," I said, trying to get through to her. "He won't just force me back with him, but you, too."

She shook her head adamantly, taking a step back. "No. They said… They said if I helped them get you back, then I could stay here. I could have Eddie."

"They lied," I cried, a sob bursting from me.

Sadie hesitated, and I launched open the door. "Eddie, help me!" I screamed.

It slipped out of my slick grasp, and Sadie banged it shut again, shoving me sideways into the end of the counter.

With a strangled cry, she lifted the knife again and brought it barreling down. I screamed hysterically and dodged the blade, falling back onto the ground.

Scrambling up, I deflected Sadie as she tried to stab me again.

Outside, I heard Eddie shout my name.

I screamed back.

Suddenly, Sadie stopped attacking me, backed off completely, threw the knife at my feet, and then she bolted out the door.

CHAPTER THIRTY-FIVE

EDWARD

How long did it take to drown?

How long until all the oxygen was burned up inside your cells? How long until your lungs shriveled and screamed, deflated and died?

It wasn't quiet down here beneath the surface. Death by Lake Loch was not peaceful. It wasn't at all how Amnesia explained the way she felt that night, how she floated peacefully, almost blissfully through a dark, quiet universe of tranquility.

Amnesia.

Reality rushed back like a ten-inch needle driven into my spine. Clarity returned, and my lungs hurt so bad I thought even if I got some air, they would still never be the same.

It didn't matter.

Half dead wasn't dead. There was still life in me.

There was still fight.

I was the only thing standing between Amnesia and this monster.

He might be strong, but I was stronger.

Using every last bit of energy I had, I twisted my entire body and bucked. His grip loosened just a fraction, and my hand shot up out of the water and claimed a handful of his balls.

I wasn't above fighting dirty. There was nothing clean about this psycho.

His hold completely dislodged, and I surged up, gasping for breath as I twisted his balls so forcefully my knuckles ached. He screamed and punched at me. I took the blows and held on. His knees buckled, but I twisted harder.

The splash he made was huge. I let him fall, releasing his nads. I took advantage of his pain to deliver a few swift punches to the side of his head, then delivered another against his cheek, the same spot I'd cracked the bone earlier.

Bubbles erupted at the surface. He propelled up, but I shoved him down.

His body fought and jerked. I felt like a fisherman trying to reel in the catch of a lifetime.

Visions of the way Amnesia looked floating in the lake swam before me. The innocent way she clung to the hoodie the first time I wrapped it around her. The first time she smiled. Her face when she talked about a banana. The way she whispered my name when we made love.

I shoved him farther beneath the surface, his kicks connecting, but I didn't care.

I pictured Sadie huddled in that hole, the see-through gown covering her body. I thought of the baby that was beaten out of her. The way she must have suffered.

With an angry yell, I picked the man up, bringing his gasping face out of the water. He sputtered and yelled.

I spit in his face. Then I punched him again. His teeth cut into my knuckles. Blood started streaming in thin rivulets across the back of my hand.

"You sick son of a bitch!" I roared, thrusting him back under the water.

To hold him down, I sat on him. He fought and struggled… until he ceased.

The second I felt his body go slack, I shoved away from him, sick.

I didn't regret killing him. Hell, it was almost too kind for a man like him.

Cold, aching, and terrified out of my mind, I yelled Amnesia's name. The water put up less resistance this time, and I rushed to the shore. I heard a muffled yell inside the house, and I knew something was wrong.

My foot hit the grass, and I started to run. A heavy, wet figure rammed into me from behind, leaping on me like an elephant wanting a piggyback ride. I made a startled sound and planted my feet into the ground, bucking upward, tossing him over my head. He landed in front of me and rolled. Chest heaving, I looked down to see him with a busted, bruising face and half the buttons missing from his shirt.

"I always come back." He started to laugh. "Always."

I punched him in the side of the head, and his laugh turned to a cough. Glancing around, I saw his boat rocking nearby, and I rushed toward it, grasped the oar, and yanked it free from its clamp.

He was on his knees when I made it back. Without hesitation, I swung the oar like a bat, landing a solid blow right to his ribs. He fell flat on his stomach, sprawling out.

I wasn't about to take any chances, so I hit him again in the back of the head. His body went immobile, and I felt around, unfortunately still finding a pulse. At least he was out cold.

For now.

The sound of a piercing scream cut through the night, and my head shot up.

"Amnesia!" I roared.

She screamed again.

The sound of the screen door banging alarmed me.

"Eddie!" she pleaded.

Bang, bang, bang.

It was as if she were trying to get out, but something was holding her back, keeping her contained.

I moved toward the sound, jerking to a stop, and every curse word I knew slipped out of my mouth. Glancing behind me at the man I wished was dead, but wasn't, I scowled.

Quickly, I grabbed his arm and started to run, dragging his body over the ground behind me like stock supply from Loch Gen.

I wasn't about to leave him so close to the shore. I wasn't giving him a chance to escape.

I let go of him halfway to the back door, not wanting to drag him too close. Even though this situation was pretty fucking dire, I still had enough wits about me to not want Amnesia to get a look at him.

I had no idea what kind of flashbacks his face would bring up, but I knew she might not recover.

Just before I made it to the porch, a blur burst out from inside, causing the door to slam against the side of the house.

"Eddie!" she yelled hysterically. "Help me!"

I barely had time to brace myself before she flung herself into my arms and practically crawled up my body. She trembled like a leaf, her face buried into my neck. Long strands of silky hair blew out over my bare shoulder. Instinctively, my arms locked around her, offering solace and protection.

Water dripped from my hair, down into my eyes.

"She's trying to kill me," she said against my neck. "Please protect me. Don't let me get hurt again."

"Shh." I soothed as movement in the doorway caught my attention and a figure staggered slowly outside. Her hand was pressed against her side, her shoulders hunched. She was hurt, bleeding.

"Amnesia," I whispered.

Sadie pulled back from my arms, her hands still clasped behind my neck. "Yes, Amnesia, Eddie," she answered. "She's trying to kill me. She wants to keep us apart."

And then I realized something.

The lake wasn't friend *or* foe. Not to me.

It was its own entity, an omega.

It had its own set of rules and balances. Its own system of justice and punishment.

It took Sadie but gave me Amnesia.

Then Sadie came back. I had one too many of its secrets.

Lake Loch might have warned me, but it wasn't without consequence. It wasn't without blame.

I was going to have to choose. Here and now. Past or present.

Sadie or Amnesia…

The girl I lost or the girl I found.

CHAPTER THIRTY-SIX

AMNESIA

I knew not to look in the yard, yet my eyes lingered there anyway.

But not at what I knew to avoid.

No, there was something even more horrific than my memories out there in the dark.

The broken make the most conniving. Perhaps because they were once victims, because devious behavior became so normal it developed into reality. A person gets very good at becoming something if they live it long enough.

Hadn't I gotten good at being Sadie?

There was a difference, though, wasn't there? A difference between being something because you didn't know any better and being something because it was all you knew. Because it was a learned behavior.

Actually, that didn't sound that different.

And it made me feel worse.

My head was throbbing. I felt confused. All my thoughts were jumbled, and the vision of Eddie—a bright spot in the dark yard—with Sadie wrapped around him as she begged for protection from me was one of my deepest fears.

Watching Eddie turn away from me. Watching him decide all he ever saw in me was Sadie sat right below remembering my past on the checklist of things I never wanted to do.

Here I was, though, staring it in the face.

I trusted him wholeheartedly. The words he whispered to me in the dark of the night, in the dawn of the morning, even in the stockroom in the middle of day, swirled around inside me, giving me hope.

He promised I was it for him. I believed him.

I wouldn't be human, though, if the sight of his first love clinging to him, crying, didn't chip away at the confidence I felt. This situation was all kinds of fucked up.

The things Sadie said to me would likely haunt me forever.

She was crazy. *No.* She wasn't crazy. Crazy (to me) required a lack of rationale. A lack of empathy and understanding.

Sadie had empathy. Mostly for herself and what she lost, but for Eddie, too. I knew she loved him. Hell, maybe it was that love that kept her from completely losing it all these years. Maybe that's why she clung to him so hard now. The thought was so sad tears sprang to my already blurry eyes.

She also understood that years of her life were stolen from her. There were moments of clarity in her eyes when she realized what she'd lost, what she would never get back.

No, Sadie wasn't crazy. She was broken. Probably shattered.

Left staring down at her shattered pieces with no idea how to put herself back together. She'd been vulnerable, and that made her susceptible to brainwashing. She was convinced the only thing left for her was to banish me back to Rumor Island and pretend none of this ever happened.

The mental abuse she endured quite possibly outweighed the physical. After all, physical wounds heal over... but the mental abuse?

It echoes inside your skin forever.

I was sorry for the way she hated me. I even understood it. Hell, in her position, I'd hate me, too. To her, I was nothing but a replacement. I escaped that island without looking back. I left her there to rot alone. To wonder. To be taunted about how I took her name. Her love. Her family and her life.

My amnesia was a get out of jail free card... but what she didn't understand was nothing in life came free.

I watched just yards away as Eddie wrapped her up tightly, making sure she was completely against his chest. His hand caressed the back of her head, sliding down the length of her long hair.

I felt I was being gutted with a knife.

Oh wait, that sort of already happened. That probably explained that pain.

Regardless, it hurt.

Though he held her, his eyes stared in mine. I was afraid to yell to him. Afraid to tell him what really happened and plead my case. She would lose her mind again. I had no idea what she would do. I didn't think she would hurt Eddie. But I wasn't willing to take the chance.

After all, it was two against one.

I knew without looking exactly where *he* lay. I knew he wasn't dead. The air still crackled with his sick and twisted energy. Just his presence made me feel weak. Made me feel scared and hopeless. How long did I spend feeling that way?

Long enough to crave death.

I was injured and bleeding. My body felt frail, perhaps my mind even frailer. If Sadie decided Eddie was somehow on my side, she could turn on him, and she would have help. I knew better than most people the kind of damage that man could cause.

Instead of saying anything, I sagged in the doorway, hand pressed against my side as blood slowly oozed between my fingers. I was getting lightheaded, woozy, and foggy. Even through it, though, I could hear her. Sadie poured out her twisted sense of truth, telling him I was playing him from the start. Telling him my amnesia had only been a game.

I asked him with my eyes, with no words, only with my heart.

Know me.

Know me without knowing, without hearing.

Know my heart.

"Where are you hurt?" Eddie asked Sadie, stroking her hair again. A part of my heart deflated. *Everything inside me hurts.*

"I'm not," Sadie answered, pulling back. His eyes shifted away from me, and I felt cold the instant they were gone. "I made it out here to you before she could do anything."

"Why is Amnesia bleeding?" he asked, keeping his voice gentle.

I perked up with renewed interest.

"Lily. I had to stab her," Sadie said. "To keep her away from me. She was trying to hurt me, trying to steal my life."

His eyes flashed to me, then quickly back to her.

"It's the middle of the night. What are you doing here?"

"I came to see you."

"Look over there, Sadie," he said, gesturing with his head.

"I don't want to," she said, her voice small.

"He's here," Eddie intoned. "Is that him?"

I had to make an effort not to look. In fact, I shrank back into the doorway.

"Yes," she whispered.

"How did you know he was coming?"

"He told me. I was supposed to be ready."

Eddie's brow furrowed. He spoke to her as though he had all the patience in the world, as though he were trying to understand her. "Ready for what?"

"For him."

As if just the mere mention of the man were a catalyst, a low groan filled the air.

"No!" Eddie's voice erupted along with the sound of pounding feet. "Get back, Am!"

My body buckled, my back hit the doorway, and began to slide down to the floor. Squeezing my eyes shut, fat tears rolled from beneath my lids, slipping down my cheeks. Seconds later, he burst up the steps, and familiar, warm hands slid around me, lifting my paralyzed form.

"He's out there," I whimpered. "I didn't look. Sadie stabbed me."

A numb feeling mixed with a muted rush of hysteria bubbled up inside me.

"I know, baby," he whispered and lifted me off my feet completely. Even as he moved so urgently, he was gentle. Always so gentle with me.

"I'm bleeding," I said, even though that was pretty obvious.

He sat me on the kitchen counter, quickly grabbed a towel, and pressed it to my side. I cried out, and he made a sound.

"I'm sorry," he moaned. "Pressure. Put as much pressure on this as possible." He pressed my hand against the towel. Breath hissed from between my teeth. A phone slapped down beside me. "Call 9-1-1," he demanded.

He gazed around, then lunged at the bloody knife lying on the floor. "This what she stabbed you with?"

I nodded. "She's so brainwashed, Eddie. They told her I left her there to die and stole her life. Stole you."

"I know," he replied, grim.

"But how—"

With the knife in hand, he lunged forward. I flinched, recalling what it was like to have it slip so easily into my body. His touch was gentle, though, as he cupped my head, pressing a soft kiss to my hairline. "I love you. So much. Don't ever forget that."

A sound like someone coming onto the porch made him jerk back.

"Eddie!" Sadie yelled, a bit of hysteria in her scream.

"You shouldn't have come for me," I whispered, afraid. "You should have just stayed with her."

With wide, angry eyes, he told me, "Do not come outside. No matter what you hear."

"But—" Oh my God, he was going back out there!

"Promise me!" he snapped.

I balked. "I can't."

"Call the cops. Stay inside," he ordered again, then rushed outside. The moonlight glinted off the red-stained blade of the knife as he went.

CHAPTER THIRTY-SEVEN

EDWARD

How do you choose between the past and the present?

You don't.

The past is gone; it isn't coming back. The future is just a promise, not a guarantee.

But the present, that was *the* choice. It was now, and without it, there would be no future.

Right now, my heart beat for Amnesia. It always would.

It was an easy choice.

I nearly collided with Sadie as I catapulted out the door.

The second I saw that hook on the back of that boat, I knew. I'd been played. We'd all been played.

Sadie included.

Though I knew she was responsible for that stab wound in my girl, though I knew she had deep-seeded hate against Amnesia, I still couldn't blame her.

She was the biggest victim of all here. Part of me would always be responsible for that.

The true villain was outside, and his arrogance would be his downfall.

The door to the house slammed behind me as I rushed outside. Knowing Am was inside, away from him, was the only thing allowing me the single-minded precision with which to end this once and for all.

I'd die before I let anyone in the house. I'd take my last breath defending her if that's what it took.

"What are you doing?" Sadie demanded, glancing past me to the door.

"It's okay now," I told her, slipping an arm around her waist. "The police are on their way."

"What?" She yanked away from me. "No!"

"They're going to help us, Sadie. They're going to take him away where he can't hurt you ever again."

"We had a deal!" she wailed, looking over toward Daniel.

"Don't look at him," I said, taking her hand. "Look at me."

She listened, her round, terrified eyes seized by my stare.

"What deal?"

"He's taking her away, back to the island, so you and I can have our life back."

"I'm not letting him take her!" I growled, momentarily losing my cool. Jesus fucking shit, I was losing my patience.

She started to cry, deep wails that frankly made me worry. "But if he doesn't take her, then he'll take me. I don't want to go, Eddie. I want to stay here with you."

"I'm not letting him take you either, Sadie. I swear it. Trust me."

"I do," she said, sobering up a little. Her head bobbed.

Daniel had made it to his feet and was staggering toward us. "They're mine!" he growled.

I shoved Sadie behind me and planted my feet, readying for another fight. In the distance, sirens pierced the night and offered some promise of an end to this all.

Daniel heard them, too. The sound stopped him cold. He glanced in the direction from which they came, then back at me. His bloody, beaten face darkened. "This isn't over yet. I always come back."

He started backing away, his steps quicker with every second, toward the lake and his boat.

Oh, hell no.

With a cry, I ran forward. He tried to scurry farther back, but his injuries slowed him down. My injuries only pissed me off.

I grabbed him by the front of his tattered, wet shirt and yanked him forward. He swung his fist around, connecting with the side of my head.

"No!" Sadie yelled.

I staggered back, and he lunged for me. Blindly, I lashed out with the knife. He grunted and fell back.

Straightening, I saw I'd sliced him, but only on the arm. Blood stained the sleeve of his shirt as he heaved, staring at me with pure hatred.

With a battle cry, Daniel surged forward, running at me like a bull charging a red flag. I moved at the last second, brought my arm up as if preparing to throw a right hook, and buried the blade in his middle.

He made a groaning sound and stumbled back. I stood there, coiled and ready, but he didn't come back. Instead, he stumbled backward, like he was trying to get away. After only a few feet he tumbled over into the shallows of Lake Loch.

Sadie screamed and rushed toward him.

I watched in horror and confusion as she fell to her knees beside the man who abused her for years, crying over him.

He moaned, and I burst forward, rushing to her side and lifting her away from him, terrified he would do one last thing to make her suffer.

"I always come back," he said, coughing. Red coated his teeth.

From up on the porch, Amnesia yelled my name.

Daniel laughed.

"Not this time." I assured and reached down, grabbing the handle of the blade and turning it.

He screamed until the sound diminished into a wet gurgle, then ultimately faded away.

Red and blue lights filled the darkness, bouncing off the side of the house. The loud sirens cut off, leaving behind nothing but the sound of Sadie crying, the wind, and the waves.

I glared down at Daniel. His eyes stared back, but they no longer saw. Water crashed over him, filling his mouth, seeping into his nose and pulling at his hair. His shirt was stained pink now, and his body only moved in the direction the water pushed him.

"Eddie!" Amnesia yelled, her voice carrying on the wind.

I spun around, glancing up to where she limped off the porch, staring down where I stood. An officer tried to take her arm, but she pushed him off, stumbling a bit, and continued toward me.

I left Daniel where he lay and sprinted toward her, stopping only when she was within touching distance. I was afraid to pull her against me. Her shirt was saturated in blood.

"We gotta get you to the ER," I said, concerned.

"Is he...?" Her eyes began to stray over my shoulder.

I went forward, wrapped my arms around her shoulders, and carefully pulled her in. "Don't look," I ordered, shielding her with my body.

"Is he dead?"

"Yes, he's dead."

"Eddie!" One of the officers jogged over. "What the hell happened here?"

"There's a dead body on the shore. He's the one who kidnapped Am and Sadie... He tried to take them again tonight."

The man immediately sent a few officers down toward the shore.

"We need a medic." I went on, pulling back so the officer could see the wound in Am's side.

"Go get that looked at. We'll talk after the scene is secure."

I didn't have to be told twice. On our way to the ambulance, Amnesia stumbled. I picked her up.

"What about you?" She winced. "Are you okay?"

"I'm okay as long as you are."

"You killed him," she murmured.

"I'd kill him again if I could."

The EMTs motioned me to put her down on a gurney, so I did. Her eyes began to stray back to the shore, and I stepped in front of her once again.

"Sadie's crying," Am whispered. "She's crying over his body."

"I know," I said, grim.

She reached out for my hand, and I gave it readily. Her shirt was cut away, baring the nasty knife wound on her side.

"Definitely going to need stitches," the medic announced.

"Go to her," she told me, squeezing my hand. "Go to Sadie."

"I want to stay with you," I murmured, feeling guilty but unable to deny the way I felt. I almost lost her tonight. It was too close.

"I'm right here." She promised. "We have a few minutes before we need to leave for the hospital, right?" she asked the EMT.

"Yeah," he answered. "We'll need to get the other victim in the back, too."

"Go to her," Amnesia urged. "She'll come if you ask her to."

I knew she would, but somehow, that made me hesitate more. It seemed wrong, almost like I was no better than Daniel and the widow. Using her. Twisting her feelings against her. I didn't want to be like them.

I wanted to help her, but I also didn't want to give her any false hope there was a chance for anything more than friendship.

"She's so confused right now." I agonized, trying to discern what to do.

A woman stepped around the side of the ambulance. She was dressed slightly haphazardly, as if she'd been in a hurry.

"Dr. Kline!" Amnesia said, surprised.

"I've been on standby since Sadie went missing. They called, said she was here?"

I nodded, but Amnesia answered, "Yes, she's very upset. *He* died."

"She stabbed Amnesia. She has no idea what she's doing," I added.

"I see." Dr. Kline frowned.

"Will you be able to help her?" Amnesia asked, worried despite the wound in her side.

"Yes. I've already made arrangements for Sadie to get the best care possible at a facility in Portland. She's going to be in good hands."

"She's going now?" I asked, feeling this was all so sudden.

"It's what's best for her. So she can't hurt anyone else or herself."

I knew it was best, but it still sucked. "I'll get her," I offered.

The EMT ripped open a large wipe and pressed it against Amnesia's side. Her breath hissed between her teeth, her eyes closed.

"It's okay," I told her, squeezing her hand, wishing I could take the pain.

Dr. Kline stepped forward, laying a hand on my shoulder. "Stay here with Amnesia. I'll get Sadie."

I pulled back, looking into her eyes.

"It's for the best," she said gently. "At least right now."

I hesitated, wanting to resist. It seemed I was somehow turning my back on Sadie.

Dr. Kline seemed to know the direction of my thoughts. "Do it for her. It will make it less confusing later. I'll be sure to call when she's more stable, more in touch with reality."

"Will she ever be?" I worried.

"I think so." The doctor smiled. "Take care of Amnesia," she said, gesturing to Am.

"Thank you, Dr. Kline," she called out.

Dr. Kline gave her a small wave. "See you at our next session."

When she was gone, Amnesia glanced at me. The EMT covered her wound and announced we were heading the hospital alone. Sadie would follow in a different vehicle.

I climbed in the back after she was comfortably situated and stared at Sadie, who was finally away from the body and now with Dr. Kline. She glanced up; our eyes connected across the yard.

I had a vision of the girl I once knew, happy and carefree. Tears burned the backs of my eyes.

Then she did something. She lifted her hand and made an X over her heart and smiled.

I smiled back. The old-school gesture gave me hope everything would be okay.

The doors of the ambulance closed, cutting off the harsh lights and the sound of people talking. I turned to Amnesia, finally alone with my girl in the center of quite literally murder and chaos.

"Thank you for protecting me." She reached for my hand.

I smiled, slid closer, and cupped her face. "Thank you for staying in the house."

"It felt kind of wimpy," she admitted.

"There is nothing wimpy about you, Am. You protected yourself for years and years with no help. You aren't alone anymore, sweetheart. You have me, and I will always protect you."

A tear ran down her cheek. I brushed it away with the backs of my fingers.

"It's finally over," she whispered.

"It's finally over," I echoed.

The ambulance started up and pulled away from the house.

"What now?" she asked, leaning her head against my shoulder.

"Now you get stitches," I teased.

"After that," she said, sitting up to give me a light shove. The motion caused her to wince.

"Easy," I cautioned, carefully lifting her into my lap.

Her fingers brushed over a few bumps and bruises on my face. She leaned up and kissed them softly.

"After that, we live happily ever after," I said, kissing her on the tip of her nose.

She smiled. "Did you get that line from a movie?"

"It's a good line. Totally applies here," I said reasonably.

"It only applies if it's true," she whispered.

Tipping her chin up with my thumb, I asked, "What do you think?"

Her brown eyes softened. The freckles across her nose and cheeks looked like stars. "True." She decided.

My lips claimed hers.

Most definitely true.

EPILOGUE

AMNESIA

We got married on the shores of Lake Loch. Right in our backyard to be exact. Our guests stood in the grass; mine and Eddie's feet were in the water.

Some probably thought we were insane to make the lake such a big part of our day. A lake that caused so much pain and turmoil. A lake that nearly robbed us of our happily ever after more than once.

But what they didn't understand…

The lake also brought us together.

Lake Lochlain was in many ways the catalyst for the wedding we stood at today.

Of course, some think the lake wasn't any of these things. It was just a lake, just a body of water with no real spirit or character. I knew better than most this was the furthest from the truth.

I could have drowned that night I jumped from the hunting stand. I was almost plucked from the depths by a madman who refused to let me go.

But I was protected.

Carried away by the waves, concealed beneath the murky depths.

And though I couldn't remember, I understood at times I'd been cradled by the water until Eddie pulled me to safety.

Sometimes when I stood on the shores and gazed out over the ever-changing current (that somehow always felt the same), I wondered if the water that surrounded my prison for many years was the very thing that set me free.

The doctors say my amnesia stemmed from trauma. My therapist told me it was my mind's way of protecting me. So many logical, sensible conclusions to explain why I couldn't remember much about my past.

I had a reason of my own, however. One that wasn't so scientific. One that would probably get me more time with the head shrink if I ever voiced the theory.

The lake.

Somehow, Lake Loch washed away everything in my past. I knew even without seeing, all my memories, my old identity, and where I came from lay at the bottom of the water. Down in its deepest depths among the largest rocks, the laziest of fish, and perhaps even the Loch Ness herself.

I was just another secret the lake would likely never give up.

And I was okay with that.

The lake could have my past. In trade, I got a future.

I was given amnesty.

Freedom.

There were remnants from before, fragments of clarity the lake showed me. They were horrible and partly unwanted, but not unnecessary.

I wouldn't understand the true gift of amnesty if everything remained forgotten.

So there we stood on the shore by the water, which on the day of our wedding was calm and peaceful. The surface so smooth it looked like glass and reflected the beautiful Maine landscape like a mirror. The early spring day was cold, but all I felt was the sun's rays shining down upon us.

As we said our vows, as I pledged to love him forever—for richer or poorer, in memory and amnesia, even after death—I looked across the water at the island and smiled.

"For the first time," the minister announced, "the beginning of a new life together—"

"A new era." Eddie cut in, reaching out to palm my softly rounding belly with his oversized hand.

A tiny flutter erupted within me, but it wasn't butterflies, not today. Today it was the stirring of our yet-to-be-born child.

(PS: That's what happens when you're so in love you never once think about birth control.)

(PSS: Sometimes not thinking—not knowing—results in something wonderful.)

People on the grass chuckled. I covered my new husband's hand with mine. "A new era." I agreed.

The minister inclined his head and smiled. "May I introduce, officially, Mr. Eddie Donovan and his wife, Mrs. Amn—"

Both Eddie and I glanced up, wondering if he would remember.

"Mrs. *Amnesty* Donovan."

Turns out Amnesia wasn't a good fit for me anymore. I was no longer a "complete memory wipe." I was full.

So incredibly full, and that in itself was my freedom.

I smiled so wide, but it was short lived because Eddie dragged me up against him and crushed his mouth over mine.

Water rushed up to our ankles, Lake Loch granting us approval. People clapped, and the cold spring breeze blew.

Behind us, the minister cleared his throat. We broke the kiss.

Eddie grabbed my hand and we turned, backs toward Rumor Island, facing forward to our lake home, our family, and our friends.

I looked first at Maggie, who was crying happy tears. She blew me a kiss, and I smiled.

Forgoing the tradition of turning around, I lifted the white bouquet of roses I held and tossed it right at Mary Beth. Her eyes widened when it fell into her arms, and I winked. I was totally betting on her and Robbie.

With one hand in Eddie's and another on the child we created, we walked out of the water and into the waiting crowd.

"Just wait until you see the cake I made," Joline said, rushing to our side. "It's the best thing I've ever done."

"I'm sure it is," I told her sincerely.

Jeremy stepped up behind her. "Good Lord, woman, leave them to bask in their wedded glow. The cake can wait." Joline gave him the evil eye, and he patted Eddie on the shoulder. "Enjoy that glow while it lasts."

Eddie turned to me, sweeping me into his chest. "I think it's never going to fade away."

Our kiss transported me to a place where we were the only two on the shore. No one else was within earshot, cake the furthest thing from my mind.

"Congratulations, sweetheart!" Maggie said, cutting into the happy bubble.

We broke apart again, reality rushing back as we were surrounded by Eddie's parents and the only mother I would ever know.

I hugged her tightly. "Thank you for everything. I love you so much." I drew in a deep breath. "Mom."

Her arms tightened around me. When she pulled back, tears streamed down her face. "You better get back. I'm going to cry all over that dress."

"I wouldn't mind."

"Come on, missus," Eddie said, taking me by the hand again. "I have a feeling if we don't go see the cake and all the catering Joline and Maple's restaurant did, we might be barred from our own reception."

"I like the sound of that," I told him.

"Being barred from our own wedding cake?" he puzzled.

"Missus," I corrected. "Being *your* missus."

Both dimples appeared and his azure eyes sparkled with the wolfish smile that transformed his face. "Good, because it's permanent."

We started following along behind the guests as they walked toward a large white tent erected right there on our lawn. Eddie paused, glancing back over his shoulder, eyes sweeping the lake and the island in the distance.

"You're thinking about her," I observed, understanding completely.

His eyes came back to mine, a little dimmer than before. "I just wish she was able to be as happy as we are. That she'd been granted some sort of…" His voice faded away as he searched for the right word.

"Amnesty?" I finished for him.

"Yeah, maybe." He agreed.

"Sadie will find her freedom." I promised. I didn't feel bad for it either, because I knew deep down inside me it was true. "She's getting all the help she needs now. It's going to take a while. Her memories and experiences will always be there. But she's a survivor. Widow West, on the other hand… I have a feeling she's probably going to spend the rest of her life in an institution. There's no saving her. But Sadie, she's going to find her happily ever after just like you did."

Eddie's arms slipped around me. Between us, my rounded belly brushed against his middle. "Like *we* did."

I nodded.

"I love you," he vowed, his lips brushing against mine as he spoke.

"Cross my heart," I whispered, delving my fingers into the dark, wild curls on his head. "Hope to die."

He smiled, pressing his forehead against mine. "You will be forever mine."

And I was.

THE END

Copycat *Joline's Monkey Bread Muffins*
'Cause she won't give me her secret recipe!

Ingredients
3 cans of cinnamon rolls (your favorite brand)
1 can of apple pie filling
½ c raisins (optional)
¼ c brown sugar
¼ c granulated sugar
1 T flour
1 t cinnamon
1 t salt
2 T melted butter
4 T milk (any kind)
muffin liner cups

Directions
Preheat oven to 350 degrees.

Place can of apples into a bowl and cut into small pieces. To the apples, add in brown sugar, granulated sugar, flour, raisins (optional), half the cinnamon (reserving the other half for the glaze), and the melted butter. Remove cinnamon rolls from cans, cut into small pieces. Combine the biscuit pieces into the apple mixture. Mix together.

Spoon mixture into muffin tins lined with foil cups. Fill each cup about three-quarters full.

Bake at 350 degrees for about 25 minutes (depending on oven).

Glaze

While muffins are baking, combine milk, powdered sugar, and cinnamon in a bowl. Mix to create a cinnamon glaze to drizzle over warm muffins when they come out of the oven. OR you could also use the icing included with the cinnamon rolls

Makes approximately 24 muffins

AUTHOR'S NOTE

We meet again. It's the end of another book for me and the end of this duet. I'm still a little fuzzy headed because I just typed the end today, and my brain is pretty mush. So let's hope I can string together a few more sentences here and let you know my thoughts.

I know this duo has a different feel from most of my other books, and it was fun to stretch in a new direction and do something a little different. I'm really honored by the readers who have been willing to embrace this story and these books, even if it's out of their norm, too.

This was definitely a challenging duo to write. Originally, I planned on Amnesia being a single standalone title. But sometimes books and characters have other ideas. The more I delved into this book, the more the plot unfolded itself and honestly... the messier it got. Ha! Halfway through writing *Amnesia*, I logged on Facebook (as one does) and saw the cover for this book. I had the same reaction to it as I did to *Amnesia*. The instant, "Oh, wow," and, "This is haunting." And instantly, I thought, *Oh my gosh, this is perfect. This isn't a single title anymore. There are two books, and this is my cover.* (This cover is designed by the same artist who designed *Amnesia*—Cover Me Darling.) I messaged the designer right away and told her it would make an awesome follow-up, and she agreed.

The second I saw this cover, the title came to me instantly as well. Sometimes that just happens.

Everything falls into place all by itself, and I'm left sitting in my chair, wondering where the hell my brain even came up with any of it. And hopefully, by now, you will know it isn't *Amnesia* on the cover of this book, but Sadie.

I like the twist that Am isn't Sadie after all and there are TWO kidnapped girls, both entirely similar in a lot of ways. I like the mystery surrounding them both and the island. The way everyone had to come to terms with the identity of both girls and how everything changed and shifted around them. It was both a challenge and a pleasure to write about a woman who didn't really have an identity, who kind of operated on the fact that she had no idea who she was or where she belonged.

At the same time, this story is a little heartbreaking, eh? And pretty dark. Darker than most of the books I've written before. Maybe that's the thing that makes it beautiful and hopefully a little haunting, just like the covers.

A few fun, random facts about a few people, etc., in this book:

1. It's set in Maine because I think Maine is beautiful, and my husband grew up there.

2. Edward is inspired by my father, who had dimples, black curly hair, blue eyes, and a square jaw. He was ornery, and everyone liked him. Everyone called him Eddie. Also, my father passed of cancer when I was eleven.

3. Joline is named after and inspired by my husband's aunt. She lives in Maine and used to work in a bakery.

4. I desperately wanted to make the monkey bread muffin recipe in the back of this book, but I haven't because I'm gluten free and these muffins are decidedly not. PS: If you try them, tell me how they are!

5. I thoroughly believe in the Loch Ness monster.

I really hope you enjoyed this story, its twists and turns, the heartbreaking moments, and the moments that made you swoon. Thank you for all the love and support you have shown the *Amnesia Duet*. Please know I am sincerely grateful and appreciative.

Now, on to the next project… which I hope you will also enjoy!

See you next book!

XOXO,
Cambria Hebert

About Cambria Hebert

Cambria Hebert is an award winning, bestselling novelist of more than thirty books. She went to college for a bachelor's degree, couldn't pick a major, and ended up with a degree in cosmetology. So rest assured her characters will always have good hair.

Besides writing, Cambria loves a caramel latte, staying up late, sleeping in, and watching movies. She considers math human torture and has an irrational fear of birds (including chickens). You can often find her painting her toenails (because she bites her fingernails) or walking her Chihuahuas (the real rulers of the house).

Cambria has written within the young adult and new adult genres, penning many paranormal and contemporary titles. She has also written romantic suspense, science fiction, and most recently, male/male romance. Her favorite genre to read and write is contemporary romance. A few of her most recognized titles are: *The Hashtag Series, GearShark Series, Text, Torch,* and *Tattoo.*

Recent awards include: Author of the Year, Best Contemporary Series (*Hashtag Series*), Best Contemporary Book of the Year, Best Book Trailer of the Year, Best Contemporary Lead, Best Contemporary Book Cover of the Year. In addition, her most recognized title, *#Nerd,* was listed at Buzzfeed.com as a Top Fifty Summer Romance Read.

Cambria Hebert owns and operates Cambria Hebert Books, LLC.

You can find out more about Cambria and her titles
by visiting her website: http://www.cambriahebert.com

MORE BOOKS BY CAMBRIA HEBERT

The #Hashtag Series
#Nerd
#Hater
#Player
#Selfie
#Poser
#Heart
#Holiday
#Bae

The GearShark Series
#Junkie
#Rev
#Swag
#Blur
#FinishLine

Standalone Titles
Distant Desires
Maneater
Whiteout
Blank

The Take It Off Series
Torch
Tease
Tempt
Text
Tipsy

Tattoo

Tricks

Tryst

Taste

Trashy

Taxi

The Heven and Hell Series

Before

Masquerade

Between

Charade

Bewitched

Tirade

Beneath

Renegade

The Death Escorts Series

Recalled

Charmed